Also by Ray Hobbs and

Published Elsewhere

A WORTHY SCOUNDREL

RAY HOBBS

Wingspan Press

Published in the United States and the United Kingdom
by WingSpan Press, Livermore, CA

The WingSpan name, logo and colophon are the trademarks
of WingSpan Publishing.

ISBN 978-1-63683-031-5 (pbk.)
ISBN 978-1-63683-974-5 (ebook)

First edition 2022

Printed in the United States of America

www.wingspanpress.com

This book is dedicated to naval aviators, past, present and, hopefully, to come.

RH

Sources and Acknowledgements

Kemp, P.K., *Fleet Air Arm* (London, Herbert Jenkins, 1954).

Bartlett, C.P.O., *In the Teeth of the Wind* (London, Ian Allan Ltd, 1974. Republished Barnsley, Pen & Sword Books Ltd, 2004).

Barber, M., *Royal Naval Air Service Pilot* (Oxford, Osprey Publishing, 2010).

Hartley, N., *Colonial Outcasts* (Morrinsville, Arrow Press Ltd, 1993).

Harding, P. *et al*, *New Zealand* (Melbourne, Oakland, London, Paris, Lonely

Planet Publications, 1977).

* * *

As ever, I wish to acknowledge the invaluable assistance of my brother Chris in the preparation of the manuscript.

RH

Author's Note

I have tried as far as possible, to keep jargon within reasonable bounds, but I feel that a word of explanation is necessary.

The Sopwith Baby Seaplane was made at the Sopwith factory at Kingston-upon-Thames and also by Fairey Aviation at their Hamble factory. The latter, which varied from the original only in detail, was called the **Fairey Hamble Baby Seaplane**. It was active on the southeast coast in the latter part of the Great War, and a painting of one such aircraft occupies the front cover of this book.

The **Navy and Army Canteen Board** performed a commendable function until the emergence of a new armed service prompted the formation of the Navy, Army and Air Force Institute, or **NAAFI.**

Curiously, the Admiralty chose to give unique names to the commissioned ranks of the **Royal Naval Air Service**, so that, in rising order, they became flight sub-lieutenant, flight lieutenant, flight commander, squadron commander, wing commander and wing captain. By contrast, the **Royal Flying Corps** retained the conventional army ranks. In April 1918, both organisations were amalgamated and rebranded the **Royal Air Force**, which assumed the Army ranks until 1919, when its commander-in-chief, General Trenchard, insisted on a system, along with a new uniform, that was intended to bear no relation to either of the former air services. The uniform was, and remains, unique, but the new system of ranks, still in force today, turned out to be a combination of the two. Trenchard also retained the RFC's motto *Per Ardua ad Astra* (Through Adversity to the Stars). They were confusing times.

The **Wardroom** of a ship or naval establishment is the officers' mess. In Nelson's time, it was used as a storage compartment for prizes until they became yesterday's excitement.

The **Gun Room** no longer exists, but it performed the same function as the wardroom for the most junior officers, although on a much more austere level, ensuring that its occupants remained keen for promotion, if only to improve their living conditions.

Take away – figuratively speaking – the wings, tailplane, fin and rudder of an aircraft, and you have the **Fuselage**.

'**Secure**' is the order to naval ratings to cease work at the end of a watch, and regard the following time as their own. It has led to a degree of confusion in the past, largely because of the Navy's habit of giving orders to new recruits in obscure navalese and explaining them later when the damage was done.

A '**Mouldy**', possibly a reference to a less than fresh sausage, was a torpedo during the Great War. The slang name that superseded it in World War Two was '**Tinfish**'. Both are surprising, as lower deck wit usually reflected greater imagination.

The practice of 'boxing the compass', i.e. dividing it into 32 points, rather than adopting the familiar compass rose, was in use by navigators at the time of the Great War. **Eight Points to Starboard** was the equivalent of ninety degrees to starboard. Much as I would like to explain the reason for its adoption, I have to confess that it is completely beyond me.

A **Flag Officer** is one who holds the rank of Commodore or higher, and is therefore entitled to have the flag, or pennant, of his rank flown when he is on board ship. It represents the Navy's acknowledgement of his importance, whilst acting as a warning to junior officers and ratings to keep their heads down.

A **Sloop** was an anti-submarine escort vessel that was smaller than a destroyer. In modern times, the type has been superseded by the frigate. Frigates, however, are expensive, so watch this space.

'**Bunts**' was the universal nickname for signalmen, or 'bunting tossers'. It is no longer used, because signalmen, like radio operators, sailmakers, powder monkeys and foretopmen, have been ousted by technology.

The '**Andrew**' was the sailors' affectionate nickname for the Royal Navy, originating in the 18th century, when press-gang bosun Andrew Miller was so successful that the Navy was said to be effectively his.

The **Voluntary Aid Detachment**, or **VAD**, was an organisation of nurses, who received the most basic training, but who made a vital contribution to patient care, often in trying conditions.

'**Pongo**' was simply the naval ratings' slang for 'soldier'.

'**Jolly Jack**', or '**Jacktar**' was to the sailor what 'Tommy Atkins' was to the soldier.

Finally, I should say a brief word about the changing value of money. On the face of it, £20,000 looks quite exciting, but it is hardly a rich man's fortune, In 1918, however, it would have been the equivalent of more than £1,000,000 today.

With those details out of the way, I hope you enjoy the story.

RH

1

THE SEAPLANE BASE, DOVER, KENT

1918

Condensation had misted up the windows of the Navy and Army Canteen on the bitter January afternoon, but the hunched shape of a lone rating was just discernible on the bench outside. Every now and again, the blustery wind blew rain directly into his face, but he seemed neither to notice nor to care.

One of the civilian canteen workers had been watching him. 'He's still there, Mrs Morley,' she said. 'Do you want me to go and find out if he's all right? It's coming on to rain again and it's a very cold wind.'

'No, Doris, I'll speak to him while you finish the dishes.' Agnes put her hat and coat on to go outside. Then, as an afterthought, she drew a mug of fresh tea from the urn, added the one spoonful of sugar allowed, and took it outside for the sailor. Closing the canteen door behind her, she hesitated, because a naval officer had stopped his motorcar to speak to him. The poor boy had already suffered harsh words from passing officers, one a naval officer and the other a Royal Marine. Unaware of their approach, he had committed the heinous offence of failing to salute them. By contrast, however, the newcomer, who had now left his vehicle, was speaking to him quietly and without evident anger, although the boy was still staring dumbly at his hands, so it was possible that he wasn't even aware he was being addressed by an officer.

'Excuse me, Lieutenant,' said Agnes. 'I've brought this boy some more tea. He received some very upsetting news this morning.'

Realising that he was in the presence of an officer, the rating tried to stand.

'Sit down,' the officer told him gently. 'You obviously have plenty on your mind without jumping through hoops as well. Stay there and drink your tea.' With a quick glance, he saw the ring on Agnes's left hand and said, 'That was very thoughtful of you, ma'am.'

'Some would say it's our function to be thoughtful, Lieutenant. We're here to provide a kind of comfort, after all.'

He nodded understandingly and, in a conversational tone, said to the sailor, 'You're one of the telegraphists, aren't you?'

'Yes, sir. Beresford, sir, nine-two-four—'

'Don't worry about your number, Beresford. Tell me about your problem instead. I may be able to help.' He took a seat beside hin. 'Of course, if you prefer it, you could always put in a request to see your divisional officer.'

The boy shook his head hopelessly. 'You can't help me, sir. Neither can my D.O.' A solitary tear rolled down his cheek as he said, 'My brother's been killed.' He added, 'In France, in the trenches.'

'I'm truly sorry to hear that, Beresford. You must be devastated. Have you requested compassionate leave?'

'Yes, sir.' His reply clearly called for effort. 'I have a warrant for a train to Whitstable.'

'What time is the train?'

'Seventeen-twenty, sir.'

The officer took out a gold hunter watch and consulted it. He asked, 'Have you the fare for the omnibus?'

'I'll walk to the station, sir. I'd rather, honestly.'

'That's entirely up to you, Beresford, but if you're going on foot, you should cut along now.'

'Aye, aye, sir.'

'I've no doubt it feels like the end of the world, and it must seem unlikely at this stage, but it will become easier in time. I can tell you that from experience.'

'Yes, sir. Thank you for....' He seemed unable to frame his expression of gratitude. Then, after a moment's thought, he said, 'Thank you, sir and you as well, ma'am, for your kindness.'

'Think nothing of it,' said Agnes.

'It's only a year ago my father was killed.' Beresford gave a weary shrug as he got to his feet. 'I suppose I'm the man of the house now.'

'Have you no one else?'

His voice broke again as he spoke. 'Two sisters, ma'am, and my mother.'

'Well, run along now. They'll need you at home.'

'Yes, ma'am. Thank you for the tea and the bread and dripping.' He saluted the officer, who returned the gesture.

When he'd gone, Agnes said, 'I'm afraid I don't know your name, Lieutenant, but you spoke in a very kindly way to that poor boy.' She added grimly, 'I have to say, your attitude was in marked contrast to that of some of your brother officers.'

'I am... unusual.' He laughed, offering his hand, and there was clearly sensitivity in his deep brown eyes. 'Fred Fuller,' he said, 'and it's "Flight Commander", not that it's of any importance.'

'I really can't get used to the RNAS ranks. I saw two rings on your epaulettes, so I called you "Lieutenant". I'm Agnes Morley, by the way. I run the canteen,' she said, looking down at her uniform and realising to her embarrassment that the fact must be obvious to him.

'And you're a credit to the Canteen Board, Mrs Morley.'

'You're very kind, but I'll be a credit to it no longer if I don't return to my duties and close for the day.' She looked up at the sky and said, 'It looks very much as if I'll be going home in a downpour.'

'Have you far to travel?'

'My home's in Whitfield.'

He looked meaningfully at the gathering clouds, doubtless sharing her conclusion. 'I'm going your way. Will you let me drive you?' He laughed when he saw her glance at the eagle brevet on his shoulder. 'Not in a seaplane,' he assured her. 'I keep a motor for excursions on dry land.' He gestured towards the stationary vehicle with its invitingly sound canvas roof.

'It's a very kind offer, Flight Commander Fuller, but I couldn't put you to the trouble.'

'It would be no trouble. I'm going to the air station at Guston, and Whitfield's not far away.'

'If you're sure it's not a lot of trouble, I'd be very grateful.'

'Then it's settled. I'll wait for you, but please don't feel that you need to hurry.'

'Thank you, Lieut... Flight Commander.' She returned to the

canteen, checked that everything was in its place, and dismissed the two members of staff, hoping they would also avoid the rain. Finally, she locked the door and walked to the parked vehicle where Flight Commander Fuller was waiting by the passenger door. 'I must say,' she said, 'this is very kind of you.'

'Not at all. I just don't want you to be caught in the rain.' He swung the starting handle. The engine coughed twice before obliging with a steady rumble. He climbed in and released the handbrake.

'Lieut... I'm sorry... Flight Commander Fuller, I'm being far too inquisitive, but something's been puzzling me.'

'Then ask away and let truth make all things plain, and don't worry about my rank. I've been called worse things than "Lieutenant", I can assure you, and I've no doubt everything will change again with this confounded Air Force Constitution Act.'

'Very well.' She had to know. 'Where are you from originally?'

'Your question doesn't surprise me. You could wonder about that until doomsday. I'm actually English, born in Hampshire, but my home, both spiritual and by domicile, is in Queenstown, New Zealand.'

'Ah.'

'I've only lived there since nineteen-ten. I returned to England in nineteen-fourteen to join in the fun, but I probably picked up a little of the accent in that time. New Zealand has a way of absorbing people without their realising it.'

The rain was increasing, and Agnes was thankful that she'd accepted his offer. 'By all means tell me to attend to my own affairs,' she said, 'but why did you have to come to England to enlist?'

'It was highly necessary. The one vital thing New Zealand lacked was a navy, and that's still the case, I'm afraid.'

'It had to be the Navy, then?'

'I should say so. Living where I did as a boy, so close to Portsmouth, I used to see warships coming and going, and I longed to be with them. I wanted to sit the exam for Dartmouth when I was fourteen, but my father wouldn't hear of it.'

'If you'd set your heart on it, it must have been an awful blow.'

'It was.'

Almost without conscious thought, she said, 'My late husband was a naval officer, a sub-lieutenant, but it was widely agreed that he had a bright future.' She sighed. 'No one could have known how brief his future would be. He was killed three years ago at Dogger Bank.'

'I'm heartily sorry, Mrs Morley,' he said quietly. 'I never realised you were widowed.'

'Thank you. I didn't really mean to tell you that. It just… came out.'

'It happens more frequently than you might imagine,' he said, making a right turn off the main road. 'It's a peculiarity I'm told I inherited from my mother.'

'Seriously?'

'Oh yes. I once spent a brief spell in the company of a Maori girl who'd had an unpleasant experience of some kind that resulted in her not speaking a word for more than two years. What a chatterbox she turned out to be. Her family were very grateful, but I'd done nothing. As I said, people just feel like talking. I can't take the credit for it.'

'You got that boy to talk this afternoon. I only knew he'd had some bad news, but he told you about it readily.'

He nodded. Clearly, it was a normal feature of his life. 'It wasn't difficult for me to sympathise with him,' he said. 'I imagine that helped.'

Agnes was conscious that she'd been asking rather personal questions, but the man almost encouraged it. 'One more question,' she said, 'if you don't mind, that is.'

'Not in the least.'

'Did you go to New Zealand with your family?'

The question seemed to amuse him. 'No, they sent me there to get rid of me. I'm a remittance man.' He shrugged. 'At least, that's what I was until my father died, and my elder brother stopped the payments. It was just as well he did, because it enabled me to return to England legally.'

It was now raining heavily, prompting a change of gear and a slower pace.

Shocked at his disclosure, Agnes asked, 'Do you mean to say that your family actually paid you to remain abroad?'

'I shan't embarrass you with the details, Mrs Morley, but yes, they did. They seemed to enjoy living in the past. For some reason, the practice has declined in popularity in the past twenty or thirty years, but they were keen enough to keep it in motion.'

'You know, I'm not as easily embarrassed as you possibly imagine, but I do seem to have touched a raw nerve.'

He laughed openly. 'No, you haven't, Mrs Morley, far from it.' Looking through the side window, he said, 'I see we've reached Whitfield. Would you care to direct me?'

'Of course.' Agnes was obliged to forget his intriguing story for the time being and concentrate on guiding him through the heavy rain and darkness to her home.

Eventually, at her request, he stopped outside a modest, detached house with a small front garden.

'I'm very grateful to you, Flight Commander Fuller.'

'One moment, if you please.' He reached behind his seat for an umbrella. 'Allow me,' he said, hurrying round to the passenger door to help her out of the vehicle and offer her his arm.

'Your courteous behaviour almost leads me to wonder if the story of your disgrace might be an elaborate tease,' she said as they passed through the gateway.

'Oh, it's true enough,' he assured her, 'but my alleged guilt is another matter altogether.' He held the umbrella above her while she opened the door to the house. 'I've enjoyed meeting you, Mrs Morley,' he said. '*E noho ra.*'

'What?'

'It's what the Maoris say when they take their leave of someone. They're very courteous, too.'

'Goodbye, Flight Commander, and thank you again.'

'You're most welcome. Goodbye, Mrs Morley.'

** ** **

The wardroom of the naval air station at Guston was especially welcoming after the blustery wind and rain, and it was a shame that Fred would have to return to Dover after dinner, but he put that thought aside and accepted a drink from Flight Commander Bill Webster.

'Thank you, Bill.' He smiled and said, 'You'll never guess what happened to me this afternoon.'

'Not without a few clues, Fred. Indulge me.'

'I met a most charming lady and drove her home to Whitfield.'

6

'You shameless Casanova. Describe her to me in exhaustive detail.'

Fred thought. 'She was wearing the uniform of the Navy and Army Canteen Board. Also, most of the time we were talking, the light was failing and the weather, as you know, was unhelpful, but I do remember that she was slender, with a lovely, trim waist, although that may have been contrived. I've no way of knowing that, and I know nothing of the devices women use in the pursuit of elegance.'

'Go on.'

'Let me think. Her hair was a kind of light red, not auburn.... I believe that people versed in such matters would call her a Titian redhead, and there was a hint of green about her eyes, if you see what I mean.'

'Hazel-green?'

'That sort of thing, yes.' He nodded. 'A most appealing lady.'

'Single?'

'Yes, but there's the rub. She's a widow, so it's possible that she's still delicate and vulnerable.'

'How recently was she widowed?'

'Dogger Bank, nineteen-fifteen.'

'Three years. Well, it could have been worse, at least from your point of view, although it was rotten luck for him. 'I seem to recall there were only a few casualties on our side. Are you likely to see her again?'

'It's always possible. She manages the junior ratings' canteen in Dover.'

Bill finished his drink and put the glass down. 'Time is a great healer,' he said encouragingly.

'That's true, but there's the complication that she knows I left the old country under something of a cloud, although I spared her the details. It was, when all's said and done, a first encounter.'

'Maybe there's no hope for you after all, Fred.' Bill picked up his glass and said, 'I see the tide's out. Let's have another.'

2

Purely by coincidence, Fred was to see Mrs Morley two days later in the base chapel. Continuing foul weather meant that all flying was cancelled, so he decided to break with habit and attend Matins, as a good officer should.

Although she was wearing a voluminous hat, presumably against the persistent rain, it was her hair that identified her. Very little of it was visible beneath the brim of her hat, but he recognised it nevertheless.

Lowering his voice beneath the organist's discreet prelude, he said, 'Good morning, Mrs Morley. May I join you?'

She looked up in surprise, recognising him immediately. 'Of course, Flight Commander. Please do.'

He placed his cap in the slot provided for hymn and prayer books, took his seat, and found the Order for Morning Service in his Naval Prayer Book.

'That's the mark of a devout man,' she observed quietly, 'finding the page as quickly as you did.' Her prayer book was unopened. 'Are you a frequent attender? I could so easily go to St Peter's in Whitfield, but I like this chapel so much, it's almost an act of self-indulgence to come here.'

'I'm usually flying,' he admitted. 'I suppose coming here when I'm grounded makes me a foul-weather Christian.'

'I'm sure it takes more than that.'

At the sound of the choir, they stood for the processional and, for the next hour, Fred immersed himself in the reassuringly familiar order of service, with its exquisite and archaic language. It was a luxury at a time when so little was certain, and a world that was once familiar was changing all the time.

** ** **

As they left the chapel, the eye of Fred's squadron commander met his.

'Good morning, Fuller.'

'Good morning, sir. May I introduce Mrs Morley, Superintendent of the Navy and Army Canteen?'

'Also,' added Mrs Morley, 'widow of the late Sub-Lieutenant James Morley, RN.'

'My condolences, ma'am.'

'Thank you…. I'm sorry, I'm still not *au fait* with RNAS insignia.'

'Squadron Commander Elliot,' said Fred, completing the introduction.

The two shook hands, and Elliot moved on to greet another officer of his squadron.

'I hope your commanding officer doesn't disapprove of your being in the company of a canteen superintendent, Flight Commander,' said Mrs Morley.

'There's no reason why he should, and as long as he thinks no less of you, I really don't care.'

'But one star seems to make a huge difference.'

'In what way?'

'You have two rings and one star above them, making you a flight commander….'

'That's right, one step above a flight lieutenant, who has no star.'

'That officer had two rings with two stars above them, making him a squadron commander, and he has to be addressed as "sir".'

'That is a courtesy I extend to him only on Sundays or in the presence of a senior officer.'

'Even so, I can't help feeling confused when you all look like lieutenants.'

'Mrs Morley,' he asked, 'will you join me for lunch? I'm sure you'll find it more agreeable than trying to make sense of the RNAS and its arcane naming of ranks.'

'You're too generous, Flight Commander, but I don't believe I'm allowed in the wardroom.'

'Today is not a guest day,' he confirmed, 'but the Corunna Hotel in Dover Town Centre is a short drive from here.'

She seemed at a loss. 'I've already benefited from your kindness. I feel it would be wrong of me to accept more.'

'On the contrary, you'd be giving me a great deal of pleasure.'

'You're a very persuasive man.'

'So you'll join me?'

'Thank you, I'll be happy to.'

As Fred led her to the Sunbeam, he said, 'There's one more favour I would ask, and that is that you use my Christian name, which is Fred.'

'I'll be glad to. Mine is Agnes.'

As they walked on, Fred was conscious that only a few years earlier, the introduction of Christian names on a second encounter would have attracted the same disapproval as the unchaperoned event itself. The war had changed society and would possibly continue to do so for as long as it lasted. He let Agnes into the car and folded his umbrella.

When he'd started the engine and joined her inside, she asked, 'Were you christened "Fred", or did the abbreviation occur naturally?'

'No, it was a deliberate change on my part. I used to be Frederick Fuller-Davies, but I decided when I was on passage to New Zealand, to jettison three syllables of my Christian name and half my surname. "Fuller" was my mother's maiden name, so I kept that, as she was the only member of my family who cared two hoots for me. Actually,' he said soberly, 'in fairness, I have to say she cared much more than that.'

'Yours was certainly a very sad start.'

'On that we can agree. Bad blood is a tradition on my father's side of the family, and one which my elder brother loyally upholds.'

'Have you seen him since you returned to England?'

'No,' he laughed, 'but, when I returned from the Middle East, I was awarded the DSC, which means little to me, but I enjoyed the thought of him reading his copy of *The Times* minutely, as he always did, and choking over his coffee when he saw the notice.' He waited for a huge, horse-drawn cart to cross the road, and said, 'Let's talk about pleasanter things, Agnes. I'm sure your childhood was Elysian compared with mine.'

'I was an only child, so I was spared sibling rivalry, and you're absolutely right. My childhood was a happy one.'

'Good,' he said, pulling into the hotel forecourt, 'I'm delighted to hear that.' He left the engine running and summoned one of the staff, who drove the Sunbeam into the hotel stable yard. Offering Agnes his arm, he took her into the lobby, where an official in morning dress directed them to the Palm Court Restaurant. An elderly waiter showed them to a table and left them with the menu after assuring them that everything listed on it was available.

'I feel that I'm forever asking you questions, Fred, but you almost invite curiosity.'

'Heaven forbid that I should ever be boring.'

'You're certainly not that,' she assured him.

'Tell me, then, what else has excited your interest?'

Agnes hesitated, as if thinking better of it, but then she asked, 'How, as a newcomer to New Zealand, did you find your way around, aged…? How old were you?'

'Eighteen. I was sent to a distant cousin, himself the grandson of a remittance man – I told you it was a family tradition – who'd built a successful trading company. I still haven't worked out what our relationship is, so I call him "Uncle Jim", and his wife is "Aunt Amelia". They're the best people on earth. They gave me a home, a job and a sense of worth. They even indulged me in my passion for flying. As importantly, they showed me that the unpleasantness, mistrust and guile we find around us are outweighed by kindness and goodwill.'

'How marvellous. I wondered at first if your past had left you sour, but now I know it hasn't.' Seemingly satisfied, she transferred her attention to the menu. 'You know,' she said, 'Living alone, as I do, I can't remember the last time I had a roast.'

'Make it a red-letter day and order one,' he advised her. 'Let today be remembered for that.'

'Thank you, I shall.'

'Are you completely alone, Agnes? I mean, have you no family?'

'No close family. My father died when I was quite young, and I lost my mother two years ago.'

'Two years? I really am sorry, Agnes.'

'Yes, my husband and my mother almost within a year.'

The waiter approached them, and they gave him their order. Fred asked, 'Does the roast turkey come with Yorkshire pudding?'

'No, sir. Yorkshire pudding is served with the beef, not with the turkey.'

'I think a break with tradition is called for.'

'I'm afraid that is the rule, sir.'

11

'So, no Yorkshire pudding?'

'No, sir.'

Fred gave the waiter a meaningful look. 'Not at any price?'

Without a change in his expression, the waiter said, 'It could perhaps be arranged, sir.'

'Excellent.'

When the waiter was gone, Agnes said, 'Fred, you're impossible. I believe you go through life getting your own way.'

Regarding her seriously, he said, 'I always make a point of having Yorkshire pudding with turkey. I enjoy them both and see no reason why they should be kept as strangers.' Reverting to an earlier subject, he asked, 'Have you no one to run your household, Agnes?'

'No, I had to learn to look after myself when I lost my husband. Staff are an expensive luxury.' She dismissed the subject and said, 'There must have been lots of remittance men who became successful. I'm thinking of innocent victims like you.'

'How do you know I was innocent?'

'Because you said so when we first met. You said something about your guilt being a matter of opinion.'

He hesitated, unsure of how his story might affect her. 'Are you easily shocked, Agnes?'

'I try to keep a sense of proportion.'

'In that case, you'll agree that wrongdoing varies in degree.'

'Naturally.'

He could delay it no longer. 'If you like to know, I was expelled from school.'

'Is that all?'

'You haven't heard everything. The assistant matron and I were found alone together, a very serious offence, even though all that passed between us was a harmless kiss. She was an innocent girl of eighteen, and I was guilty of sullying her reputation.'

'What happened to her?'

'She was initially dismissed from her post, but I managed to convince the headmaster that it was only at my repeated and forceful insistence that she'd joined me, so he took a more lenient line with her, conceding that she was in need of guidance and protection rather than punishment. He was a man of the cloth, you understand.' Adopting a rueful look, he added, 'But that didn't prevent him from giving me the severe beating he thought I deserved.'

'I'm sorry about the beating, and I don't believe for a second that you put pressure on her.'

'You're right to doubt it, Agnes. Coercion is alien to my character. I simply felt I owed it to the girl to get her reinstated, and the truth should never stand in the way of a worthy argument.'

She looked relieved. 'It was a worthy argument indeed, Fred, and you're a worthy scoundrel. 'You do seem adept, as well, at putting forward a telling case.'

'I'd wronged her and I had to make amends.'

She shook her head in protest. 'What you did was questionable, I agree, but you did the honourable thing in pleading her case.'

'The headmaster said it was the first honourable thing I'd done. He didn't know me all that well.'

'And your family sent you to New Zealand because of that?'

'It gave them the excuse they needed. I'd been at loggerheads with my father and my brother for some time, but seven generations of the Davies family had been educated at Tenbury School, and now, in one careless escapade, I'd brought disgrace on the venerable pile and on the family as well.'

Tentatively, she asked, 'Where did your mother stand in all this?'

'She was spared the unpleasantness, having died seven years earlier.'

'I'm sorry, Fred. I'd no idea.'

'No, you hadn't, so there's no need to be sorry.' To move the conversation on, he said, 'I remember my mother with great affection. Those who knew us were kind enough to say I'd inherited some of her qualities, and I hope that's true, although my indiscretion would certainly have shocked her.'

'Fred,' she said in a way that sounded almost motherly, 'you made a silly mistake, but you did more than atone for it, at least, in my opinion.'

'I suppose so, and you're very kind, Agnes.'

The subject was forgotten, at least for the time being, when the waiter arrived with their order.

When the main course materialised, they were less than surprised to see Fred's roast turkey sharing a plate with a fair-sized Yorkshire pudding.

** ** **

'And now you're going to drive me home. I feel utterly spoiled.'

'If it's been such a long time since you were spoiled, Agnes, it's surely overdue.'

'You're very kind.' She gathered her skirts so that he could close the door.

He started the engine and climbed in beside her. 'I've enjoyed every minute,' he said, and he meant it.

As they left the town centre and climbed the hill, Agnes asked, 'Will you return to New Zealand when the war's over?'

'Of course I will. It's my home, the best place on earth.'

'What's it like, I mean, physically?'

' "Beautiful" doesn't begin to describe it. Its mountains, forests and lakes are absolutely breath-taking, and the sea is as clear as glass. I have some photographs in my cabin that I took from the air—'

'From the air?'

'Yes, it's a hobby of mine. I brought them over to show the Navy what I had to offer. I'd heard of colonials being turned down by starchy senior officers, so I showed them I could fly and take pictures from the air.'

'Good for you.'

'I was thinking,' he said with new enthusiasm. 'If we can meet again, I'd like to show you those pictures. They're only photographs, of course, but how much colour do you need to see mountains and forests in snow?'

'None, I imagine.' She was quiet for a spell, and Fred was afraid he'd been a little too ambitious with his suggestion, but then Agnes said, 'Maybe we could have afternoon tea some time when we're both free, and then I'd love to see your photographs.'

'That's an excellent idea, Agnes. Thank you, I'll look forward to that.'

'How can I send you a message?'

'Just drop it in at the wardroom or even at the Main Gate. The weather's set to improve, they tell me, but I shan't be flying all the time.'

As they drew closer to Whitfield, Agnes asked, 'Why did they bring you home from the Middle East and post you to Dover, or was that a good thing?'

'It was a very good thing. Mesopotamia's an unhealthy place, but the reason they posted me was that I'd spoken my mind, as usual, and that doesn't go down well with senior officers. Home Establishment is easy compared with the Middle East or the Western Front, but the powers that be took the line that I'd be less of a nuisance here, and particularly on a seaplane base.'

'Why on a seaplane base?'

'Some senior officers take the Army's view and think that the seaplane's day is over, so they give us all the tedious, routine jobs to do, although, even then, we sometimes surprise them.' He drew into the side of the road beside Agnes's house and took out the umbrella. He offered her his arm, and they walked along the path to the door.

'Thank you for a delightful meal and an entertaining time, Fred. If I don't see you in the meantime, I'll send you a note.'

'Thank you for the very real pleasure of your company, Agnes.' He touched his cap.

'Are you going to bid me that native farewell again?'

'Of course. *E noho ra*, Agnes. Goodbye.'

'Until next time.'

'Until next time.'

3

The seaplane left the ramps and Fred was conscious immediately of the movement of the sea beneath the floats. A green flare burst overhead and, seeing only open water, he opened the throttle and headed for the harbour mouth. Once past the Eastern Fortress, he gave the engine full throttle. The air speed indicator needle flickered and began creeping clockwise. As it registered the optimum take-off speed, he eased back the joystick and felt the aircraft break free of the water's drag. Now airborne, he continued to climb, watching all the time for other aircraft.

The Short Type 184 was a magnificent seaplane, stable and reliable at a time when reliability was an emerging luxury. It was ideal for spotting, reconnaissance and anti-U-boat patrols; it could even launch an aerial torpedo, but it carried only one machinegun, and that was the domain of the observer, wireless operator or gunlayer, who normally occupied the after cockpit. On this occasion, Fred was alone, his task being to deliver the aircraft to the station at Dunkerque and to return with one of the single-seater Fairey Hamble Baby Seaplanes. He could only hope he wouldn't meet an enemy scout, as the single-seat fighter was known, on the way over. Whichever name they were given, just one would be more than a match for the slower, cumbersome Type 184, with no forward-firing gun.

It was a slow climb, but he eventually arrived at an economical altitude and settled on his course for Dunkerque, occasionally wiping the oil film from his goggles with the silk scarf that had become part of the flying kit. It had originally been adopted as protection against chafing by over-starched collars, although Fred made a practice of flying collarless. A senior officer might accuse him of being improperly dressed, but Fred had seen bodies of aircrew washed ashore, and the experience had taught him the important lesson that he, too, could find himself in an unforgiving sea, where a linen collar would shrink all too quickly and strangle him before he could unfasten the front stud.

The distance to Dunkerque was about fifty miles and, even with the south-westerly breeze against him, Fred was there in a little over forty-five minutes. He flew over the harbour to display his 'friendly' markings, and a green flare invited him to approach the seaplane station.

** ** **

After a surprisingly good lunch in the wardroom, Sam Curwen, a Canadian Fred had met on a previous visit, told him the secret.

'Shortage of food is a problem here, as well, Fred,' he said, 'but the French farmers sometimes come up trumps. Follow me.' He led the way to the galley, where the crew were hard at work washing the utensils. He called a Chinese galley boy over.

The boy came to him. 'Yessir?'

'Those hams I brought in this morning. Where are they?'

'Here, sir.' The boy indicated the meat safe.

'Give one to this officer.'

'Aye, aye, sir.' He took a large piece of ham from the meat safe and reached for clean muslin to wrap it.

'Before you do that,' said Fred, 'will you cut a steak off it, about so thick?' He showed him.

'No savvy, sir.'

'Cut there,' Sam told him. He watched the boy sharpen his knife and cut a generous steak off the ham.

'Wrap it up together.'

Again the Chinese boy seemed not to understand.

Sam made himself understood, partly by sign language, and the boy wrapped the ham and the steak together.

'Give him half-a-dozen eggs,' said Sam, showing him six fingers.

'Aye, aye, sir. Haffa duzzy eggs, sir.' He put the eggs into a strong paper bag.

'Thank you,' said Fred.

'Yes, thank you. Good boy.'

As they left the galley, Sam said, 'It's always a good idea to treat the Chinese gently. I remember a junior officer in the Royal Marines insulting a Chinese laundryman on one occasion. When he picked up his shirts from the laundry, they were as creased as hell, and one of them had a scorch mark left by an iron. They have their little ways of repaying an insult, and who can blame them?'

It seemed obvious to Fred, but he left that unsaid. 'Thank you for the ham and eggs, Sam,' he said.

Sam put a finger to his lips. 'I only brought them in this morning,' he said, 'so no one will be any the wiser, but it's still our secret.'

'Agreed, Sam, and thank you.'

They shook hands and Fred made his way to the landing, where the Fairey seaplane was waiting for him.

'It's fuelled up and armed, sir,' an air mechanic told him.

'Thank you. Will you pass this box up to me? It's quite fragile. There's a bottle as well.'

'Aye, aye, sir.' The rating waited for Fred to take his seat in the cockpit, and then handed the cardboard box containing the ham and eggs to him and then a bottle of cognac that he'd bought.

'Thank you. I just have to find a place for it.' He looked around the cramped cockpit with no immediate success. In the end, he wedged the box and bottle into the space beneath his seat. It was a tight fit, but all the more secure for that. 'Ready,' he told the air mechanic. Two more ratings stood beside the aircraft, ready to launch it.

'Switches off.'

'Switches off, sir,' confirmed the mechanic.

'Draw in.'

'Drawing in, sir.' The mechanic turned the propellor so as to draw petrol vapour and air into the combustion chamber.

'Contact.'

'Contact, sir.' The air mechanic swung the propeller. It coughed, but didn't catch, so he swung it again, and the engine started with a healthy roar. Fred gave the 'chocks away' signal, and the ratings pulled them out and pushed the seaplane down the ramp. He waved his thanks to them. It wasn't part of the drill, but those who observed it were remembered for it.

Once airborne, he climbed to eight thousand feet and levelled out. He was very fond of the Type 184, but he knew that the Fairey Hamble

Baby was faster and more agile. It couldn't carry anything heavier than two 65 lb bombs, but something had to be sacrificed for speed.

He'd been flying twenty minutes or so, when he caught sight of a destroyer, most likely of the Dover Patrol, and he wondered a little about the trials of serving in a ship of such meagre size.

The rattle of a machinegun interrupted his thoughts. He looked around and saw above him the familiar fat-belly fuselage of an LFG Roland. It was time to address the difference in altitude, so he opened the throttle and pushed the Baby into a half-loop, rolling out of it at the top and heading westward. The enemy aircraft was ahead of him, but now a little below. Its pilot wasn't in a hurry to change direction, as the sun, now beginning to wane to the west, was behind him. There was another rattle of machine-gunfire, and holes appeared in the fabric of the Baby's upper wing.

Fred began to throw the seaplane into a series of banking turns, first to starboard, then to port, never flying straight or level, but the pilot of the LFG continued to follow him, even though his enforced manoeuvring had forfeited to Fred the advantage of coming out of the sun. Fred saw his opponent raise an arm to shield his eyes, and he knew that the Hun was temporarily blinded. He pulled back the lever of the synchronising gear that enabled him to fire through the arc of the propellor without damaging it, and fired a long burst with the Lewis gun, during which he saw his bullets tear into the LFG's engine. Within seconds, flames were leaping from the enemy aircraft's fuselage. Watching it descend towards the sea, Fred located the destroyer and flew down to read its pennant number whilst returning the waves of the cheering officers and ratings on the bridge.

The LFG was now in the water, and the destroyer had altered course to pick up its pilot, supposing he were still alive.

With so much fuel spent in dogfighting, Fred had to continue on his way. He could only wonder at the state of the merchandise beneath his seat.

** ** **

His first call on arrival at the seaplane base was the galley, where he surprised the chief cook by giving him the ham minus the steak. He asked for muslin and wrapped the steak in it. Incredibly, the eggs

19

had survived the aerobatics during the dogfight, and he left the parcel temporarily in his cabin while he reported to the Squadron Office.

Squadron Commander Elliot asked, 'What time did you touch down, Fuller?' It was a loaded question.

'Fifteen-fifteen.'

Elliot consulted the large clock on the bulkhead and said, 'That was twelve minutes ago. Where the devil have you been since then?'

'In the galley, delivering tomorrow's breakfast.'

'What?'

'I was given a ham at Dunkerque. I think you'll enjoy it, and I'm sure everyone else will.'

'Don't be impertinent, Fuller. What else have you to report?'

'One enemy aircraft destroyed, an LFG Roland. The event was witnessed by a destroyer.' Fred tore the page from his notebook and passed it to Elliot. 'There's its pennant number.'

Elliot took the slip of paper with an ill grace. 'You're experienced and senior enough to know better than to go picking fights with enemy aircraft,' he said. 'Your task was simply to deliver the Short and return with the Fairey.'

'Nevertheless, the Hun fired at me. Had I not returned fire, I should have been unable to deliver the Fairey, because it would have been floating in the English Channel, a sorry and soggy monument to slavish obedience.' Ignoring his superior's angry reaction, he went on. 'I should like to claim the victory and see the watch bill for the week, please.'

Elliot contained his irritation and contrived, instead, a bored tone. He asked, 'How many is that now, Fuller?'

'I'm not a trophy hunter, as you know, but this one makes twenty-two.' He knew Elliot's tally was much lower.

'I see. The watch bill is on the bulkhead.'

'Thank you.' Fred studied the notice on the bulkhead. He was down for anti-U-boat patrol for the remainder of the week, but he would be free on Sunday.

'Off you go, Fuller.'

Fred saluted and left the Squadron Office. It was a little after fifteen-thirty, ample time to see Agnes before she closed the canteen.

It occurred to him that he should have washed before making

his way to the canteen, but he wanted to give her the ham and eggs while they were fresh. He knew very little about the care of food, and preferred to err on the side of safety. His appearance was less than salubrious after the flight, but he was sure Agnes would make allowances.

He pushed open the door and held up a restraining hand to the ratings who were about to stand. 'At ease, lads,' he said, 'I'm only visiting.' He turned to the counter, where Agnes and one of her staff were staring at him in something akin to alarm.

'It's only the intrepid aviator,' he assured them, realising that his oil-blackened face and white, goggle-shielded eyes must give him the appearance of a fugitive from a minstrel show. It was no wonder they were alarmed.

Sensing her supervisor's need for privacy, the girl went about her business.

'Fred,' said Agnes, 'why is your face so dirty?'

'It's oil from the aircraft's engine,' he explained. 'I've only just returned from France, and I decided, in these straitened times, to bring you an offering.' He handed her the bag and the bottle of cognac. 'The eggs came close to being scrambled this afternoon, but they survived. So did the bottle.'

'Good heavens! Thank you.' It was as if he'd delivered riches, which, in view of the current situation, they no doubt were.

'There's a gammon steak in there as well,' he told her.

'Thank you. I wasn't expecting—'

'The best presents are the unexpected ones.'

She looked around her and motioned towards the door.

'Fred,' she said when they were outside, 'these things are like manna from Heaven.'

'In a sense, I suppose they are.'

'Of course. Silly of me.' She seemed to brace herself before speaking again. 'If you're free, would you like to come to afternoon tea this coming Sunday?'

'I am free, and I can't imagine anything I'd like better, Agnes.'

'About three-thirty?'

'On the dot, and I'll wash before I come. I'll leave my helmet and goggles behind as well.'

'I'm sure you will. Thank you again for the ham and eggs and the cognac,' she said, smiling. 'They're a lovely surprise.'

He returned to his quarters for a bath and to write his report.

** ** **

He'd just finished dressing when he received a visit from one of the new flight sub-lieutenants, an awkwardly enthusiastic youth with a name connected in some way with the porcelain industry.

'I say, sir, is it true?'

'That Nanny's drawers are blue? That they start round her tum and envelope her bum and cover her stocking-tops, too?'

'No, sir. I meant that you got a Hun this afternoon.'

'Yes, Doulton, it's true.'

'Actually, it's Rockingham, sir.'

'I'm sorry, Rockingham, Aren't you glad your name's not Dresden? In the current climate, you'd have had very few friends.'

'That's all right, sir. I certainly would, but is it true, as well, that it was your twenty-ninth kill?'

'No, it was my twenty-second victory. I don't call them "kills", Rockingham. Come in and take a seat. There's something you should know.'

The boy entered the cabin and looked around for a chair.

'Sit on the bunk. I'm not using it, as you can see.'

'It's awfully good of you to spend time with a new chap like me, sir.' Rockingham sat excitedly on the edge of Fred's bunk, looking as if his housemaster had invited him for tea.

'It's highly necessary, because if no one curbs your silly, schoolboy notions of duelling in the skies, you people will simply go off and get yourselves killed. The Hun's an old hand at the game and he has a trick or two up his sleeve, believe me.'

'But you got that one this afternoon, sir.' The boy's eyes were glowing with admiration.

'Only because I, too, have had some experience. I began flying three years before the war, and I've been on active service since early nineteen-fifteen, Rockingham. I spent time in France and then the Middle East, fighting the Turks, but now, I'm here to fly anti-submarine patrols, and so are you. This is your job.'

22

'But, sir—'

'No, Rockingham. Listen to me.' He was beginning to wonder if he could ever persuade this youth to put aside his foolish ideas of glory. 'I only became involved with the LFG because he fired first. If he hadn't been stupid enough to draw attention to himself by engaging me, he might still have been alive.'

'Everyone's talking about your latest kill, sir.'

'So I'm the talk of the gun room, am I? I'd rather that were not so, and I'd still rather you didn't refer to my victories as "kills". I never set out to kill anyone. I know the word's used in France, but that's where a pilot's lifespan can be counted on the fingers of two hands, and I'm talking in terms of days rather than years.' He had to remember that the youngster wasn't long out of school. It was less than surprising that he was full of romantic notions about the knights of the air, and duels fought among the clouds. He'd probably collected cigarette card pictures of 'aces', many of whom had since been killed. 'Listen to me, Rockingham, because all I'm trying to do is to save your hide. We are here to fly anti-U-boat patrols. It's highly necessary and just as important as doing battle with the Marinefliegerabteilung.'

'Sir?'

'The naval arm of the German air corps, Rockingham, and most likely your nemesis if you don't listen to me and remember what I'm saying.'

'Yes, sir.'

'So, having made the point that you'll live a damned sight longer than anyone on the Western Front, let me advise you to settle for it, and remember that you're helping to save the country from starvation.'

Rockingham looked downcast. 'I feel foolish now, sir,' he said.

'It'll wear off,' said Fred gently, 'but the memory of it may just stand you in good stead.' He stood up and said, 'Now, cut along to the gun room and tell the others to stop talking tommy-rot as well.'

'Aye, aye, sir.'

'Chin up, Rockingham. Everyone's allowed to behave like an ass once in a while, even the aces you idolise.' He added modestly, 'Even I'm allowed a red face occasionally.' He watched the boy go, chastened and disappointed, but he told himself, better a disillusioned youth than a lamb to the slaughter.

A Worthy Scoundrel

He was looking forward to Sunday all the more, now. As well as spending time with Agnes, he would be spared, albeit temporarily, the jealousy of superior officers and the naivete of vulnerable schoolboys.

4

Agnes was wearing a lilac dress trimmed with a white neckline and white lace cuffs. Her hair was carefully pinned, and Fred wondered briefly, although privately, how it would look unfettered.

'Simply to look at you, Agnes, is a tonic.' He took her hand and kissed it in greeting.

'You're too kind, Fred. Do come in and let me take your things.' She took his greatcoat, cap, scarf and gloves. 'Make yourself comfortable in the dining room,' she said, pointing the way. 'I'll hang these up and brew the tea. The kettle's almost boiled.' She added apologetically, 'Because of the shortage of wood, I'm afraid there's no fire in the sitting room.'

Fred took his briefcase with him into the small dining room, with its velvet curtains and table laid for tea. The most welcoming feature, a log fire, was burning in the oak-framed fireplace. In all, the scene was infinitely more cheerful than the one he'd left behind at the seaplane base.

He looked further and saw photographs, including one, presumably, of the late Sub-Lieutenant Morley. Not surprisingly, he looked youthful; not as young as Rockingham, but the two images created, momentarily, an uncomfortable association. Agnes's late husband had been one of only fifteen fatal casualties at Dogger Bank, which had been a British victory. It was a stroke of irony that seemed to make his death all the more poignant.

The rattle of a cup and saucer alerted him to Agnes's reappearance, this time with a tray of tea things.

'Let me take that,' he said, relieving her of the burden. 'Where would you like me to put it?'

She smiled, possibly at the naivete of his question. 'On the table behind you, if you will.'

Fred turned and placed the tray on the dining table.

'I have just two more things to fetch,' she said.

'Let me help you.'

She laughed. 'There's nothing heavy, unless you count the cake, which is rather heavier than either Mrs Beeton or I intended.'

'I'm nevertheless at your disposal.' He followed her to the kitchen, where she showed him a plate of muffins and a Madeira cake on a stand. 'I'm glad I volunteered,' he said. 'You could never have managed these things alone.'

'I'll bring a toasting fork. That won't be too heavy for me.'

'Bring two if you have a spare one,' he said.

He carried the muffins and the cake to the dining room and put them on the table, next to the tray.

'How do you like your tea, Fred? I'm afraid lemons are impossible to find nowadays.'

'It's no matter. With milk, but no sugar, please.'

'This is one task I can perform,' she said, pouring tea into two cups.

'I think you're doing yourself an injustice.'

'You haven't tried the cake yet,' she told him nervously.

'Never mind the cake for now. Are we going to toast the muffins?'

'Would you like them toasted? I brought toasting forks.'

'In that case, let's do it together.' He offered his hand for support while she lowered herself to the floor and arranged her skirts by the fireside.

'To say you were banished to the colonies in disgrace, Fred, you're the most courteous man I know.'

' "Dastardly but dignified" they call me.'

'I don't believe you,' she said, fixing half a muffin to her toasting fork.

'Nevertheless, that's been the story of my life. I've been unfairly criticised, as you know, and it doesn't end with my family.' The delightful memory of his recent encounter with Elliot sprang to mind, and he said, 'My squadron commander is positively eaten up with jealousy.'

'The man we met outside the chapel?'

'The very same.'

'But why?'

'I suppose he lacks my handsome profile and urbane persona. Who can blame him for resenting those things.' He turned his half-muffin and began toasting the other side. The log settled in the grate, creating a minor shower of sparks that clung tenuously to the fireback before being snatched upward by the draught.

'I haven't done this since I was a girl,' said Agnes, possibly having settled for the fact that a sensible answer to her question was not forthcoming.

'Neither have I.'

'But you were never a girl.' Her eyes mocked him.

'It was such a long time ago, I'll have to take your word for it.'

'The butter's on the table.'

'Let me give you a hand up.'

'You spoil me, Fred.' She nevertheless took the hand he offered.

'Did you go to school, Agnes?' He motioned to her to help herself to butter.

'No, I had a tutoress, a very clever woman. She taught me English, arithmetic, Latin, history, geography, music and the needle arts. There were just two things that, because of my station in life, I was never required to learn, and they were cookery and baking, as you will discover if you try the cake.'

'You're afraid of that cake, aren't you? It's become an ogre in this very room.'

'You've noticed.' Looking at his empty cup, she asked, 'Would you like some more tea?'

'Yes, please, and by the way, these muffins are excellent.'

'I bought them from the baker.' She regarded them wistfully and said, 'I should have bought a cake from him as well.'

'That cake has assumed a threatening importance quite disproportionate to its size, and the only way to lay that kind of fear is to challenge it head-on.'

'How?' She eyed the cake nervously.

'By cutting into it and calling its bluff.'

'Do you feel the risk is justified?'

'I do.'

She took a knife and a napkin and cut slowly and deliberately into the cake. 'It cuts well,' she commented, making a second cut, 'but that doesn't mean a thing.' She transferred the wedge of cake to his plate. 'I baked it longer than Mrs Beeton recommended,' she confessed. 'I didn't want it to be underbaked,' she said, adding unsurely, 'if there is such a word.'

'I'm sure there is,' he told her soothingly. He examined the piece of cake closely and broke off a corner, which he put into his mouth.

Agnes watched him with discernible dread. 'Don't feel that you have to be diplomatic,' she said.

'This is not a bad cake,' he told her when he could speak, 'although it's too dry to be a good one, so maybe you did overbake it a little, and I'm still confident that the word exists.'

'Oh dear.'

'There is a remedy,' he assured her.

'Is there?'

'There is indeed, and the answer is on the table before you.' He transferred some butter from the dish to his plate and proceeded to butter the cake while she watched him in disbelief. Finally, he tried a piece.

'Put me out of my misery, Fred. I so wanted this tea party to be a success and not made a mockery by the cake.'

'Banish your misery, Agnes. The improvement is remarkable. Try it yourself.'

'Really?' She reached out and took his hands, realising immediately what she'd done. 'I'm so sorry. I was rather excited.'

'Please don't apologise. As for the success of the occasion, that's never been in doubt.'

'Hasn't it?'

'Not for a moment.' He reached for his briefcase. 'Would you like to see these photographs I've brought?'

'Oh yes, please.' She buttered a piece of cake, still looking uneasy.

He took out a collection of half-plate prints, handing them to her in turn. 'That first one's Milford Sound,' he said, 'and here's another, but taken at a lower altitude.'

'My goodness, how wonderful! Those rocks are absolutely sheer.'

He waited until she was ready to see more. 'These are the Cathedral Caves. You can only get into them at low tide. I took this one,' he said, handing her another, 'in Wanaka.'

'Those mountains are just… magnificent.'

He continued to show her pictures of mountains, lakes, forests and bays. 'All these photographs I took over South Island,' he said. 'North Island's less than fourteen miles across the Cook Strait, and it would mean nothing at all to a pilot nowadays, but it was a different matter before the war.'

'I didn't know it was possible to take photographs and drive an aeroplane at the same time,' she said.

'It takes skill,' he told her, holding a serious expression as long as he could.

'I know you're joking, but it must. I mean, how do you get a steady picture when you're flying at goodness-knows-what speed?'

'You're so high in the air that the ground doesn't seem to rush past you. It looks quite still, and you can get a long exposure.'

She nodded. Whether or not she really understood was uncertain, because she changed the subject by saying, 'I remember your telling me you brought these to help you get into the Navy. I imagine photographs from above must be quite useful in wartime.'

'They should be, and I shouldn't tell you this, but I don't care. A chap in the RFC once told me that they take pictures of gun emplacements and troop movements all the time, but whether the High Command take any notice of them or not is a mystery, although the evidence is far from encouraging.'

Remembering her duty as a hostess, Agnes asked, 'Shall I make some fresh tea?'

He looked at his pocket watch. 'If you're happy with that,' he said, 'but I don't want to overstay my welcome.'

'You're not likely to do that. I'll fill the kettle, and if there's anything else you'd like, just tell me.'

When she returned, he said, 'Much as I enjoyed your greatly-improved cake, I'd rather like another muffin, please.'

'I think I'll have one too, when I've made some tea.'

She returned a few minutes later, and they left the table and went to the fireside once more to toast the last two muffins.

'I can't tell you,' she said, 'how special this is….' She stopped, realising she was repeating herself.

'You haven't toasted muffins since you were a girl, I know, and I haven't since I left New Zealand, so it's special for me, too.'

'I'm glad you found a proper home there, and I'm glad you came back to help with the war, too.'

'Yes, they might have struggled without me. My squadron commander would disagree, but he has no imagination.'

'You know what I mean.' Remembering something she'd heard, she said, 'One of the boys who come regularly to the canteen said you'd shot down an enemy seaplane.'

'It was an aeroplane, actually.' He smiled mischievously. 'That's how your eggs narrowly avoided being scrambled.' As an afterthought, he added, 'Your gammon steak only just escaped perforation, as well.'

'How can you joke about it?'

'It was less dangerous than you'd think, Agnes. It was the Hun's fault. He started it, so I had to respond. According to my squadron commander, I shouldn't have got into a fight with an enemy aircraft, but he wasn't there, so he hadn't a clue.'

'Maybe he was just jealous because he's not as handsome and sophisticated as you.'

'That's all it is. I suffer for my flawless Grecian features and my engaging demeanour.'

'It serves you right for being so conceited about them.' She looked at his cup and asked, 'More tea?'

'One more,' he said, 'and then, with the greatest regret, I must leave you.'

Pouring the tea, she asked, 'Why did you have to go to France, or shouldn't I ask?'

'Last week?'

'Yes.'

'Nothing important. I had to deliver a seaplane to the base at Dunkerque and bring back another, that's all.' He leaned towards her confidentially and said, 'If I have to go again, I'll bring you something different, but I shan't know what it will be until I arrive there. It'll be a great big surprise.'

'It's very kind of you.' Then, changing the subject abruptly, she asked, 'Have you seen the boy whose brother was killed?'

'Beresford? Yes, he's back in harness and he seems to be coping well. I had a few words with him when I saw him.'

'I'm glad. All I could do was give him tea and bread and dripping. It was all he wanted.'

'All the same, it helped.' He looked again at his watch and said, 'It's time I was elsewhere, Agnes. Thank you for a very special treat.'

'Thank you too, Fred. I'll get your things.'

She helped him on with his coat and handed his gloves to him. 'Oh, there's your scarf as well.' She took it from the hook.

'Thank you.' He draped it round his neck. 'Agnes, if I'm being too presumptuous, just tell me and I'll not trouble you again....'

'What do you mean?'

'In my apologetic way, I'm working up to asking you if you'll join me for dinner some time, now that the restaurants don't seem quite so embarrassed by the shortage of food.'

'I'll be happy to.' She was smiling.

He took her hand again and kissed it. Then, on an impulse, he leaned forward and kissed her cheek. '*E noho ra.*'

She seemed unperturbed. '*E noho ra.*'

'No, you're the one who's staying, so you say, '*Haere ra.*'

'There's a lot to learn. Until the next time, Fred.'

'Until the next time, Agnes. I'll be in touch.'

5

FEBRUARY

The wisdom of deploying unarmed reconnaissance aircraft on anti-U-boat patrols was more than questionable, at least, to Fred's way of thinking. A U-boat's speed was negligible, so the procedure on sighting one was to transmit its position and course to Dover by wireless so that a destroyer could be directed to intercept it. It seemed to Fred that it would be much simpler to launch a torpedo against a surfaced U-boat, but Squadron Commander Elliot disagreed. The increased fuel consumption when carrying a torpedo or bombs, he argued, curtailed the Type 184 seaplane's duration, and time spent in reconnaissance was clearly precious. They had to agree on one principle, however, which was that the aircraft's most effective role, by its very presence, was to force the U-boat to submerge to a depth that precluded mischief.

An anticyclone had settled on south-east England, making the temperature unusually warm for February, and the change was particularly welcome. Fred had been able to shed two layers of clothing, and the freedom of movement it afforded was an additional luxury.

Half a mile to starboard, Rockingham was following a parallel course, whilst Ferris, the other new pilot, was momentarily obscured by cloud, but he reappeared after a few seconds, thankfully also on course.

Fred opened his pocket watch, currently dangling by its chain from the instrument panel, and noted the time. The flight had been on patrol almost two hours, and he was about to tell Albert Dixon, his observer, to fire the recall flare, when Albert's voice came through the Gosport tube.

'U-boat on the starboard beam, Fred, about a thousand yards!'

Fred looked along the bearing and saw the white wake of the

U-boat. It must have surfaced and then seen the aircraft. It wouldn't be on the surface for long. 'Fire the recall, Albert, and then get the position and course off to Dover Patrol HQ.'

Two consecutive flares shot into the sky, ordering Rockingham and Ferris to return to base. Fred hung around long enough to see that they did so, and then followed them. If he'd had bombs or, better still, a torpedo, he could have dealt with the U-boat in the short time it was on the surface, but the orders were as inflexible as the squadron commander himself.

The safety of his flight members was his responsibility, and one which he regarded as sacrosanct. He had only a sub-flight with him that morning, but the other two pilots were young and inexperienced, so he felt the responsibility all the more keenly, taking up station about five hundred yards astern of Rockingham so that he could watch them both put their machines down in Dover harbour.

A green flare burst over the slipway, and Ferris touched down quite capably, continuing to his berth. It was now Rockingham's turn, but he seemed to have other ideas because, instead of following Ferris into the harbour, he regained altitude and turned towards the west. Fred was now divided in his anxieties for Rockingham's safety and his own ability to put down before running out of fuel. With no fuel contents gauge, he could only calculate roughly what remained in his tank from the time spent in the air, and his deliberations left no room for joyriding or whatever Rockingham had in mind.

Rockingham was now flying over the town and turning southward, as if intending to make a complete circuit. Eventually, he turned again, causing Fred to take evasive action, and made his descent untidily into the harbour. Now that he was down, Fred could return gratefully to the seaplane base.

When his aircraft had been winched up and its wings folded, he went straight to the gun room, where he startled a group of midshipmen by demanding, 'Is Flight Sub-Lieutenant Rockingham here?'

The group of midshipmen parted to reveal Rockingham, who now looked shocked and nervous.

'If this is because I got rather close to you on my way in, sir, I—'

'That's only a tiny part of it, Rockingham. Unless you wish to be roasted in public, you'd better step out here.' Turning to the midshipmen, he said, 'The rest of you, get on with what you're supposed to be doing.' He stepped outside the gun room and waited until Rockingham had closed the door behind him and stood sheepishly before him.

'What was the purpose of your aerial display, Rockingham?'

'I'm sorry, sir. I couldn't resist a final joyride. It's such a beautiful morning—'

'Would you describe yourself as a child of nature?'

'Not really, sir.'

'So it wasn't filial loyalty that made you behave like an irresponsible, inconsiderate half-wit.'

'What, sir? Oh, I see what you mean, sir.'

'How much fuel did you have in reserve?'

Rockingham's eyes flickered with guilt. 'I don't know, sir. There's no way of knowing, is there, sir?' Too late, he seemed about to see the possible consequence of his stupidity.

'You had no way of knowing. You could very easily have run out of petrol and come down in the town, possibly killing or maiming innocent people as well as destroying a valuable aircraft.'

Rockingham hung his head miserably. 'I know I've been an ass and I'm sorry, sir.'

'I haven't finished with you yet. How much fuel do you imagine I had?'

'O Lord, sir, I really have been a complete ass, haven't I?'

'I'm glad you realise that, Rockingham. Now, you're as green as grass, but you can't help that. Otherwise, you're not a hopeless case, and I'm not going to refer you to the squadron commander, so there's no need to pack your trousers with blotting paper yet.'

'I'm ever so grateful, sir.'

'I'd rather you were ever so sensible, Rockingham. More than anything, I want you to realise that this is a war, not an inter-school cricket match, and that there's no excuse for following your devices and desires, not to mention playing bloody silly pranks. There must be absolutely no joyriding at all! Is that clear?'

'Yes, sir.'

'Carry on, Rockingham.'

'Aye, aye, sir, and thank you, sir.'

'Step out of line again and you'll have nothing to thank me for.'

He continued to the Squadron Office, where he found Elliot in his habitually judgemental state of mind.

'I have two questions, Fuller. Where have you been until now? Also, what was the purpose of that ridiculous display?' He motioned unnecessarily towards the window.

'And I have but one explanation, which should nevertheless answer both your questions. I have been dispensing advice to Flight Sub-Lieutenant Rockingham, who was so fearful of making an untidy and possibly dangerous put-down that he elected to make an extra circuit to correct his approach.'

'How long does it take you to impart a word of advice, Fuller?'

Fred looked up at the bulkhead clock. 'In this case, only about five minutes.' He added by way of explanation, 'I was being particularly succinct.'

'I think you were being self-indulgent, Fuller.'

'The advice was purely for his benefit.' Before Elliot could muster another attack, he went on to say, 'As you know, I have seven years' experience as a pilot, and it's my duty to give youngsters such as Rockingham the benefit of my wisdom.'

Finding himself in a state of checkmate, Elliot tried another line of attack. 'Fuller, do you no longer feel that it's necessary to address me as "sir"?'

'I wouldn't go as far as that, exactly.'

'Well, don't you think you ought, even occasionally?'

'Occasionally, yes.' Fred counted silently up to seven and said, 'Sir.'

'Go about your duties, Fuller.'

'Aye, aye... sir.'

** ** **

'Perhaps bizarrely, I feel that respect, and I mean *true* respect, should be earned, Agnes. When I was at school, I addressed the masters as "sir" to avoid the beating that was the accepted punishment for not doing so. That was fear. Only two of them earned my respect.' He and Agnes were in the Palm Court Restaurant of the Corunna Hotel, and Fred had just told the story of his encounter with Elliot.

'I'm glad you didn't report that boy for his silliness.'

'He was lucky. As much as for any other reason, I was loath to give Elliot the satisfaction of reprimanding a member of my flight.' He picked up the wine and asked, 'May I?'

'No, thank you.' Agnes was more interested in the rift between Fred and Elliot. 'You've joked about his jealousy,' she said, 'but what really is the bone of contention between you?'

For the moment, Fred feigned hurt. 'Do you mean you don't find me more handsome and charming than he is?'

'Who could deny that? Even so, I sense something much deeper between the two of you.'

'There's nothing deep about Elliot, Agnes,' said Fred, refilling his glass. 'He's as superficial as a coat of varnish. No, he simply resents the fact that I have more experience, and that I've achieved more than he has.'

'In that case, why does he outrank you?'

'He's a professional RN officer who's never left the country, whereas I'm a temporary gentleman and a colonial.'

'You're an Englishman,' she protested.

'And I don't care two hoots. I'm not trying to make a career in the Navy. When the war's over and won, please God, I'll go back to New Zealand and concentrate on becoming a true colonial.'

'I believe you will.'

'I'm determined, Agnes.' He put his hand on hers before realising what he'd done and withdrawing it guiltily. 'I'm sorry,' he said.

'There's no need to apologise.' Clearly, his future in the service was still on her mind, because she said, 'There was something you said when we first met, something that puzzled me. It was when I kept addressing you by the wrong rank.'

'That's nothing to worry about.'

'No, but it puzzled me all the same. It was about the Air Force Act that went through Parliament last year. You said it would create further confusion.'

'In more senses than one,' he confirmed. 'When you consider that the Admiralty and the War Office haven't been able to co-operate with each other since the war began, the creation of a central air force makes an uncomfortable kind of sense, but can you imagine the disagreements that must inevitably take place?'

'No, but it's beyond the scope of my experience.'

'Have some more wine, Agnes. I don't want to drink it all.'

'Oh well, just a little, then.'

He topped up her glass. 'All right. Can you imagine the Navy, with its four hundred years of tradition, agreeing with the Army when they come to name the ranks and rates in the new service? As well as that, can you see them agreeing on the new uniform?'

'Now that you mention it, no, I can't.'

'And that's a mere bagatelle compared with some of the decisions that will have to be made. The biggest stumbling block, however, is going to be right at the top.'

'Whatever do you mean, Fred?'

'General Trenchard is Chief of the Air Staff. He has absolutely no time for the Navy, and he regards naval flying as a military irrelevance.'

'I'd no idea.'

'It's inside information that's come down the grapevine, but it's certainly food for thought, if you'll allow me to mix metaphors.'

Realising that, once again, his hand was on hers, he removed it, but she took it back. 'If it helps you to express yourself,' she told him, 'you're welcome to touch my hand.'

'You can tell I'm only a temporary gentleman.'

'I know differently, Fred, and I'd like to know how you feel about this central air force.'

'As I said, it makes sense after all the disagreements, but I came here to join the Navy, not some new army in disguise, and I do care about the future of naval flying. Whatever Trenchard believes, there will be a need for air power at sea, and for pilots and observers who can recognise what they're looking at, who can tell a battleship from a destroyer, and who can calculate the position and course of a ship at sea and estimate its speed.' He looked down, aware that he'd taken her hand between his. She seemed unfazed by it.

'How is it likely to affect you?'

'Goodness only knows. I just hope we can win this war quite soon, so that I can go home and leave them all to organise their new air force.' He looked around for the waiter. 'Would you like coffee, Agnes?'

'Shall we? It's such a treat now that there's none in the shops.'

Fred summoned the waiter and ordered coffee.

'I'll miss you when you return to New Zealand,' she said. 'My friends are scattered all over the country. Getting to know you has been rather special.'

'You could always give New Zealand a try. There are worse places to live.'

'Don't joke about it, Fred. In fact, let's not talk about it. I'm sorry I mentioned it.'

'All right, it's a forbidden subject from now on.' Partly in an effort to introduce a new one, he asked, 'When did you last have leave?'

'It was so long ago, I can't remember. In any case, it's not a great deal of use to me nowadays.'

The waiter arrived with the coffee. When he'd gone, Fred said, 'They say that a change is as good as... something or other, and it must be true, or people wouldn't keep saying it.'

'What do you have in mind, Fred?'

'For the sake of doing something different, and if you could get a few days' leave, we could maybe go to a London theatre or something like that.' He felt suddenly awkward. 'Not that I'm suggesting anything at all improper,' he assured her.

'That's a good idea, Fred. I've done so little with my time over the past few years, and I never doubted your intentions for a second.'

'It's something we can plan, and I'm bound to get leave. It just has to coincide with yours.'

'It shouldn't be difficult.'

They talked until Agnes looked at the time and decided it was time to go. Fred paid the bill, the waiter brought their coats and hats, and they went out to where a member of the hotel staff had parked the motorcar.

'It must be an awful nuisance,' said Agnes, 'having to wind that big handle each time you want to start the engine. It seems such hard work.'

'Until someone invents something better, it's the only way. To start an aircraft,' he told her as he released the brake, 'someone has to swing the propellor.'

'Isn't that dangerous?'

'Not if the chap swinging the prop remembers to let go.'

'That's silly.'

'It's truer than you think.'

They drove to Whitfield, enjoying the mild air while they could. Eventually, Fred parked outside the garden gate.

'There's no need for an umbrella this time,' said Agnes. It was a welcome change.

Fred opened the passenger door and helped her out. They walked up the path together.

'Thank you for a perfectly lovely evening,' she said.

'Thank you for being a part of it. I'll make enquiries about leave and let you know what happens.'

'Good.' She turned the key in her door.

'*E noho ra.*'

'*Haere ra.*'

'You remembered.'

'Of course.'

He took her gloved hand in his and kissed her cheek, hesitating for a second and then kissing her again. 'Until next time, Agnes.'

'Until next time, Fred.'

6

George Makepeace, a second-generation Australian from Brisbane, and Fred's opposite number in 'A' Flight, was already in the squadron office when Fred arrived. Elliot had summoned them to tell them about a matter of 'operational importance.'

On hearing the door open and close, George turned and said, 'G' day, Fred.'

'Good morning, George. Good morning, Squadron Commander Elliot.'

'I'm glad you could find the time to attend this meeting, Fuller. We've been waiting for you so that we can begin.'

'Only about two minutes,' George told him comfortingly.

'That's beside the point, Makepeace. He's late and therefore guilty of an unpardonable lack of consideration.'

Fred thought it was time he said something. 'I apologise to those seriously affected by my delayed arrival,' he said, looking at the bulkhead clock, 'because two minutes represent... well, two minutes. There's no denying it, is there?'

'No denying it at all,' agreed George in his habitual deadpan manner, 'not for one minute.' He considered that briefly and added, 'Or two minutes, if it comes to that.'

'Oh, for goodness' sake, you fellows. Let's get on.'

'Just one minute,' said Fred, 'and I mean one minute, not two. You haven't yet heard why I was two minutes late.'

'Perhaps you'd like to tell me, and then we can get on with the meeting.'

'It's this bloody war. It keeps finding jobs for me to do.'

'You know, Fred,' said George, 'I find the same bloody thing. Day after day after bloody day—'

'Will you both stop this ridiculous rambling and let me begin?' Elliot's impatience had finally given way to anger. 'I told you both that I had something of operational importance to make known to you, and I think you'll agree when I tell you that the Type One-Eight-Fours are to be withdrawn from anti-U-boat patrol.'

Neither of the officers was entirely surprised; Elliot's dislike of the Type One-Eight-Four was well-known, but to mothball them was ludicrous.

George asked, 'To be replaced with what, exactly?'

'You'll be flying the Fairey Hamble Baby. It carries two sixty-five-pound bombs and still has a duration of two hours.'

'Whereas,' said Fred, 'the One-Eight-Four carries a fourteen-inch torpedo or a five-hundred-pound bombload, either of which only reduces its duration to two hours.'

'The "Hamble" is faster and more agile than the One-Eight-Four,' insisted Elliot.

'How fast and agile does it have to be,' asked George, 'to attack a U-boat making less than seventeen knots on the surface?'

'It lessens the risk of the U-boat diving before it can be attacked.'

'That's bloody ridiculous.' George shared Fred's rebellious nature, to the extent that Elliot had been known to complain loudly about the 'disruptive colonial element' in his squadron.

'You two can argue as much as you like, but the fact remains that you'll be flying the Hamble.'

'They don't want to win this bloody war,' said George, as if the possibility had only just occurred to him. 'They're sending out seaplanes with toy bombs and no wireless capability, presumably hoping that the Hun U-boat crews will die laughing.'

'Be fair, George,' said Fred. 'A sixty-five-pound bomb placed next to a U-boat's hull could give the skipper a very nasty headache, so that he'd have to take a powder and lie down in a darkened bunk space, thereby depriving the U-boat and its crew of leadership.'

'You've got a fair point there, mate,' said George. 'I wonder if our superiors are secretly hoping for that outcome.'

'Another thing that's occurred to me,' said Fred, ignoring Elliot's visibly mounting fury, 'is that – and I offer this suggestion with full and proper respect – it's just possible that a mistake was made in drafting the order, and that instead of "operational importance", it should have read "operational impotence". It makes a deal more sense.'

'It makes total sense to me, mate.'

Controlling his ire with difficulty, Elliot said, 'I think you'd both better leave now and give the information to your flight members.'

'You know,' said George, 'I can't help thinking that if you'd summoned them as well as us, it would have saved a lot of time and effort.'

'In this tiny office?'

'I don't know,' said Fred. 'It would have been cosy, admittedly, but better for morale, I'd say.'

'But only up to the bit about mothballing the One-Eight-Fours,' said George. 'That would really have upset them.'

'That's still on the cards.'

'Go,' ordered Elliot.

George made for the door, but Fred remained behind to say, 'I need to ask you about something.'

'It had better be something sensible,' warned Elliot.

'It's very sensible,' Fred assured him. 'I want to request a short period of leave.'

'Well, all I can say is that you've gone the wrong way about it this morning.'

'That's all right. If you feel disinclined to co-operate, I can always call on Wing Commander Bryant. When he realises that I've had no leave since....' He searched his memory. 'I can't remember how long it's been, but I'm sure he'll be sympathetic.'

With defeat staring him in the face, Elliot relented. 'All right,' he said, 'I'll put in a request on your behalf for a seventy-two-hour pass.'

** ** **

Later in the week, Fred called at the canteen and found Agnes alone, her staff having gone home.

'I've just heard that I've been given leave,' he said after delivering a discreet and chaste kiss on her cheek.

'How long?'

'Seventy-two hours. I just hope it's not too soon for you to arrange leave for yourself. It's officially from next Friday, so I could get away on Thursday evening.'

'It shouldn't be difficult. The Canteen Board are quite accommodating, and you're not the only one who's not had leave for quite some time. I'll send in my request tomorrow morning.'

He looked around the empty canteen and asked, 'Are you about to close for the day?'

'Yes.'

'Will you let me drive you home?'

'It's a lot of trouble for you, Fred.' Nevertheless, it was clear that she was tempted.

'If you remember, we had this conversation earlier, and I told you it was no trouble at all. Also, if I were to go back to the wardroom now, I'd only have to make conversation with Squadron Commander Elliot, and we've seen enough of each other to last us both a lifetime.'

'All right, you've convinced me. Thank you, I'd appreciate your driving me home.' She took her coat from its hanger and allowed him to help her into it. Finally, she took her hat and set it on her head, checking her reflection in the window.

'Perfect,' he said, favouring her with a salute.

'Don't be silly.'

'Madam, your carriage awaits.' He waited for her to lock the outer door, and offered her his arm.

As he reached inside the Sunbeam to advance the ignition, she asked, 'Why do you do that?'

'It makes it possible to start the engine from cold. It takes a little time to burn the fuel, and this,' he said, touching the ignition switch, 'just makes sure it's burning when the piston is at the top and ready to deliver maximum power.'

'I didn't understand a word of that.'

'You don't need to. If you're going to drive a motor, you just need to know that it's necessary to advance the ignition before starting the engine.' He swung the starting handle and the engine came to life.

'Would you like to learn to drive, Agnes?' He asked the question as he settled in the driving seat and released the brake.

'I don't know. It doesn't seem terribly ladylike, somehow.'

'I wouldn't tell anyone, and you don't want to be weak and feeble all your life, do you?'

'How dare you? I'm not at all weak and feeble. I'll have you know, I'm a supporter of the Suffragette Movement.'

'Are you?' It was surprising news.

'Well, I signed their petition.' She looked at him via the corner of her eye and asked, 'Do you disapprove of that?'

'Why should I? Women have the vote in New Zealand. Why shouldn't they have it here as well?'

'Have they?' It was clearly a surprise.

'Yes, since eighteen ninety-three. Enzed's a very forward-looking country.'

'Good heavens. I never realised that. I mean, that women had the vote there.'

'It's not really surprising,' he said, pulling out into the main road, 'when you consider that it happened at the other side of the world and before you were born.'

'How do you know it was before I was born?'

'I was one year old at the time. I'm twenty-five, almost twenty-six, and I'm sure you're younger than me.'

'What makes you so sure?' She seemed to be in an argumentative mood.

'I wouldn't dream of asking a lady's age, but you're so young-looking, I'm convinced you're nowhere near as old as I am.'

'Shall I put you out of your misery, Fred?'

He turned his head and saw that she was smiling. 'There's no need,' he told her. 'It can be your secret for as long as you like.'

I don't care about keeping it a secret. 'I'm twenty-four.'

'Now you have surprised me.' He looked at her, and then looked again. 'I thought you were tall for your age,' he said.

'You chump.'

As they approached Agnes's house, she asked, 'May I offer you tea before you go back to socialise with Squadron Commander Elliot?'

'Thank you, Agnes. A cup of tea will steady me before that dire event.' He helped her out, closing the passenger door behind her, and they walked together up the path.

'I hope I can get leave,' she said, 'although it shouldn't be a problem.' She turned the key in the lock and pushed the door open.

'What kind of entertainment would you like to see in London?'

'Almost anything, I suppose.' She let him help her out of her uniform coat and placed her hat on its hook. 'Let me take your things,' she said.

'Thank you, but you're too late.' He hung his coat and cap beside hers.

'Come through to the kitchen and we'll talk while I make tea. I'm an awful hostess.'

'You're an excellent hostess.'

'I bored you about the cake I'd made.'

'I was never less bored in all my life. You're a superb hostess.'

'You're evidently convinced of it, Fred.'

'I don't want to be anywhere else, and that must be the ultimate proof.'

She filled the kettle and set it on the range. 'I'll still take some convincing. I think you're just being kind.' She seemed to tire of the subject, because she asked, 'Are you keen on operetta, or do you feel that it lacks gravitas?'

'Is he the Spanish tenor who's all the rage just now?'

'No, and you know perfectly well what I mean.'

He considered the question and said, 'I'm not a purist. I'm happy with anything as long as it's done well.'

'I have this morning's *Daily Sketch*. We could possibly find something worth seeing.'

'You see? You can even provide a newspaper at the critical moment. If that doesn't make you the perfect hostess, I'm sadly mistaken.'

'Oh, don't start that again.'

'I must, because I can't allow you to go on believing less of yourself than you deserve. Now, how can I persuade you? Let me count the ways.' He adopted a pensive look.

'That sounds suspiciously like Elizabeth Barrett Browning.'

'She went through a similar exercise,' he agreed, 'and answered her particular question in fourteen lines, but let me begin. You're an excellent hostess because you know how to welcome a guest without being too formal, thus demonstrating that your welcome is undeniably genuine.'

'That's only one way.'

He affected a suitably stern look and said, 'I haven't finished yet.

'When I came to tea, you evoked feelings I hadn't known for years. Toasting muffins by the fire carried me back to one of the best times of my life.'

'It did as much for me.'

'And you shared it.' He paused, thinking about his next point.

'You've used up all your arguments, haven't you?'

'No, I haven't. You excelled in a vitally important way, and that was evident when I had to force myself to leave and return to the base. The whole experience was as enjoyable as that.'

'As enjoyable as that?' She was clearly surprised. 'What can I say?' She picked up the kettle of boiling water and scalded the tea. 'You're quite serious about all that, aren't you?'

'Absolutely. Are you going to let me carry the tray?'

'After such an accolade, I feel I should carry it myself, but you'd only mount another incontestable argument as to why I shouldn't, so yes. Please do carry it into the sitting room. I'll get the newspaper.'

Fred placed the tray on the low table and waited.

'I've found the theatres page,' she said, 'but before we do anything, let me pour.' She lifted the teapot lid to inspect the brew, voiced her satisfaction, and poured for them both.

'I imagine *The Arcadians* is no longer running,' he said.

'Not since before the war.'

'Good, it never appealed to me.'

She gave him an odd look. 'Do you always choose by elimination?'

'No, I didn't want to throw cold water over something that might have appealed to you.'

'You're a chivalrous soul, Fred.' She ran her eye further down the page and said, 'I've read conflicting reviews of *The Lilac Domino.* Have you heard anything?'

'Only that Elliot saw it on his last leave and bored everyone in the wardroom with it to the extent that any topic of no interest whatsoever is now referred to as a "lilac domino".' He added, 'But don't let me put you off.'

'I wasn't convinced.' She continued her search, suddenly punctuating it with, 'Oh!'

'Yes?'

'*The Maid of the Mountains* is very popular.'

'It's probably too highbrow for Elliot, which is a recommendation in itself, although it's my belief that he'd struggle to follow the plot of a children's pantomime.'

'Be serious, Fred.'

'All right. If it appeals to you, I'm certainly game.'

'Are you sure?'

'Convinced. I'll see if I can get tickets. Which theatre is it?'

'Daly's in Cranbourne Street, Leicester Square.'

'Leave it to me, Agnes.'

She folded the newspaper and said a little shyly, 'There's also the question of hotels.'

'Trot out your question regarding hotels.'

Her shy look persisted. 'Oh dear,' she said. 'It's just that, if we were to book rooms in the same hotel and be seen in each other's company, it might look a little….' She left her disquiet unspoken.

'I hadn't considered that, Agnes. You're quite right. I'll book two hotels not too far apart.'

'I'm sorry to be difficult.'

'You're not at all difficult. It makes perfect sense.'

With that concern resolved, they both relaxed, and chatted easily until the time came for Fred to leave, and Agnes took down his coat and cap.

'I'll make arrangements tomorrow,' he said, 'and keep you informed.'

'That sounds terribly official.'

'It's as important as that.' Holding her gently by the shoulders, he kissed her on both cheeks. 'Until the next time, Agnes.'

She smiled happily. 'Until the next time, Fred.'

'*E noho ra.*'

'*Haere ra.*'

7

gnes peered at the line of cabs and said, 'Horses seem to have regained popularity since I was in London.'

'I'm surprised they can still find them,' said Fred, 'but with petrol so scarce, it's as well that they can. I imagine the Army will have inspected them and left only the oldest and least fit for the cabbies.'

A cab drew away, taking the people who'd been in front of them, and another drew up beside them.

'Brown's Hotel, and then The Piccadilly Hotel, please,' he told the driver.

'Brown's Hotel and the Piccadilly Hotel, guv'nor,' repeated the driver, taking their luggage. The horse changed feet noisily, as if impatient to be off. Fred helped Agnes into the vehicle and signalled their readiness to the driver.

'It was a stroke of luck, our being granted leave at the same time,' said Agnes.

'In my case, it certainly was. They're giving priority to chaps at the Front, but the wing commander took pity on me when he saw how little I'd had in the past year. Naturally, Elliot was miffed. He'd been hoping my request would be turned down.'

'What a disagreeable man he is.'

'As well as being a fool, but let's not concern ourselves with him.'

The driver interrupted their conversation by saying, 'I can't do this journey as quick as I used to, guv'nor. This old gel ain't all that fit nowadays, an' she's all I've got.'

'Well, slow down,' said Fred. 'There's no hurry, and we don't want a dead horse on our conscience.'

'No, we don't.' Agnes closed her eyes tightly at the thought.

'Right you are, guv'nor. We're nearly there, anyway.'

In a very short time, the cab entered Albemarle Street, and the driver called, 'Brown's Hotel, guv'nor.'

Fred climbed down, retrieved Agnes's luggage and helped her out of the cab. 'I'll be back shortly,' he told the driver. 'I'll take these in.'

'Right you are, guv'nor. Much obliged to you, I'm sure.'

Fred carried Agnes's bags into the hotel reception area and registered her. Opening his pocket watch, he said, 'I'll come for you at seven and take you to dinner. If you need to speak to me in the meantime, I'll be at the Piccadilly Hotel.'

'Thank you, Fred.' She inclined her head and accepted a kiss.

'I'll see you soon.'

'Until then.'

Satisfied that he'd done all that was necessary, he returned to the waiting cab. 'The Piccadilly Hotel, please, and do spare the horse. There's absolutely no hurry.'

'Right you are, guv'nor. It's a pleasure to serve a naval officer and a gen'leman.'

** ** **

'Have I left something undone?' Fred looked down at his evening dress studs and waistcoat. He'd had been aware of Agnes's scrutiny ever since they'd left their coats at the cloakroom.

'No.' She laughed. 'It's the first time I've seen you out of uniform, and you look even finer in evening dress.'

He leaned towards her as far as the table would allow, and said softly, 'You look captivating.'

'Thank you, Fred, but you told me that already.'

'No, I said you looked enchanting, and I was right on both occasions.' She was wearing a deeper shade of lilac than before, but her dress was still trimmed in white. It seemed to be a theme.

'I'm glad you could take a rest from wearing your uniform,' she said.

'Yes, I imagine the silly, spoilt creatures who amused themselves by distributing white feathers have possibly learned their lesson by now.' He turned his head to see the waiter approaching their table.

Agnes asked, 'What is he carrying? It's not our first course, surely.'

The waiter stopped at their table and placed a corsage of three red roses in front of her.

'Thank you,' said Fred. 'That's excellent.'

'The pleasure is ours, sir.'

'Yes,' said Agnes, somewhat bemused. 'Thank you.'

'Your first course will be along shortly, sir.' The waiter withdrew, leaving Agnes puzzled.

Fred asked her, 'Do you know what today is?'

'Thursday, of course.'

'Thursday, the fourteenth of February,' he prompted.

'Oh.' Realisation made her gasp. 'It's St Valentine's Day! Thank you, Fred. It's lovely!'

'And so are you. Are you going to wear it?'

'No, I'd rather keep it where I can see it and enjoy it.'

There was a burst of unusually loud laughter from a nearby table. Fred looked across at their uniforms. 'Americans,' he explained.

'Have you met any Americans yet?'

'A few,' he said. 'They've taken over the aerodrome at Swingate.'

The waiter arrived with their first course and asked if they required anything else.

'No, thank you,' said Fred. 'We have everything we need.' He waited until they were alone and said, 'The cab driver who took us to our hotels made a point of saying I was a "gen'leman". Not everyone says, "please" and "thank you", you understand, but I'm a colonial, and we're non-conformists to a man.'

With a teasing smile, she said, 'You're a lesson to us all, Fred.'

He leaned forward again to say, 'I don't think the waiter will be as impressed as the cab driver was.'

'What's happened?'

'I just heard one of the Americans address him as "boy". I think some preparation might have been in order before they left their shores.'

'How awful. I've only ever seen them in the pictures, so I didn't know what to expect.'

'They're always much quieter in the pictures, aren't they? It's either that, or you can't hear them for the piano.'

Agnes gave him an impatient look and said, 'There's no sound with the pict…. Oh, you're impossible.'

'The chaps from Swingate were all right. One thing I have to say about them, though, is that they're remarkably confident.'

'Why is that remarkable?'

'Just that they're so sure of their chances against an enemy they met for the first time in October. We may not be all that fond of the Hun, but we respect him as an adversary, and they would if they had any sense.' He picked up the bottle of wine and topped up their glasses.

'I'm sorry, Fred. I've made you think of the war, and we're here to relax and forget about it if we can.'

'I'm always relaxed in your company, Agnes. I just wish....'

'What do you wish?'

He waved his hand impatiently in the direction of the musicians. 'I wish they'd find something else to play. I'm sick of "Keep the Home Fires Burning".'

'So am I.' Despite her ready agreement, it was clear that Agnes's thoughts were elsewhere. 'Did you mean that about being relaxed in my company,' she asked, 'or were you being silly?'

'I can't help being silly,' he said, 'but yes, I meant it.'

'I'll accept that as a compliment. Thank you.' She laid her knife and fork together on her plate. 'And that was most enjoyable,' she said.

'Which is more than can be said for the music.' It seemed that Fred's patience was about to be rewarded, because the number was clearly coming to its end. 'What now, I wonder?'

'Be patient and you'll find out.'

The first bars of 'Let Me Call You Sweetheart' led Fred to ask, 'Do you waltz?'

'I have, but not for some time.' If she were reluctant, she gave no sign of it.

'Will you grant me the pleasure of this dance?'

'Of course.' She allowed him to lead her on to the dance floor, and soon they were moving together to the graceful violin solo.

Fred knew from her expression that she was enjoying every beat, and so was he. He was enjoying the music, the dance and simply being in contact, albeit discreet contact, with Agnes.

At the end, they returned to their table.

'I've heard tell there's a new dance,' she said. 'It's called the "Foxtrot".'

'I've heard of it too,' said Fred, 'but that's all. I haven't a clue how it's done, but maybe it's one of those things that can wait until after the war.' His life was currently busy enough.

** ** **

The following evening, at the theatre, Fred looked along the row at the other members of the audience taking their seats, and said, 'I'm afraid I don't possess a pair of opera glasses.'

'I've never used them,' said Agnes.

'You must have excellent vision.'

'Fortunately, I have, but that's not the reason.'

Fred waited politely for her to continue.

'To see a spectacle on stage too clearly is to penetrate the make-believe. In that way, opera glasses defeat the object of theatre-going, which is surely to indulge in that fantasy.'

'As always, Agnes, you make perfect sense.'

The fantasy was about to begin, because the conductor could be seen making his way to the rostrum to begin the overture. For Fred, it was always the most exciting part of an evening's entertainment. As he gripped the arm of his seat, he was conscious of Agnes's gloved hand on his. He sandwiched it with his other hand, knowing that she was content for that intimacy to take place.

The plot was contrived, and the music was light and lacking any real depth, although he enjoyed a few of the songs. 'A Bachelor Gay am I' appealed to him particularly. In all, however, the experience was a good one because, in all that time, he'd given no thought at all to the war.

When the curtain calls were done, the audience stood for the National Anthem before making for the exit, and Fred found it necessary to put his arm around Agnes to guide her through the crush. She seemed not to mind.

Later, in the cab, she said, 'I must say, I enjoyed *The Maid of the Mountains*, partly because it was my first visit to a theatre in four years, but mainly because it was a refuge and a diversion.'

'That's just what it was,' agreed Fred. He said no more, because he was newly conscious of the driver trying to calm the horse. Something had disturbed the unfortunate animal, and he was struggling to bring it under control. It was unusual, because cab horses were generally docile and immune to external disturbances. Fortunately, they were now in Albemarle Street, and the driver managed to bring the cab to a halt outside number thirty-three.

'Brown's Hotel, guv'nor,' he reported.

As Fred helped Agnes out of the cab, the driver said, 'The horse knows some'ink we don't, guv'nor. It wouldn't surprise me if them Huns are about to pay us another visit.'

'Thank you, driver.' Fred paid him. 'Keep the change and pay some regard to that unfortunate animal.'

'Much obliged to you, guv'nor. Goodnight, sir. Goodnight, ma'am.' He took the reins in both hands and concentrated his efforts on controlling the nervous horse.

Agnes asked, 'Why did you let him go, Fred? I was expecting you to take the cab to your hotel.'

'I want to be sure you're safe. Also, something's put the wind up that horse, and I didn't want to be a party to keeping the poor animal on the streets at this time.' He gave her his arm, and they were about to enter the hotel, when Fred picked up a sound that was all too familiar. 'The cabby was right, Agnes,' he said. 'It was the sound of aero engines that scared the horse. I think we're about to receive visitors.' The sound was growing louder.

Agnes made no comment but clung instead to Fred's arm. She was no stranger to air raids; Gotha heavy bombers had been over Kent and done widespread damage, but for this to happen after a relaxing evening at the theatre made the experience uglier than ever.

'I'm going to stay with you until they've gone,' Fred told her.

'How long will that take?'

'Not very long. They've come from France and they're limited by what fuel they can carry.'

Residents were picking up their belongings and hurrying to wherever they felt safer. A hotel porter said to Fred, 'You're welcome to use the hotel basement, sir. That's where most residents are going.'

'Thank you,' said Fred, 'but I don't think it'll be any safer than this lobby. We'll just find a corner away from a window and see out the raid from there.'

'As you please, sir. Can I bring you anything?'

Fred looked at Agnes, whose face was white. 'You'd like coffee, wouldn't you, Agnes?'

The sounds of several explosions could be heard, and she nodded, scarcely able to speak.

'Yes, coffee for two, please.' He guided her to a corner sofa. 'Something stronger might have been welcome, but they're not allowed to serve spirits at this time.'

'Aren't they?'

It was likely, judging by Agnes's strained expression, that she asked the question purely without thought.

'The Defence of the Realm Act,' he reminded her, 'prohibits the sale of strong drink at certain times.' He inclined his head upward and smiled briefly at the irony of the ruling. 'Even at times when it might be beneficial.'

Several more explosions caused Agnes to flinch and hold more tightly to his arm.

'We're unlikely to take harm here,' he said, 'and the raid can't last much longer.'

'I've heard they carry huge bombs,' she said.

'Fiddlesticks. They carry sixty-pound bombs, and there's a limit to the damage they can inflict.' His mind returned momentarily to his last meeting with Elliot.

'I'm glad you're here, Fred.'

'Good, because I'm going nowhere until this raid is over.'

The porter appeared with a tray of coffee things. 'I've brought you some biscuits, sir, madam. I thought they might help sustain you in the circumstances.' A series of explosions in the distance seemed to reinforce his concern.

'How very thoughtful. Thank you very much for that.' Fred looked at the bill and put his free hand in his pocket.

'Are you a resident, sir?'

'No, I'm not. This lady is, but I'll pay for this.' He put some money on the plate with the bill. 'Keep the change.'

'Thank you very much, sir,' he said, adding as an afterthought, 'There is still room in the basement, in case you change your mind, sir.'

'Thank you, but we'll be just as safe here.'

'Very good, sir.' The porter retired, leaving them alone in the lobby.

As Fred poured the coffee, Agnes asked, 'Why do you say we'll be as safe here as in the basement?'

'We'll actually be safer here. To be trapped underground would be less than amusing, but try not to think about it.' A string of explosions followed, none of them close by, but making his advice nonetheless difficult to follow. As a distraction, he offered her the plate of biscuits.

'No, thank you. I couldn't eat anything.'

'It's going to be all right, Agnes,' he said putting his arm around her shoulders for comfort. 'They'll be on their way shortly. Trust me, as one who's been on the other side of this business.' For additional reassurance, he said, 'No Hun wants to come down in the English Channel for want of fuel.'

'I believe you, Fred.'

'Snuggle up. What comfort I can give is entirely at your disposal.' There were more explosions to the west, or so it seemed to Fred, and they made him hold her more tightly.

'I'm glad we ate before we went to the theatre,' she said.

'Yes, we'd have missed supper and been very hungry by this time. Are you sure you won't have a biscuit?'

'Quite sure, thank you.' She clung to him more closely, as if his body could provide adequate shelter from a bomb.

'They're going home,' he told her. The noise had all but stopped.

'Are you sure?'

'Sure as I can be.' He kissed her forehead as if he were comforting a child, and she turned up her face so that it seemed the most natural thing to kiss her cheek as well. 'Sure as I can be,' he repeated. Almost without thinking, he allowed his lips to touch hers, lightly at first until, sensing compliance, he kissed her parted lips slowly and gently. After a few seconds, they drew apart, and he said, 'I'm sorry. I didn't intend that to happen.'

'I'm glad it did,' she said. 'It's better than listening to London being blown to pieces.'

'Much better, and I was right.' He motioned upward. 'They have gone home. Sadly, so must I. At least, I must return to my hotel and leave you to benefit from a proper night's sleep.'

'Must you go so soon?'

He put on a thoughtful face and said, 'I'll stay with you until the residents come up from the basement.' He kissed her again to confirm it.

'Will you be able to get a cab at this time?'

He took out his watch and opened it. 'It's only ten minutes to midnight,' he said.

'I thought it was much later than that.'

He felt the coffee pot. 'It's still warm,' he said.

'Oh, good. I couldn't face it earlier.'

'Would you like a biscuit as well?'

'Yes, please. I seem to have regained my appetite.'

8

The first person to greet Fred on his return to the base was Flight Lieutenant Arthur Reynolds. He seemed unusually reserved.

'Good morning, Fred. Did you have a good leave?'

'Excellent, but you're not your usual chirpy self, Arthur. What's on your mind?'

'Bad news, Fred. I'm afraid we've lost a man and a machine.'

'Bugger. Who?'

'Rockingham. We were attacked by an Albatros. The usual thing. The Hun reckoned on making a quick kill before heading for home. I signalled the flight to join me – I reckoned we could at least send him on his way – but Rockingham disregarded my flare and went after him. It was like David and Goliath, except that Goliath inevitably won. Not only that, as Rockingham dived towards the sea with his machine in flames, the Hun followed him, firing at him all the way down and even when Rockingham's machine was sinking. He just went on firing. I know it doesn't excuse Rockingham's folly, but it was cold-blooded murder on the part of the Hun.'

'And the Hun made his escape?'

'We couldn't catch him, Fred. You know the Albatros.'

'No, there was nothing more you could have done, Arthur.' He put a consoling hand on the flight lieutenant's shoulder. 'When did it happen?'

'Yesterday forenoon.' He said pensively, 'Elliot's going to write to Rockingham's mother.'

'That'll be cold consolation. I'll speak to Elliot. With any luck he won't have written the letter yet, and I'll be able to persuade him to leave the task in more sensitive hands.'

'Good luck, Fred. Elliot's looking for a convenient scapegoat. I only escaped by the skin of my teeth.'

'I can handle Elliot.'

It seemed that Fred would have his chance to prove his claim sooner than expected, because the wardroom door opened to admit Elliot, who spotted him immediately.

'Fuller, come to my office.'

Fred shrugged and followed his squadron commander to the office, where he found Wing Commander Bryant waiting. He came to attention and saluted.

'At ease, Fuller. First of all, did you have a good leave?'

'Excellent, thank you, sir.'

'I'm sorry I couldn't give you longer, but priority must go to the chaps in France.'

'I quite understand, sir.'

'Good. Now, regarding Flight Sub-Lieutenant Rockingham, I've spoken with Reynolds, who was leading your flight in your absence, and I'm beginning to see the general picture. What sort of chap was Rockingham?'

'He was a boy, sir, with a schoolboy's quixotic ideas of glory in the skies. Of course, I did my best to disabuse him of that nonsense.'

'Are you sure, Fuller?' The question came from Elliot. 'I'm told Rockingham hero-worshipped you because of your latest auspicious success in aerial combat.'

'I imagine Fuller's success owed more to skill than good fortune, Elliot.' The wing commander's intervention was both timely and welcome.

'Last month, Rockingham came to my cabin to ask me if the buzz about my twenty-second victory was true, sir. I'd been obliged to defend myself against an LFG Roland, and he was terribly impressed, but I went to some trouble to warn him against seeking the bubble reputation. I made it clear that his duty was to search for U-boats, and that was all. I'm truly sorry that he was killed, because, for all his boyish silliness, he was a pleasant lad. I shall naturally write to his next of kin, that is if Squadron Commander Elliot hasn't already done so.'

The wing commander turned to the latter. 'Well, Elliot?'

Elliot was clearly recovering from the Wing Commander's slap on the wrist. 'I had the matter in hand, sir,' he managed to say, 'but

Flight Commander Fuller is welcome to discharge that duty. He knew the man, after all.'

'What I don't understand,' said the wing commander, 'is why a pilot in a Type One Eight Four would go after an Albatros.'

'He was flying a Hamble Baby at the time, sir,' said Elliot reluctantly.

'On anti-U-boat patrol? Why, for goodness' sake?'

'The Hamble is a superior aircraft, sir.'

'In some capacities, admittedly. In the anti-U-boat role, it's as much use as a novice in a knocking shop. What happened to the Type One Eight Fours?'

Elliot had broken into a sweat. 'I had them taken out of service, sir, as they were too slow and cumbersome for the task.'

'Nonsense. You'd better put them back into service and send them on patrol, armed, I suggest, with torpedoes. Is that clear?'

'Yes, sir. The only snag is that they're all due for servicing.'

'You know what to do about that.' The wing commander picked up his cap. 'Get them serviced and back on patrol.'

'Aye, aye, sir.'

'I'll arrange more leave for you when I can, Fuller. I realise you've had precious little during the past year.'

'Thank you, sir.'

'Carry on, both of you.'

'Aye, aye, sir.'

'Aye, aye, sir.'

Fred left Elliot to lick his wounds and went in search of Arthur Reynolds.

He found him in the seaplane hangar, talking to one of the air mechanics. Two Wrens nearby, were examining the torn fabric of a seaplane's wing. They saw Fred approaching and retreated to a respectable distance, followed by the air mechanic.

'The Type One Eight Fours are to be reprieved,' said Fred. 'Wing Commander Bryant took a dim view of Elliot's latest initiative, if I can call it that. He even gave him a flea in his ear while I was in the office.'

'Do you mean it was actually Elliot's idea all along?'

'It had to be. Only a chump like Elliot could dream up something like that.'

'That's true enough.'

'I suppose we'll have to use the Hambles this morning, as the One Eight Fours need servicing, but that can't be helped.' As another thought occurred to him, he said, half to himself, 'It might not be such a bad thing in the short term.'

'Thank goodness Wing Commander Bryant got involved.'

'I agree.' Fred was thinking about his latest idea. 'Arthur,' he said, 'could you identify the Albatros that shot Rockingham down?'

'I could do it from the depths of slumber, Fred. It's not the first time I've seen it stooging around, or the second. It has a sky-blue fuselage, fin and rudder, and silver wings. The black crosses on the fuselage and on the wings are simply black on blue or silver without background. Oh, and there's another thing. The pilot wears a scarf, like ours, but sky-blue as well. Most unusual.'

'Thank you, Arthur. If you see him again, give him a wide berth.'

'With pleasure, Fred. I've seen what he can do.'

** ** **

'B' Flight were rewarded within half-an-hour of relieving George Makepeace's Flight, when they sighted a surfaced U-boat approximately five miles off the French coast. Fred fired a red flare to alert the rest of the flight, and dived on it immediately, releasing both sixty-five-pound bombs. Two more of the flight were able to make their attack before the U-boat dived for safety. Unfortunately, with no wireless facility, Fred was unable to transmit the enemy's position and course, so he signalled his flight to continue the patrol, its presence usually being sufficient to keep any U-boats submerged.

From the commencement of the patrol, he'd been keeping a lookout, not simply for U-boats, but for enemy aircraft as well. He was particularly anxious to spot the sky-blue and silver Albatros before it was able to attack the flight from a strategic position, and to deny it that advantage, he began climbing, thankful that he was now free of his bombload.

The Hamble was outgunned, outclimbed and slower than the Albatros, but it was unlikely that the Hun pilot could match Fred's experience of aerial combat. Scout pilots generally led a mayfly existence, constantly challenged as they were, like the gunfighters of the Wild West, by those who wanted to prove themselves. Rockingham wasn't the only adventurer to have taken to the skies; there were many who were more accomplished but no less misguided, and a national idol could quickly become the subject of a telegram to a grieving relative.

After six minutes, the altimeter showed something over two thousand, five hundred feet, about half a mile. In an almost cloudless sky, the flight was clearly visible below, and Fred had an unimpeded all-round view. He contented himself by flying figures of eight over the patrol and keeping a keen lookout for his adversary.

His initial reward came after less than ten minutes, when a speck in the distant sky grew rapidly into an aircraft with the unmistakeable combination of a sky-blue fuselage and silver wings. Its pilot had evidently seen the Hamble, and was climbing to create the advantage of altitude. It was all the same to Fred, who waited for him to make his approach. When it came about, he twisted, turned, rolled and occasionally side-slipped, although he was careful not to lose too much height. Essentially, he would employ any device to avoid flying straight and level until he was in position to shoot. In that way, he might pass through the Hun's gunsights for a split second at a time, but no more than that.

They circled, wheeled and manoeuvred for what seemed an age, sometimes close enough for Fred to see the pilot's blonde moustache and sky-blue scarf, with the Hun firing his twin Spandau machineguns when he saw his target, only to have it snatched from him a moment later; in fact, it was happening so frequently that it occurred to Fred that his quarry might soon run out of ammunition. The thought was purely academic, however; the Hun was a murderer, but Fred would never shoot when he was changing magazines, because to fire at an unarmed man would also be murder.

The bursts of machine-gun fire were becoming more frequent, and it was evident that the Hun was losing patience.

'Yes, you bastard,' said Fred, 'you're not fighting a schoolboy, now.'

The Albatros half-looped and rolled out in the manoeuvre that had become known as the Immelmann Turn, after the sometime ace who'd invented it. It was clear that the Hun intended to approach from astern, but he'd all-but telegraphed the intention to Fred, who made a tight, banking turn, and pulled the priming lever on his synchronising gear.

As the Albatros made its turn, Fred fired a long burst, seeing his bullets hit their mark. Within seconds, the Hun pilot was holding up his hands to shield his face as flames leapt from the stricken engine. The Albatros turned its nose to the sea and dived, the flames consuming the whole of the fuselage, and Fred watched the starboard mainplane break away as the aircraft hit the waves. The pilot would have no chance of survival.

Fred turned to re-join his flight.

** ** **

He found Elliot in the Squadron Office.

'Well, Fuller?'

'One U-boat attacked. Three aircraft took part. I also wish to claim an Albatros Mark Five. The fight was witnessed by the rest of "B" Flight.'

'What?' The question was clearly the prelude to an outburst of recrimination.

'Didn't you hear me?'

'Yes, I heard you. Are you saying you defied my orders to pick a fight with a superior enemy, and all to enhance your personal record?'

'No, on four counts.'

'Fuller—'

'No, listen to me, Elliot. It's time you did some listening for a change.'

'You're forgetting yourself, Fuller.'

'No, I'm not. You accuse me of defying your orders, which I didn't. I acted in the interests of my flight.' He could see that Elliot was about to interrupt, so he waved him to silence. 'Secondly, you accused me of picking a fight. You weren't there, Elliot, so how can you possibly know that? I took on the Albatros to protect the flight. As for the enemy being superior, what gives you that idea? The Albatros is superior to the Hamble, I'll admit, but the pilot was anything but superior. In fact, if they continue to send pilots like him into the air, we've won the war for certain.'

'Damn it, Fuller!' Elliot seemed about to burst.

'Now, I could be accused of taking on that Hun to avenge Rockingham's murder, but the situation would remain the same. I had to take him on in order to protect my flight.'

It seemed that Elliot was not going down without a fight. 'I still say you defied my order, Fuller.'

Fred sighed. 'You don't listen, do you, Elliot? I've already answered that allegation, but let's address your fourth ludicrous charge, that I did it to enhance my reputation, to chalk up my twenty-third victory. Listen, Elliot, the only problem my record presents is that you resent it. You're a very jealous and insecure man, Elliot. I don't know how old you are, but you have a great deal of growing up to do.' He picked up his cap. 'Now, I'm sure you have more important tasks in hand than bandying wild accusations, and I'm going to have a bath, so I'll bid you good day… sir.' He would make his report in writing, and a copy would go to the Wing Commander, as usual. If Elliot wanted him disciplined for telling a few unpleasant truths, he might find he was wielding a double-edged blade.

9

The Wing Commander's reaction to Fred's report was less than Elliot had hoped, and he was so disenchanted with Fred's company that he readily gave him dispensation to be absent from dinner in the wardroom.

He called for Agnes, and they drove to the Corunna Hotel, where he'd reserved a table.

The waiter, who had adopted them as regular diners, showed them to their usual table and left them with the menu, informing them regretfully that the duck was no longer available.

'You're in a thoughtful frame of mind, Fred.' Agnes was very sensitive to mood. It was a quality that Fred had already recognised and had come to value.

'I try to be thoughtful,' he said.

'And you are, but I mean you have something on your mind,' she insisted.

He wondered how best to dismiss the subject without being abrupt. 'A procedural matter,' he said. 'It's tiresome and tedious, but it's all over now, so there's no problem.'

'It's affected you,' she observed. 'You were very quiet on the way here.'

'Was I? I'm sorry, I didn't mean to be a wet blanket.'

'That's not how I would describe you.' She placed her hand on his and said, 'Don't you want to get it off your chest?'

'You don't give up easily, Agnes.' He hesitated. It was hardly a suitable subject for a lady's ears, but she was insistent, so he gave in. 'Whilst you and I were travelling back from London,' he said, 'my flight went on anti-U-boat patrol, and they were visited by an Albatros, by which I don't mean a huge bird, but a fast, manoeuvrable and well-armed Hun scout.'

'I'm sorry to interrupt you, but what is a "scout"? It sounds like a reconnaissance aeroplane.'

'Originally, they were, but they're now single-seat fighters.'

'Do go on.'

'Well, Arthur, my number two, quite rightly signalled the flight to form up with him so as to deter the Hun from attacking. Unfortunately, a boy called Rockingham saw his opportunity to make a name for himself and threw down the gauntlet.'

'How did he do that?'

'He flew towards the Hun.' He shrugged. 'That's all it takes.'

She nodded sadly. 'I imagine he was unsuccessful.'

'That's right. He was eighteen years old, and he'd no experience of aerial combat. I'd already spoken to him about his silly romantic notions of jousting in the skies, but it had no effect. At all events, the Hun shot him down.' He hadn't wanted to relate the next part, but now it seemed necessary. 'He followed the wretched boy down, shooting all the time. It was nothing less than murder.'

'Oh, Fred. I'm sorry.'

'It wasn't really my problem. I've suffered a jolly sight less than poor Rockingham.'

'But you've taken it to heart,' she said, squeezing the hand she was holding.

The waiter arrived, and they gave him their order.

'Some good came of it,' he said. 'Anti-U-boat patrols are to be escorted by scouts, now, from Guston, which makes a repetition unlikely.'

'Oh, good.'

It occurred to Fred that it must be hard for her to understand such things, so it was very much to her credit that she insisted on knowing the details.

'The upshot of it was that I had to doff my cap in front of the Wing Commander and be reprimanded. It was the mildest of slaps on the wrist,' he assured her.

'Why did you have to be reprimanded?' Her tone suggested that she found even the thought of it unacceptable.

'Ah, well, because I went after the Hun pilot and shot him down, and because I'd blotted my copybook with Elliot.'

'Your dreadful squadron commander?'

'The same, yes.'

She seemed puzzled, and confirmed it when she asked, 'What was wrong with shooting down an enemy aircraft in wartime? I thought that was the accepted idea.'

'Elliot had ordered us not to become involved with enemy aircraft, but to concentrate on searching for U-boats. He accused me of all kinds of nonsense that included furthering my personal glory. I told him to grow up, and he reported me to the Wing Commander.'

'You don't have to look far for trouble, do you, Fred?'

'I do tend to give it a helping hand,' he admitted.

Squeezing his hand again, she asked, 'What did the Wing Commander say?'

'He recognised the fact that I couldn't avoid the Hun, he congratulated me on overcoming a superior aircraft, even if its pilot needed a few lessons in aerial combat, and then he told me I mustn't speak again disrespectfully to Elliot.' He laughed shortly. 'I even have to address him occasionally as "sir".' More soberly, he said, 'I've written to the boy Rockingham's mother. He had no father.'

'Is that your responsibility?'

'No, I volunteered. It was preferable to leaving Elliot to do it in his usual insensitive way.'

'Commanding officers' letters are important,' she said, clearly remembering. 'They arrive when wives and mothers are at their most raw and vulnerable.'

It was Fred's turn to squeeze her hand. 'Let's consider my experience resolved and closed,' he suggested. 'It was never my intention to upset you or make you feel sad in any way, and it never will be.'

'I know.' She smiled as she said it.

They let the waiter set out their first course. When he'd gone, Agnes said, 'What a wonderful time we had in London. I keep thinking about it just to keep the memory fresh.'

'I'm glad. We must do it again.'

'Do you really think we could? That would be marvellous.' She seemed about to laugh, and then thought better of it.

'What's so funny?'

'I was only thinking about you telling the cab driver to take better care of his horse.'

'Was that funny?'

'No, it was noble and kind, and completely unexpected.'

'It wasn't a good night for cab horses,' he reflected.

'Or for people. Paddington Station was damaged as well.'

'My sympathy,' he told her, 'was with the horses. People were out and about by choice, but the horses had no say in the matter.' He considered it further and said, 'When people are threatened, they can rationalise their fear. They can usually weigh up the risks and see a way forward, but animals can't. They only know terror, and that leaves us with a great responsibility.'

She regarded him seriously. 'Fred,' she said, 'you're truly noble.'

'My family goes back a long way, but there's nothing remotely noble about them.'

'You know what I mean. When we were at Brown's during the air raid, you were so protective.'

'It's not difficult. You were frightened, and I had to make you feel safer, that's all.' He added, 'But you're right, and you weren't even a cab horse.'

She laughed. 'So can you accept that you're noble?'

'If you say it, Agnes, I accept it.'

They chatted easily until it was time to leave, and they drove back to Whitfield.

As Fred pulled up outside the house, Agnes asked, 'Would you like to come in for a while. I have the cognac you brought from France.'

'How tempting. Yes, I'd like that very much.' He switched off the engine and helped her out of the motor.

As they walked up the path to the house, Fred said, 'When I suggested that we regard my recent adventure as over and dealt with, I realise I'd touched on a painful memory. I hope you didn't think I was being dismissive about your loss. I'd never do that knowingly, but I can be clumsy at times.'

'I didn't think that, and I know you wouldn't.' She put the key in the lock and opened the door. 'As for being clumsy, who's perfect? Do come in.'

He helped her out of her coat, and they hung up their things.

'I can't offer you coffee,' she said, taking down two brandy glasses, 'because there's none to be had.'

'It's all the fault of the Kaiser and Squadron Commander Elliot. You are absolved.'

'Where does Mr Elliot come into it?'

'Oh, he gets in the way of our attempts to quell the U-boat threat. Frankly, I think he should be court-martialled and shot. As a matter of fact, I'm not doing much this weekend, so I could do the job myself.'

'You do talk nonsense. Will you bring the bottle? We're in the sitting room this time.'

Fred picked up the bottle of cognac and followed her into the sitting room, where a small fire lay in the grate. 'He asked, 'Would you like me to revive this?'

She turned, and saw that he was referring to the fire. 'Yes, please. That would be very nice indeed.'

He placed two small logs over the glowing embers and was soon rewarded as flames flickered around them.

'Will you open the bottle, please? I'm not strong enough.'

He looked at the bottle, realising that the cork was surrounded by foil. 'I see why you were struggling,' he said, using his pocket knife to cut through the foil. He eased out the cork and poured two measures.

'This is luxury,' she said. 'So many things have become impossible to find.'

'I'll find you some coffee,' he told her, joining her on the sofa.

'Are you going to France again?'

'No, French coffee's half chicory. You don't want that. I'll get some from the wardroom.'

'Don't make trouble for yourself with that Elliot man, whatever you do.'

'There'll be no trouble, Agnes. Whatever I take from the wardroom I charge to my account and then I pay for it.'

'Oh, good.' With her mind set at rest, Agnes tasted her cognac. 'This is glorious,' she said, 'and this is the first time I've tried it, but I suppose it's always been a male preserve.'

'What you do in your own home is your affair,' he assured her. 'In any case, I don't subscribe to that nonsense, coming as I do from a liberal society.'

'Yes.' His remark reminded her of a previous conversation. 'I was very surprised when you told me that women had the vote. I suppose that's only white women, of course.'

'No, Maori women have had the vote for about twenty years now.'

'Good grief.' She almost spilled her drink in surprise.

'By and large, we respect the Maoris and, by and large, they respect us.'

'No wonder you're so noble, coming from a noble community.'

'You wouldn't say that if you saw the goings-on in the pubs sometimes.'

'I've never been inside a pub.'

'Quite right.'

She looked at her drink thoughtfully, prompting him to say, 'A penny for your thoughts, Agnes.'

She seemed to shake herself back into full consciousness. 'I'm sorry. I was thinking about the air raid in London.'

'What prompted that?'

'I've been thinking about it all day – two days, really, since the papers showed all those pictures of the damage it caused.' It had evidently left a deep impression on her.

'Put it behind you, Agnes. We escaped it.'

'I know. You were wonderful in the hotel lobby.'

'I told you, I just wanted you to feel safer.' He held out his arms to her. 'It was frightening for you, but I'm used to loud explosions. I've been around them for some time now.'

It was as if the memory of it prompted her to relive the experience, and she laid her head on his shoulder as she had in London.

'You're safe now,' he told her. 'Nothing's going to hurt you.' He kissed each cheek, and then, quite deliberately, her lips, a development that seemed to please her. She made no protest, either, when he gathered her into his arms, but accepted his kisses readily.

After some time, she said, 'I wondered if it would happen again. It did in London, but I was afraid it might have been a passing thing.'

'I didn't want to scare you away.'

'You're not going to do that.'

He kissed her willing lips again.

'I'm afraid I'm not very experienced,' she said shyly. 'James and I were as innocent as each other, and we hadn't been married long when he was killed.'

The thought of it made him hold her more tightly, and he wondered a little about her diffidence. 'You're allowed to join in nowadays,' he assured her. 'It's a twentieth century thing.'

'But how?'

'Just do as the urge dictates.' He kissed her again, teasing her lips, first one and then the other. After a while, she began to do the same, and continued with some eagerness until, as if by unspoken agreement, they joined in a long, searching, probing kiss.

'That was lovely,' she said eventually.

'So it was.' Regretfully, he took out his hunter to check the time. He shook his head sorrowfully, saying, 'The time has come. Goodbye, Agnes, I must leave you.'

'If you'd called me "Dolly", I'd have worried.'

'Oh, I left her years ago.'

'Was she good at kissing?'

'No, that's why I left her, whereas you've taken to it quite naturally.'

'Are you serious?'

He kissed her again. 'Listen, Agnes, it's a natural thing that just develops. Don't think of it as a skill that has to be learned.'

'I'm quite relieved to hear that.'

'Like most young women, you've grown up protected, and there's nothing wrong with that. It's the way society works. That you were married for so short a time was just rotten luck for you both.' Confident that he'd made his point, he stood up. 'Reluctant though I am to leave you, duty calls.'

She went with him to the door and helped him with his coat, cap and scarf. 'Thank you for another memorable evening,' she said. 'When shall we meet again?'

'I'm stood down at the weekend.'

'Oh, let's meet.'

'I'll call at the canteen and we can make arrangements then.' He bent and kissed her again. 'Until then. *E noho ra.*'

'Until then. *Haere ra.*'

10

The entertainment at the Royal Hippodrome Theatre in Snargate Street was a light-hearted revue featuring the few acts that had escaped military service. In all, it was entertaining but superficial, perhaps more noticeably so after *The Maid of the Mountains*, but it was, as Agnes pointed out, a diversion at a time when such luxuries were needed.

At supper afterwards, Fred was visibly thoughtful.

'A penny for them,' offered Agnes.

'I was wondering what kind of homeland our soldiers and sailors are going to return to when the shooting and shelling ceases.'

Clearly, his reply wasn't what Agnes was expecting. 'What made you think of that, Fred?'

'Have you noticed that every restaurant and theatre we've visited recently has displayed signs saying "Officers Only"?'

'Yes, I have, but those soldiers and sailors who might use restaurants in peacetime can't afford them on service pay.'

Fred picked up the bottle and refilled their glasses before speaking. 'You're a fair-minded person, Agnes,' he said eventually, 'so I'll put this argument to you. It's true that most restaurants and theatres are beyond the means of the lower deck and "other ranks", as I believe the Army calls them, and the general preference may well be for more familiar diversions, but my objection is one of principle, to the signs themselves, which are saying, in effect, "The lower orders are not welcome here. It's perfectly right for them to die in their country's service, but they mustn't forget their rightful place in society." '

'I understand what you're saying now, Fred, and I see your point. Those signs are insulting.' She even looked penitent as she said, 'I just hadn't thought about it that way.'

'I don't believe I did until I went to live abroad.' Reflecting further, he said, 'I think sometimes about young Beresford, the wireless operator who'd lost his father and brother.'

'So do I, Fred.'

'He's helping his widowed mother as much as he can with what the Navy pays him, because she'll get next to nothing from this ungrateful government, as you know.'

Agnes nodded her agreement. 'I'm fortunate in not having to rely on a war widow's pension,' she told him quietly.

'I'm glad.'

'Is Mrs Beresford struggling?'

'She can't be finding it easy, but now we're using the Type One Eight Fours again, I've co-opted him as my wireless operator, so he'll get a little extra pay for that.'

'Oh, Fred, most of that meant nothing to me, but I know it was a deed worthy of you.'

'He's a good hand, so it made sense. As soon as I can have him promoted to leading telegraphist, I shall.' He shook his head, as if ridding it of gloomy thoughts, and said, 'So far, I've cast a cloud over the proceedings, and I apologise for it. Let's talk about happier things.'

'Don't worry about it, Fred. It's enough for me that you care about mankind, not to mention frightened horses and the Beresford boy. That alone makes you special in my eyes.'

'Cats and dogs too. Don't forget them.'

'Cats and dogs?' She smiled in spite of her bemusement, apparently confident that his explanation would be quite acceptable.

'I care about them. We keep both at home, and they're like friends, even though they're working animals.' Leaning across the table confidentially, he said, 'And I'm pleased that I'm special in your eyes.'

She smiled in a way that made her eyes twinkle. 'You knew that already.'

'I was hopeful, yes.'

The waiter brought their main course, inhibiting further confidences, at least for the time being.

Agnes asked, 'What do you do, exactly, in New Zealand?'

'Everything. I work in the store, in the warehouse, in accounts, I visit customers and I negotiate with suppliers.' He smiled modestly. 'Not bad for a middle-class ne'er-do-well trained to do nothing at all.'

'No one could call you a ne'er-do-well, Fred. It sounds as if you work jolly hard.' It seemed that she was prepared to defend him on any score.

'I do, but not all the time. As you know, my hobby is flying, and I've done a lot of that.'

'How did you get started?'

'I just said I wanted to learn to fly, and Uncle Jim and Aunt Amelia paid for me to learn. It was a birthday present.'

'How generous.'

'They're extremely generous. They bought me an aeroplane after that. That was for Christmas. You see, for whatever reason, they have no son or daughter of their own, so they adopted me – unofficially, of course – but as far as I'm concerned, they're my family.'

'Of course they are, and a wonderful family too.'

He was thoughtful again. 'We make a habit of this, Agnes,' he said.

'A habit of what?'

'Talking about me and my background. Can't we talk about you for a change? I'm sure it would be interesting, and I wouldn't feel quite so selfish.'

'I'm not at all interesting,' she said, placing her knife and fork neatly together on her plate. 'I was respectably brought up, educated by a tutoress, I became engaged to the son of one of my father's professional acquaintances, we were married for less than two weeks before he had to join his ship, and I was widowed shortly afterwards. Being independent, I joined the Canteen Board more for something to occupy myself than for any other reason. The only interesting thing that's happened to me since then was meeting you in January.'

'I'm truly sorry that you were married for such a short time,' he said, taking her hand. 'However, I disagree strongly with you about being uninteresting.'

'How can you say that, Fred?'

'Simply because of the way you appeal to me. A great many people are complicated by life's experiences and therefore they're difficult to fathom, and then, when I learn more about them, I find

I'm disappointed. Some are simply complex; others are dull. You are different. Some person, some influence, or maybe a combination of influences, has made you both fascinating and engaging, someone I'm sublimely happy to know and whom I want to go on knowing.'

She made no reply, but simply looked at him as if he'd said something strange and difficult to understand.

'I'm sorry if I've disturbed you,' he said, at a loss for anything more soothing to say.

'You haven't disturbed me, Fred. That was the loveliest compliment I've ever been paid, and it was such a surprise.'

'I have more, just as sincere as that one.'

'I don't think I could cope with any more tonight.'

'Could you cope with dessert?'

She considered it for a second and said, 'Perhaps just coffee.'

'That reminds me. I brought you some coffee. I left it in my motor.'

'In that case, shall we have it at my house?'

'That's an excellent idea.' He signalled the waiter for the bill, paid it and escorted Agnes to the cloakroom, where they retrieved their outer garments.

As they left the restaurant, Agnes asked, 'Where does the Navy find coffee?'

'Like most things, it comes by sea, in convoys. It's another example of the unfairness of life. People are going without, but the wardroom must have its luxuries. The same applies, I'm told, to the Army, but fear not. The RNAS and the RFC will only behave irresponsibly until the first of April.' He opened the passenger door for her.

'What happens then?'

He turned the handle and started the engine. 'Irresponsible behaviour will become the province of the Royal Air Force.'

'Oh, I'd forgotten about that.'

'I hadn't. I'd do anything to miss the first of April.'

'Don't say that, Fred. You'll tempt Providence.'

They drove to Whitfield in companionable silence, content simply to be in each other's company. When they arrived, Agnes let them into the house and took the packet of coffee beans from Fred, who then went to the sitting room to revive the fire.

'It's going nicely,' he reported on his return.

'Thank you, Fred.' As she turned the handle of the grinder, she said, 'I was so pleased when you told me what you were doing for the Beresford boy.'

'It won't make him rich, but it might help ease his family's finances.'

'It was so awful, watching him outside the canteen, that day. I'll never forget it.' She took the drawer from the grinder and emptied the grounds into the percolator. 'I really should admit defeat and hire a cook,' she said, 'albeit a part-time one. I'm hopeless at these things. It just seems so selfish on my part to have someone cook just for me.'

'I thought you were coping rather well, but if you were to hire a cook, you'd be providing employment for someone who needs the income, and I don't need to remind you that there's no shortage of war widows.'

'I hadn't thought of it like that.' She set the percolator on the range and asked, 'What do you do about cooking in New Zealand?'

'We manage. When we're very busy, a woman comes in to cook for us, but Aunt Amelia likes to keep her hand in.'

'I'd be a complete disaster.'

'No, you wouldn't. These things can be learned.' He held out his arms to her and they kissed, not as they had at first, but quite naturally, and they continued to do so until the coffee was ready. 'This is one art you've mastered in a very short time,' he assured her.

'Now, that is good news.'

They carried the coffee things, the cognac and the glasses into the sitting room, where flames were once again leaping up the fireback and creating a shifting frieze of shadows on the walls of the half-lit room. Agnes poured coffee and then cognac before resting her head against Fred's shoulder.

'Fred,' she asked, 'would you ever consider staying in England?'

'I'd consider it, yes. I try not to dismiss anything out of hand, but I have to say I don't think I'd consider it for long.'

'In a sense, you turned your back on your old country, yet you travelled across the world to fight for it. Doesn't that amount to a paradox?'

'Not really. The Kaiser's a bully, and I dislike bullies. All I'm doing is helping to put him in his place.'

She shifted to make herself more comfortable. 'Do you really dislike this country so much, or is it simply that New Zealand appeals more strongly?'

'Both those things, really. New Zealand is a wonderful, forward-looking country, the place where my life really began, and now that the sourness I felt at being rejected by my family has subsided, I can make a clear-headed comparison between the two societies.' He tasted his coffee and made a gesture of approval. 'I left behind one in which parents pay a nanny to care for their children and keep them out of sight until they're old enough to enter the next stage in their loveless lives. That's when boys are sent away to school to learn a regimented way of life and be beaten when they transgress. You know how girls are educated, and I'm thankful you weren't damaged by the process.'

'Not everyone lives like that, Fred,' she said, squeezing his arm reassuringly.

'No, they're sent to fight in appalling conditions, and when they're fortunate enough to be given home leave, they're told they're not welcome in certain places of entertainment.'

'That's still rankling with you, isn't it?'

He smiled apologetically. 'I'm sorry, I've done it again.'

'You have a conscience that you bear for thousands of others. That needs no apology.'

'But I've no right to treat you as an audience for my angry outbursts.' He put his coffee cup down and looked at her directly. 'You deserve better than that.'

'If that's what you believe, who am I to disagree?' They kissed at some length until eventually, she said a little coyly, 'Before I was married, I was taught that a woman should adopt a passive role in physical matters.'

'Is that what your tutoress called it? "Physical matters"?'

'It was my mother, who had a euphemism for every occasion and especially for intimate occasions.'

He kissed her again by way of a reminder that times were changing. 'We received similar guidance from our housemaster, the Reverend H R Palfrey. His choice of euphemism was so creative that, after he'd dismissed us, we returned to our classes no better informed than we'd been before his homily.'

'Did you ever come to understand what he was saying?'

'Yes, I learned about it eventually, but I shan't embarrass you with the details. Instead, let me devour you one last time.' They kissed with the kind of gusto that would surely have caused great offence to the Reverend Palfrey.

'Shall I see you tomorrow?'

'You can bank on it.'

** ** **

Agnes lay awake for some time, thinking about the evening's conversation, and particularly about Fred's joking reference to his housemaster. It was the first time in her life that a man had even referred obliquely to such an intimate matter, and that had been a surprise in itself. James had been as shy as she was to talk about such things, and they'd been equally inhibited during the brief time they'd had together.

All the same, Fred was an honourable man, and he was probably right in saying that society had moved on since Victorian times. Her mother's strictures were born of the Victorian era, and much had changed since the days of her youth.

Something else that created unease was the way their relationship had developed quite naturally to the stage of intimacy it had, as if they were assured of a future together, and that was by no means certain.

11

MARCH

The warm, dry weather of early February had receded and. now, heavy rain and a cold wind had arrived to greet the new month.

'Come inside quickly,' said Agnes, visibly alarmed by the sight of Fred's inverted umbrella.

He hurriedly pulled it back into its normal shape and folded it as he stepped indoors.

'Let me take your coat and cap.' She took his cap from him and hung it up.

'I'm surprised I still have a cap,' he said, unbuttoning his coat. 'At all events, this is a good weekend to be stood down.'

'Why do you say that?'

'There'll be no flying today or tomorrow, or for as long as this wind continues. Happily, the sea state in the Channel will also make the U-boat skippers keep their heads down.'

'Come through, Fred, and I'll make coffee. I've lit a fire in the sitting room, but I think it needs your magic touch.'

He went into the sitting room to find the fire struggling to take hold, just as Agnes had said. Like her, he'd grown up with servants to light the fires, but he'd learned a great many new skills in New Zealand, of which fire-lighting was one of the least demanding. He re-arranged the kindling and laid two of the lesser pieces of wood over it, so that, in a matter of minutes, the fire was ready for a heftier log.

'Oh, thank you, Fred,' said Agnes, standing in the doorway, 'that's wonderful.'

'Another time,' he said, 'I'll show you how to do it. It's easy enough.'

'Like so many more things I have to learn.'

'You've learned to make coffee. That's a good start.'

'But what use is that when it's too strong to drink? It happens so quickly, and I'm sure no one else has that problem.'

'They no doubt had someone to show them. Let's go to the kitchen and see if it's ready.' He followed her to the kitchen and found that the coffee was, in fact, percolating. He took it off the heat and asked, 'Have you a large jug?'

'I think so.' She opened a cupboard and took down an earthenware jug. 'I think I should wash it,' she said. 'I haven't used it for a long while.' Peering inside it, she said, 'I don't think I've ever used it.'

When the jug was clean and dry, Fred decanted the coffee into it. 'It'll be all right now,' he said. 'It's the percolator that makes it stronger.'

'I'd no idea.'

'But now you know. Let's take it through to the sitting room.'

'That's another thing,' she said, joining him in the sitting room. 'At one time, I'd have called this a drawing room. Isn't that awful?'

'Not in the least,' he assured her. 'We are what we're made, at least until we take over the responsibility for our own actions. You've already begun to do that, so you're well on the way to becoming the complete person you want to be.'

'You flatter me, Fred.'

'Speaking of adjustment, I remember talking with an Irish girl, who came with her employers to live in New Zealand. She'd spent her early years in a remote part of western Ireland before going into service as a housemaid in Dublin.' He accepted a cup of coffee from Agnes. 'Thank you. She told me that on her first day in the job, her mistress had told her to put the light out in the drawing room before going to bed. It must have been awful for the poor child. She looked for the wheel to turn down the wick, but there was none. She looked for a tap because she'd heard of gaslighting and she knew the gas came through a pipe with a tap, but tap there was none. Then she tried blowing it out, as she would a candle. She removed her shoes and stood on the table, blowing for all she was worth, but nothing happened. The poor girl had never heard of electricity.'

'How awful. We never think of these things, do we?'

'I was only thinking of it at the time, because she'd come to the store for a new wick for an oil lamp. I remember saying to the girl,

79

"Don't try to blow this one out. You'll blow oil everywhere." She knew I was joking.'

'Good. It would have been awful if she'd thought you were laughing at her.'

'Make fun of the poor child? I wouldn't dream of it.'

'No, I know you wouldn't.' She joined him on the sofa and looked towards the window. 'This weather's not going to change for some time,' she said.

'Let's just stay here and enjoy the warmth and the knowledge that we don't have to go out in the wind and rain. Let's enjoy the sound of it battering the windows. We'll be like the Three Little Pigs.'

'What on earth made you think of pigs?'

' "No, by the hair on my chinny-chin-chin, I will not let you in." '

'That's silly,' she laughed.

'Being silly just once in a while is good for the soul.' He put his arm round her. 'Snuggle up and help me defy the storm.' As he spoke, the wind rattled the sitting room shutters.

'What have I to do?'

'Say the magic words with me, the words the third little pig shouted to the big, bad wolf.'

'But I don't know the story.'

'Don't you? He was genuinely surprised. 'How fortunate it was that I came today. I'll tell it to you.' He waited until he was sure she was ready, and then began the story. She was a rewarding listener and she heard the story to its end, interrupting him only four or five times.

'That was lovely,' she said.

'It's a good story,' he agreed. 'I once told it to a Maori boy to cheer him up. He'd just fallen from a tree and broken his arm.'

'Did he enjoy it?'

'It's difficult to say. He didn't really understand it.'

For the moment, she looked concerned. 'Wasn't his English good enough?'

'It wasn't that. No, the reason he didn't understand it was that there are no wolves in New Zealand. He'd never heard of them.'

'Oh dear.'

'When you think of it, it rules out most of the Grimm brothers' fairy tales where Maori children are concerned. Snuggle up.'

'I'm snuggling up, Fred. I can't get any closer to you.'

'Good, I've got you just where I want you.' He bent his head to kiss her slowly and with much feeling. After some time, he asked, 'Do you remember asking me if I'd ever consider staying in England?'

'Yes, I do.'

'Well, it's my turn to ask you if you'd consider going to live in New Zealand.'

She hesitated awkwardly and said, 'I thought we'd agreed not to discuss that.'

'Ah.'

'What does "Ah" mean?'

'It means that I've got a feeling this conversation isn't exactly taking the route I had marked out for it.'

Agnes looked down at her hands but said nothing.

'You see, you've come to mean a great deal to me, and I think you feel much the same about me. I was working up to asking you if you'd consider coming with me to New Zealand as my wife. I can offer you a good life, I stand to inherit the company, so you'd never want for anything. As for all those things you say you can't do, we could always get someone in to do them.'

'Oh, Fred.' She continued to look down at her hands. 'Maybe it was my fault for encouraging you.'

'You haven't.'

'I never asked you not to… be intimate. I just allowed it to happen, and now I see that I was wrong to do that.' She looked at him for the first time and said, 'Had circumstances been different, I might easily have given you a different answer, but you're asking me to leave everything that's familiar and to travel twelve thousand miles to a strange country.' She hesitated again. 'I can't even contemplate such an enormous step.'

'I see.' He withdrew his arm and stood up. 'I don't want to embarrass you further,' he said quietly, 'so it's by far the best thing for me to leave now. I'm sorry I put you in an awkward situation.'

'You didn't, Fred. I'm just as much to blame for the misunderstanding.'

'It really wasn't what I'd intended.' He turned towards the door. Seeing her get up to follow him, he said, 'I'll see myself out. You shouldn't come to the door. You'll be soaked.' He went to the hallway and took down his coat and cap. 'I'm sorry, Agnes,' he said, putting them on. 'Fool that I am, I completely misjudged the situation. Good bye.' He opened the door and hurried through the driving rain to his faithful Sunbeam.

** ** **

Agnes stood by the door, devastated. In a matter of seconds, she'd hurt the person who meant most to her. Even worse than that, she was convinced she'd encouraged him in his pursuit of her affection. In truth, she'd tried repeatedly to resist his physical attentions, but the awful fact was that whenever desire had clashed with reason the latter had proved woefully weak. She returned to the sitting room, tearful and deeply ashamed of her weakness. Wind and rain continued to hammer with unrestrained spite against the shuttered windows, but she was only half-conscious of it, and paid little regard to anything beyond her wretchedness.

** ** **

Fred drove slowly back to the seaplane base, not so much because of his mood, but in response to the rain that lashed his windscreen. From time to time, he slowed down almost to a crawl to avoid running off the road, so impaired was his view.

Eventually, however, he reached the base and signed himself in. Then, reluctant to face his brother officers in the wardroom, he went straight to his cabin and hung up his tunic before subsiding wretchedly on to his bunk.

'Had circumstances been different....' That was what she'd said, presumably meaning that if his home had been in England, the problem would never have arisen. He could understand her reluctance to leave the country of her birth; he'd never had to make that choice, and he could only wonder how he might have reacted in similar circumstances. As things stood, however, whilst he would be prepared to forego a great deal to spend the remainder of his life with her, he drew the line at deserting Uncle Jim and Aunt Amelia, the first people, since his mother's death, to show him kindness. On reflection, he decided, the word 'kindness' barely began to describe their treatment of him. To lose Agnes was too awful for words, but he could never desert them.

12

Rockingham's replacement had not yet arrived, so the flight was short of a pilot, but it hardly mattered. With a little adjustment to the flight plan, five could do the work of six. So far, however, the U-boat captains seemed unaware that the weather had taken a welcome turn, because they all appeared to be submerged.

The trouble with aerial reconnaissance, at least from Fred's point of view, was that it allowed too much time for thought. It was quite possible to keep an eye out for U-boats at the same time as thinking one's own thoughts, and he'd done too much of that lately. One positive step he'd taken was to apply for a posting, and he expected to hear about it quite soon. There had never been any question of it happening. Elliot wanted rid of him and had barely suppressed his delight at the prospect of his departure. Fred was looking forward to it, although not for any positive reason. He simply wanted to be somewhere where the Navy and Army Canteen wasn't there as a permanent reminder of his foolishness and his loss. There was also the possibility of a posting to a seaplane carrier, and that would take him even further away from his current situation.

He looked at the hunter that dangled from his instrument panel. 'A' Flight should be along soon, and then Fred and his flight would be able to return to base. Above him, Sopwith Camels from Guston kept their vigil. They, too, would be expecting their relief.

A thump on his shoulder made him turn to see Beresford giving him the crossed-fingers sign that meant that enemy aircraft were in the vicinity. It was often easier to communicate that way than with the Gosport tube, which had to compete with the noise of the engine. He looked upward and, sure enough, a pair of Fokker scouts were being engaged by the Camels from Guston. Suddenly, the air was filled with the sound of machine-gunfire as the Fokkers and Camels wheeled, dived and rolled to get into an attacking position. It was too distracting when the task of the One Eight Fours was to search for U-boats.

There was a deafening roar as one of the Fokkers dived in flames towards the sea. A glance aloft told Fred that the Camels were once again taking up station. It meant that the other Fokker had run for home. The Fokker D VII was faster than anything the British had, so it would make its escape easily enough. More importantly, however, it meant that the search could continue unmolested.

Presently, George Makepeace arrived with 'A' Flight, and Beresford fired the flare, ordering 'B' Flight to return to base. Fred led them back to Dover, watching each of them put down safely in the harbour, before he did the same.

With its wings folded, Fred's machine was pushed into its hangar space and made ready for servicing and refuelling. When he'd thanked the ground crew, he turned to Beresford, who was removing the code book and associated matter. He asked, 'Have you heard anything about your leading rate yet, Beresford?'

'Not yet, sir. Maybe they don't think I've got enough seniority.'

'I left them in no doubt about your ability.'

'Thank you, sir. That'll be a great help.'

They walked out of the hangar together, and Fred asked, 'What will you do after the war, Beresford?'

'There's plenty for me to do at home, sir. We have a smallholding, and it's hard work for my mother and sisters.'

Fred thought of the father and brother being killed in the war. 'I imagine it is,' he said.

'Oh well, sir, we only appreciate what comes our way by hard work.'

'That's true.'

'I'm off to get washed now, sir, an' then I think I'll go up to the canteen for a mug of tea.'

'You do that, Beresford, and well done this afternoon.' Mention of the canteen was not what Fred had wanted to hear, but Beresford wasn't to know that.

'Thank you, sir.'

'All right. Secure.'

'Aye, aye, sir.'

Fred continued to the Squadron Office, where he found Squadron Commander Elliot.

'Well, Fuller?'

'No U-boats sighted, but two enemy scouts engaged by aircraft from Guston. One Fokker shot down, the other made a strategic withdrawal.'

'I see. By the way, Fuller, your application for posting has been rejected.' Clearly Elliot shared Fred's disappointment.

'Why?'

'How the hell should I know? Ask the Wing Commander, not me.'

'All right.' Fred picked up Elliot's telephone.

'I wasn't being serious when I suggested that, Fuller.'

'You're such a serious person, Elliot, it's hard to know when you're not being serious.' He eyed him quizzically. 'Do you actually jest, or do you just wax guardedly whimsical from time to time?'

A Wren's voice asked him what number he required.

'Hello, my dear. Flight Commander Fuller here. Would you be kind enough to connect me, please, with Wing Commander Bryant?'

'Certainly, sir. I'll try his extension for you.'

'Thank you so much.'

Elliot asked, 'Do you know how to give a coherent order, Fuller?'

'Yes, Elliot, Do you?'

'By Jove, Fuller, one of these days you'll go too far.'

'Hopefully as far as New Zealand. Then we'll both be happy.'

A voice came on the line. 'Hello, Fuller. Wing Commander Bryant here. What can I do for you?'

'Good morning, sir. I'm just wondering, sir, why my application for posting was rejected. Squadron Commander Elliot has just told me about it, and he hasn't a clue.' As he spoke, he could see Elliot fuming. It was a good feeling at a time when he needed one.

'Yes, I'm sorry, Fuller. The fact is you're an experienced and skilful pilot as well as a valued flight commander, and I just can't let you go at this stage. I told all this to Elliot. I don't know why he's being so coy about it, but there it is.'

'Thank you, sir. It's disappointing, but at least I know my efforts are appreciated.' He looked straight at Elliot as he said it.

'They certainly are, Fuller. Carry on.' As a hurried afterthought, he said, 'Oh, put Elliot on the line, will you?'

'Ay, aye, sir.'

As he left the office, he could hear Bryant's voice saying, 'Elliot, when I tell you something, I don't expect you to disclaim all knowledge of it.' He smiled, as he always did when Elliot caught the rough edge of Bryant's tongue.

** ** **

That evening in the wardroom, George Makepeace made a point of speaking to Fred. 'What is it, Fred? You're not the happy bloke you used to be.'

'My application for posting has been turned down, George.'

'That's a fair cow, mate, but why are you so keen to leave us?'

'It's not you or anyone else in this establishment, George…. At least, I'd be glad to leave Elliot behind, but no, it's a petticoat problem, really.'

'Bad luck. Let me buy you a drink.'

'Thanks, George. Gin would oil the wheels, if you don't mind.'

George called the steward over and ordered two gins. When they were alone, he said, 'It's none of my business, but what's the problem with the lady?'

Fred wondered how he could condense the problem, rather than bore George with it. Finally, he said, 'She seemed happy enough with me, but she can't face pulling up her roots and going to live in Enzed.'

'Poms do get worked up about distance, don't they? Maybe it's because it doesn't exist over here. I mean, let's face it, you can't go far without finding yourself in the sea.' He appeared to give the matter some thought and then asked, 'Have you considered staying here after the war?'

'It's crossed my mind, George, but my aunt and uncle in Enzed have given me everything. I can't run out on them.' He smiled guiltily. 'I won't go on about it.'

'No, fair goes, mate. The least I can do is help you get stunned.'

'Just as long as I'm sober by the end of the Afternoon Watch tomorrow, George.'

'I'll make sure of it, mate. I've got the patrol before yours.'

** ** **

The following lunchtime, Fred received a letter that had been delivered by hand. It was addressed in a woman's handwriting. The only woman he knew in England was Agnes, so he wasn't so much surprised as curious about its content.

5th March, 1918.
Dear Fred,
I feel so wretched after our conversation on Saturday that I have to offer some explanation. It's very difficult for me to express this on paper rather than face to face with you but, in the absence of that luxury, I feel I must.

Your acts of affection were something I'd never before experienced, and I freely admit that I welcomed your attentions. Had that not been the case, I should probably have behaved more modestly from the outset.

I have to admit, also – and I am deeply ashamed to do so – that I did entertain the possibility of persuading you to remain in England after the war. Knowing how you feel about New Zealand and about your aunt and uncle, I can only offer my heartfelt apology for that unworthy thought, and I hope you can find it in your heart to forgive me.

Our time together was delightful, and be assured that I am genuinely fond of you. As I told you on Saturday, had circumstances been different, my answer might also have been different from the one that has caused us both such regrettable distress.

May God watch over you and bring you home safely from this war.
Yours with great affection,
Agnes.

He read the letter several times before taking paper, pen and ink from his locker.

6th March, 1918.
Dear Agnes,
Thank you for your note, which was delivered to me this morning.
It was generous of you to make matters plain, but I have to say that nothing in your explanation surprised me.
I realise that your wish was for me to remain in England, and I find that quite understandable. For my part, I wanted to persuade you, as

you now know, to come with me to New Zealand, so I think that puts us on equal footing if, indeed, any guilt exists. If you are less than innocent, then so am I.

As for my advances – if they pleased you, let them become a fond memory, and I shall do the same, because I am no less genuinely fond of you.

I wish you health and happiness, and if some fortunate man should succeed where I failed, I wish you well in that union also.

Yours with the greatest affection,
Fred.

He blotted his note, folded it and placed it in an envelope, addressing it to: *Mrs Agnes Morley c/o The Navy and Army Canteen.*

Looking at his watch, he realised he had five minutes in which to join his flight in the hangars, so he left the note on his table, resolved to deliver it on his return.

He donned his flying kit and hurried down to the hangars, where he found Beresford waiting for him.

'You shame me, Beresford,' he said. 'I should have been here before you.'

'I'm an early riser, sir, being a smallholder.'

Fred knew that was a nonsense. Junior ratings were routinely shaken each morning, loudly and vulgarly by loud and vulgar petty officers. Something puzzled him, however. 'Beresford, why did so many members of your family enter military service, when you could have served your country as providers of food?'

'We reckoned we could do both, sir, and so far, we have.'

'I admire you for that, Beresford.'

'Thank you, sir.' He waited for Fred to climb into his cockpit and then hoisted himself into his own. The crew unfolded the wings and locked them into place.

'Switches off.'

'Switches off, sir.'

'Drawing in.'

'Drawing in, sir.' The air mechanic turned the propellor to draw fuel into the cylinders.

'Contact.'

'Contact, sir.' The air mechanic swung the propellor, and the engine caught immediately.

One by one, the aircraft of the flight entered the water, gathering speed until they could take off. Fred watched them, finally opening his throttle and following them into the harbour and thence into the air, where he established his place at the head of the formation.

13

It seemed that the tactic of rendering U-boats inactive simply by maintaining an aircraft presence was having remarkable success, because 'B' Flight had been on patrol for more than an hour without a sighting. Visibility was good, particularly after the foul weather of early March, and Fred felt satisfied that the search was being well carried out.

Unfortunately, as he'd found previously, the inactivity of the anti-U-boat patrol allowed too much time for reflection and introspection, and he soon found himself revisiting his last meeting with Agnes. It was wasted energy, he knew, but self-discipline was remarkably difficult in the circumstances. He forced himself to concentrate on his stretch of water, until a change in the engine note alerted him to a possible fault. He looked up to the radiator, which was situated above the engine and just forrard of the upper wing, where an angry release of vapour told its own story. The engine had overheated, and in a remarkably short time. It was already faltering.

Holding the joystick with his left hand and pulling off his right gauntlet with his teeth, he scribbled a note to Beresford. It read: *From G101 to Base. Engine failure 10 miles due S. of Lydd.* He held it up, and Beresford took it. Meanwhile, the engine was protesting more violently than ever. Then, with a feeble grunt, it stopped altogether. Fred turned to the Gosport tube and yelled, 'Hold on tight. We're going down.'

He held the seaplane in a shallow dive, flattening out as it approached the water, then gliding parallel to the surface. Finally, he eased the stick back to adopt a tail-down attitude, watching the wave formation for the best place to put down, and brought the floats into contact with the water. A plume of seawater flew over each of the main floats, and the aircraft hove-to very quickly. He'd been able to give Beresford barely enough time to trail the wireless aerial beneath the aircraft and send the signal. He just hoped enough of it had reached base, or that someone had seen G101 go down, because, now that the aerial was beneath the surface, it was quite useless.

** ** **

Officers' Steward Long, whose valet services Fred shared with George Makepeace, arrived to clean Fred's cabin and make his bunk so that it was ready for night-time. He picked up the various items of laundry and stowed them in the basket provided for that purpose before starting work on Fred's uniform shoes. When he'd worked up a commendable sheen, he re-laced them and left them at the foot of the locker. It was while he was remaking the bunk that he noticed an envelope addressed to Mrs Morley at the canteen. The fact that she and Mr Fuller were in some way connected was common knowledge among the ratings who used the canteen, so the steward placed it in the inside pocket of his jumper. He would deliver it later, when he went for his stand-easy. He was looking forward to that. They usually had currant buns at the canteen on Wednesdays.

** ** **

'I got the signal off by the time we ditched, sir, but I can't be sure they received it.' Beresford sounded apologetic.

'It wasn't your fault, Beresford. I'll have a look at the engine when it's had time to cool down, and see if there's anything obvious.' If there was a chance of their returning under their own power, he had to investigate it, although the likelihood was that the engine was seized and would never run again.

'It would have to happen on a Wednesday, sir.'

'Have you a preferred day of the week for ditching?'

'No, sir. It's just that we usually have currant buns on Wednesdays.'

Fred felt beneath his seat for a paper bag. 'There you are, Beresford,' he said, taking a bun from it and handing the bag containing the other to his wireless operator. 'Now you can be thankful you ditched on a Wednesday.'

'Thank you, sir. Are you sure, sir?'

'Fairly sure, Beresford. If I were you, I'd eat it before I change my mind.'

'Thank you, sir.'

'You're welcome.' When Fred had eaten his, he looked up at the radiator again. He had to check the engine, if only to confirm what he already suspected. Grasping the nearest half-strut, he climbed out of the cockpit and lowered himself so that he was standing on the starboard main float with the disquieting thought that it was all that separated him from the English Channel. With his right hand, he took the side panel off the engine compartment and peered into it in the fading light. He shook his head in response to an enquiring look from Beresford. The oil feed pipe was broken, no doubt having scattered the precious oil over the English Channel. Fred hauled himself back into the cockpit.

'What did you find, sir?'

'The oil feed pipe's fractured, and the engine's most likely seized. There's no shortage of water here, but there's no oil, and even if there were, the engine's not in a fit state for us to get excited.' He looked up at the darkening sky. 'It looks as if we're going to be here all night – at least.'

'All night, sir?'

'At least, Beresford.'

There was a brief silence, and then Beresford said in a sickly voice, 'I'm afraid I'm going to waste that currant bun, sir.'

'In that case, heave to leeward.' He pointed in the direction the wind was taking. 'That way you'll get rid of it for good.'

Beresford made no reply, but vomited over the side.

'That's the spirit. Get rid of it.'

'Don't you get seasick, sir?'

'I did at first, but when you steam across the world and back, you get used to the ship going up and down.'

Beresford heaved again.

'You've got all night to practise. You'll be all right by morning.'

'I hope I'm not going to do this all night, sir.'

As a cloud of spray swept over them, Fred said, 'Let's hope you're not, Beresford, but seriously, you mustn't fall asleep, either.'

'I'll keep watch for any passing ships, sir.'

Fred smiled at his innocent zeal. 'I'm sure I can rely on you for that, but you have to stay awake to survive. You're going to be cold and wet, and the greatest temptation is to say, "Bugger it" and let yourself nod off. That's when your body closes down, and rescuers find a casualty with a blissful expression but not a breath in his body. Trust me.'

'If you say so, sir.'

'I do. Your family has lost more than its fair share of men, and I want to deliver you back to your mother in one functioning piece, so mark my words.'

'Aye, aye, sir.'

'Very good.' Darkness was falling, and the sea was livening. 'We must keep talking, Beresford. Anything but sleep. Tell me about your smallholding.'

'There's not much to tell, sir. We've got two cows and a calf, a few pigs and some chickens. We grow vegetables rather than cereals, and somehow, we make a living, sir.'

'I'm delighted to hear it, but with two cows and a calf, how do you produce calves without a bull?' He wasn't all that interested, but Beresford was, and it might keep him awake.

'We pay a local farmer to let us take our cows to his bull, sir. It means everyone gets what they want.'

'Including the bull and the cows, I suppose.'

'I doubt that, sir. It's all over in a trice with them, sir. Farmers tell me its nothing at all compared with…. You know, sir, what makes people keep doing it. I wouldn't know, myself.'

'How old are you?'

'Nineteen, sir.'

He was another boy who stood every chance of forfeiting his life in the war before ever experiencing the joys of manhood. 'You will one day,' he told him; at least, he hoped he would.

'If you don't mind me asking you, sir, what time is it?'

'Just a minute.' Fred opened his hunter and squinted at it in the failing light. 'Wait. There's an electric torch here.' He took the torch from its clip and shone it on his watch. 'It's almost eighteen hundred.'

'The end of the First Dog Watch, sir. They'll know we're overdue.'

'Yes, but they won't begin searching until daylight tomorrow. A search in darkness is nothing but a fool's errand. I'm sorry, Beresford, but there it is.'

'A ship of the Dover Patrol might pick us up, sir.'

'You never know.' Situated as they were, halfway across the Channel, they were as likely to be picked up by an enemy U-boat, but he left the thought unspoken. There was no sense in alarming the boy.

'How did you get to be a pilot, sir?'

'That's a long story. You'll have to keep chipping in, just to let me know you're awake.'

'I'll do that, sir.'

'Good lad. Well, I decided I wanted to learn to fly. This was in nineteen-eleven, in New Zealand.'

'New Zealand, sir?' He sounded incredulous.

'Yes, that's where my home is. Anyway, I learned in my spare time, and then, when war came, I sailed to England to join the RNVR.'

'Is it expensive, travelling by sea, sir?'

'It can be, but I worked my passage.' It was blatantly untrue, but Fred felt awkward talking about his comfortable existence to a boy whose family were only scratching a living.

'What did you do, sir?'

'I stoked the boilers. It was hard work, I can tell you. It kept me warm, though.'

'I can see how it would do that, sir. What I was really wondering, though, was, how did you get into the RNAS, sir?'

'By sheer brass neck. I marched into the recruiting office and I told them. "I want to join the RNAS," I said. "I can fly, and here are some photographs I took from my aeroplane." They couldn't really argue with that, could they?'

'No, sir. They'd have been daft if they had.' After a moment of silence, he said, 'Some of the lads at the base tell me I'm lucky to be flying with you, sir, and I think I am, too.'

'Perhaps not at this very moment, but the situation could still improve. All the same, thank you for the compliment.'

'Credit where credit is due, sir. What are we going to do next?'

'Have you finished heaving?'

'I think so, sir. I should be about empty now.'

'I think you should, Beresford. While there's no one around to complain, we could sing. How about "Daisy Bell". You must know that.'

' "A bicycle built for two", sir? Yes, I know it.'

They carried out an assault on the old favourite from the music halls, and Fred's reference to the absence of complainants seemed quite apposite, as neither of them was at all vocally gifted, but it filled a need.

' "Keep the Home Fires Burning", sir?'

'No, anything but that.'

'You choose, sir.'

'All right, let's be really crass and have a go at "Mademoiselle from Armentieres" with all the coarse verses we can remember.' He thought it might distract his mind from the very real danger of the aircraft succumbing to the battering of the waves and disintegrating before they could be found.

They did, and the licence the situation afforded seemed to empower them in some way, so that they sang lustily and with great enjoyment despite the increasing cold and spray thrown up as each wave encountered a float.

'Do you know "I'm Shy, Mary Ellen", sir?'

'I don't know the verse, but I can manage the chorus.'

'I only know the chorus, sir.'

'All right, then. Here goes.' They sang the chorus of the well-known song with gusto, actually remembering more of the words than they thought they knew.

'What about "If You Were the Only Girl in the World"?'

'All right, sir.'

They gave the song their usual treatment.

Beresford suggested 'It's a Long Way to Tipperary,' and Fred wryly agreed that it was, but they sang it nevertheless.

' "K-K-K-Katy".'

'All right, Beresford. "K-K-K-Katy", it is.'

They went on to sing that, and then "Pack up Your Troubles in Your Old Kitbag" and many more, and when they could think of no more songs, they tried playing 'I Spy with My Little Eye', but soon gave up, hampered as they were by an expanse of sea, darkness and spray, which offered little in the way of observable objects. Instead, they fell back on the game 'What Am I Thinking Of?' It called for each competitor to think of a noun, to give an unhelpful clue – animal, vegetable or mineral – and allow twenty questions. In this way, they remained awake and ever hopeful as the night wore on, and until the first streaks of sunlight became visible.

** ** **

Officers' Steward Long had shaken Flight Commander Makepeace and was about to perform the same service for Flight Commander Fuller, when he remembered the letter he'd found in the latter's cabin. He hurried along, rehearsing his apology, and arrived at the cabin to find it empty. Moreover, the bunk had not been disturbed. It was very odd. He was about to leave, when the chief steward appeared in the doorway.

'It's your lucky day, Long,' he said, 'even if it ain't Flight Commander Fuller's.'

'What do you mean, Chief?'

'He went out on patrol yesterday afternoon, and he ain't been seen since, so you don't need to do nothing here. You'd better go along to the wardroom and give 'em a hand-out with breakfast.'

'Yes, Chief.' He would have to deliver the letter later.

** ** **

'Are you still awake, Beresford?'

'Yes, sir. Only just.'

'Prop your eyes open. Make an effort.'

'Aye, aye, sir.'

Fred rubbed his eyes and quartered the horizon as best he could. His head ached after the night of sleepless vigil, and his vision was slow to clear. He looked around again and fancied he saw a speck in the sky. It was difficult to tell with tired, sleepy eyes. 'Beresford,' he said, 'will you pass me your night glasses?'

Beresford handed the binoculars over, and Fred focused them on the speck, which revealed itself to be an aircraft.

'Can you see anything, sir?'

'An aircraft. It's too early to tell whether it's friendly or not.' He continued to peer into the morning light until he could make out more of the aircraft's characteristics. Suddenly, he was excited. 'By jingo, it's a One Eight Four!'

'One of ours, sir?'

'Yes, unless the Hun's started using them too. Give them a white flare, Beresford.' He waited, and nothing happened, 'What are you playing at, man?'

'My hands, sir. They're so cold, I can't find the trigger.'

'Pass it over to me.' He sympathised with Beresford in his predicament; his own hands were numb inside the gauntlets that were supposed to protect them. Carefully, he took the Very pistol from Beresford and fired a flare high over the sea and in the direction of the seaplane, which was now easily recognisable for what it was.

The seaplane came down low and swept past them, the pilot and wireless operator waving encouragingly to them, and Fred read *G102* on the side of the fuselage. It was Arthur Reynolds, his flight lieutenant. Fred couldn't help shouting, 'Good old Reynolds!'

As the seaplane turned, it was possible to see something trailing beneath it that was creating its own tiny wake between the waves, and then it disappeared.

'He's paying out his aerial, sir,' reported Beresford excitedly. 'He's going to report our position!'

The seaplane rocked its wings as a parting salute and began to climb again. All the two had to do now was wait for a ship to arrive. It might take a long time, but at least, their position would be known.

** ** **

Agnes was behind the counter at forenoon stand-easy when the first of the ratings arrived. They headed straight for the counter, but one of them, a steward she'd seen on several occasions, seemed to be waiting for something or someone. She left the girls to serve the ratings while she spoke to him.

She asked, 'Is something the matter?'

'No, ma'am.' In a lower voice, he said, 'There's a letter for you from Flight Commander Fuller.' He took it from his jumper and handed it to her. Her heart quickened as she took it. It looked a little creased, but she made no comment. Instead, she asked, 'Did he ask you to deliver it?'

'No, ma'am. I haven't seen Mr Fuller since yesterday morning. I found it in his cabin in the afternoon when I went to make up his bunk an' all. I'm afraid I forgot about it when I came yesterday, but you weren't here, anyway. I'm sorry, ma'am.'

'There's no need to apologise. Did you say you hadn't seen him since yesterday morning?'

'No, ma'am, I haven't.'

A nearby rating asked, 'Who's that, "Shorty"? Flight Commander Fuller? 'E went out on patrol yesterday and 'e never come back. They're out there, lookin' for 'im. Beresford an' all.'

Agnes felt cold blood rushing to her extremities. 'How long has he been missing?'

The rating who'd delivered the news looked thoughtful. ' "B" Flight went on patrol yesterday afternoon, during the First Watch,' he said. Looking at the bulkhead clock, he made a calculation. Finally, he said, 'Nineteen hours 'e'll have been gone.'

**** **** ****

A smudge of smoke on the horizon grew into an approaching ship. Fred stared through the binoculars, trying to identify it. 'It's a warship,' he said, 'so it's most likely to be one of ours.' He stared a little longer and said, 'It is one of ours.' He seized the Very pistol again and fired a flare ahead of the warship. 'It's coming for us, Beresford,' he said. 'We're in luck.'

The warship, which turned out to be a destroyer, covered the distance as only a destroyer could. When it was almost alongside, Fred shouted, 'Don't come too close. I have a "mouldy" on board!'

An officer on the bridge shouted back, 'I'll lower a boat.'

The sea boat was hastily manned and lowered. The leading seaman on board brought it to the after end of the aircraft, away from the dangerous end of the torpedo, and Beresford scrambled on board first. Fred had to crawl into the after cockpit and then along the fuselage, holding on with numbed fingers, until he could board the boat.

When they were safely on board the destroyer, Beresford was taken below, and Fred climbed the ladder to the bridge, where he shook hands with the captain. 'I'm obliged to you, sir,' he said with some feeling.

'Not at all. Welcome aboard. I expect you'd appreciate a spot of breakfast.'

'I should, heartily, sir, and so would my wireless operator, but first things first. As I told you earlier, sir, my aircraft has a torpedo on board and, rather than leave it as a floating hazard to shipping, I wonder if your gun crews might welcome some target practice.'

'A wise suggestion,' said the captain. Turning to the voice pipe, he gave the order, 'Turn eight points to starboard.' It would enable him to put some distance between his ship and the aircraft.

When the distance was complete, the captain passed the order to open fire on the luckless seaplane. Fred had known and flown G101 for some considerable time, and the process gave him no satisfaction beyond that of knowing that the torpedo would no longer present a danger to shipping. He could hardly bear to watch, but he forced himself to witness the destruction of his faithful friend. With the third salvo, a shell detonated the torpedo, causing a gigantic explosion, and Fred paid his respects, holding his salute until only a few items of wreckage remained on the surface.

** ** **

Agnes continued to perform her duties mechanically whilst, behind the calm and business-like facade, she was experiencing a torrent of emotions. Guilt, regret, horror and a sense of acute loss presented themselves repeatedly in a kaleidoscope of torture that gave rise to unanswerable questions. Had Fred's state of mind following their last meeting contributed in some way to his misadventure? Had his power of concentration been impaired by the distraction? Had he gone to his death feeling rejected? Of course, there was always a chance that he would be found. By definition, seaplanes floated on water, and that must increase the possibility of his survival.

Conjecture was a pointless and self-defeating pursuit. The only sensible course was to wait until she heard something definite. Steward Long had promised to find out what he could, but he wouldn't be back until the end of the First Watch at four o' clock. Meanwhile she forced herself to concentrate as much as she could on her work.

She felt a quickening of her pulse when the first of the junior ratings arrived, but Long wasn't with them. With only Doris available for work, she was obliged to help with the tea, and that, at least, provided her with something to occupy herself.

Eventually, Steward Long arrived, although he waited, as he had that morning, until Agnes had worked her way through the queue of demanding sailors.

Mercifully, he came straight to the point. In a low voice, he said, 'They're all right, ma'am. A destroyer picked them up this morning.'

'Oh, thank you. Are they really all right?' She tried to sound calm, but her heart was pounding.

'There's nothing that a hot bath and square meal won't put right, ma'am. They say the seaplane went down due to engine failure.'

'That is such a relief, Steward Long. Thank you.'

'It's no trouble, ma'am. I've left a hot water bottle in his bunk. It's as much as I can do, so I'd like a cup of tea now, if you'd be so kind.'

'Of course.' She waved his penny aside. 'Have this one on the house.'

'Thank you, ma'am. I'm obliged to you.'

Relieved of her burden, Agnes waited for the last of the ratings to leave. They were allowed no more than fifteen minutes for their stand-easy, but it seemed an age. Eventually, they went, leaving her and Doris.

'Ma'am?'

'Yes, Doris?'

'Do you mind if I go when I've done the washing-up, ma'am? I have to call in on my mother. She's not been all that well.'

'Of course, Doris. Leave the washing-up to me. I hope your mother improves quickly.' Although Doris couldn't possibly know it, it was a relief.

'Are you sure, ma'am?'

'Yes, off you go, Doris.'

'Thank you, ma'am. Thank you most kindly.' Doris put her uniform cap and coat on and left, closing the door behind her.

Agnes stood with her back to the sink and with her eyes closed. For the first time since losing James, she began to sob, continuing to do so unrestrainedly until she was convinced she had no tears left to shed. She would write a note to Fred when she arrived home, but first, she had to give herself time to become calm and settled.

14

Fred was grounded for the next three days, and Steward Long failed to appear the next morning. When Fred was sufficiently awake, he consulted his hunter and found that he'd slept almost three hours past the usual time for Long to call him. He'd just closed his watch and settled comfortably back on the pillow, when Long arrived with a cup of tea.

'Good morning, sir, and welcome back.'

'Thank you, Long. Thank you, also, for the hot water bottle I found in my bunk and for allowing me to sleep until this disreputable hour.'

'You needed the rest, sir.'

'How very thoughtful of you, Long. I imagine breakfast is long gone?'

'Breakfast in the wardroom, sir, yes, but the chief cook tells me he will be happy to make special arrangements in your case.' He felt inside his jumper and took out an envelope. 'Also, I was asked to give you this, sir.'

'Thank you, Long.' Fred put it on the table beside him. 'You know, I'm surrounded by the very best of people.' He saw the curtain twitch and, recognising the twitcher, qualified his observation with, 'But there's always an exception. Thank you again, Long. Carry on.'

'Aye, aye, sir.' Long departed, making way for Squadron Commander Elliot.

'Good morning, Fuller.'

'Good morning, Elliot. The procession of well-wishers seems endless.'

'I'm actually here to remind you of your responsibility to report to me after each patrol.'

'And I thought you'd hurried over to express your heartfelt relief at my deliverance from Davy Jones's Locker. Oh, the bitterness of life. However, I can give you my report now. We found no U-boats, at least while I was with the flight, but I did find a fractured oil feed pipe. I found it whilst standing on a float in the middle of the English Channel and peering into the engine compartment, and that was when I realised the game was up. Does that satisfy you, Elliot?'

Elliot was beginning to bristle. 'Whether it does or not, Fuller, I will remind you that I am superior to you in rank—'

'If in absolutely no other respect.'

'Let me finish, Fuller. I was about to say that the significant difference between you and I—'

'Don't you mean. "you and me"?'

'Damn it, Fuller! You know what I mean. Isn't it high time you repented of your rebellious, colonial ways and addressed me as "sir"?'

Fred adopted a pensive look. 'I had it in mind to leave it a while longer, so that you would appreciate it more fully' he said, 'but I can see that it's causing you no end of misery. Would it make you happy if I called you "sir"?'

'Of course it would.'

'Would it make your cup run over with unalloyed joy if I played the old retainer, tugged my forelock, bent the knee and addressed you as "sir"?'

'Damn it, Fuller, will you take this seriously?'

'Oh, that's asking too much, but now that I know how vitally important it is to you, I'll try, every once in a while to bring a smile to your careworn features by using the desired form of address... sir.'

Seemingly at a loss for a suitable retort, Elliot looked at his watch and said, 'You realise you've missed breakfast, don't you?'

'Sadly, I fear that may well be the case... sir.'

'Well, you've only yourself to blame.'

Fred looked suitably penitent until Elliot had left, and Long returned to say, 'I've run you a bath, sir.'

'Long, you continue to amaze me, and I'm as grateful as ever. Thank you.'

** ** **

Half-an-hour later, Fred sat down to a substantial breakfast made all the more enjoyable because Elliot had come into the wardroom just as Long was serving it. His disapproval was not difficult to discern.

Having eaten, Fred poured himself a second cup of coffee and, whilst doing so, remembered the envelope Long had given him. The diversion of his impish exchange with Elliot had driven all other thoughts from his head. He took it out and recognised Agnes's handwriting. As far as he was aware, everything that needed to be said had been said at least once, so it was with mild curiosity that he slit open the envelope to read the letter.

8th March, 1918.
Dear Fred,
I cannot express my joy and relief on learning that your rescuers had found you safe and well. I had no idea for most of today whether you were alive or dead. All I knew was that you'd been missing for nineteen hours. Also on my mind was the memory of our last meeting, and the thought of your going, for all I knew, to your death, having experienced rejection at my hands was too much to bear.
What I said to you when we last met remains unchanged, but I do have a suggestion to put to you. It's not the kind of thing I can express adequately in writing, so I wonder if we might meet once more. I shall be at home at the weekend. Could you possibly call at the canteen, so that we can make arrangements? Of course, if you'd rather not, I shall understand. I wait to hear from you.
Yours with great affection,
Agnes.

Surprised that Agnes knew of his misfortune, and somewhat intrigued by her reference to a 'suggestion', he returned the note to his pocket and finished his coffee. In a very short time, he realised, the canteen would be full of junior ratings enjoying their forenoon stand-easy, so he would leave his visit until that was over.

** ** **

Agnes must have seen him approach the canteen, because she came outside to meet him, presumably in the interests of discretion.

'Fred, how are you?' There was still a note of concern in her voice, despite the relief she'd mentioned in her note.

'I'm in robust health, thank you. And you?'

'I'm well, thank you.'

'And I'm glad to hear it. Thank you for your note. I'm excused flying duties until Monday, so I can meet you at any time over the weekend.'

'Oh, Fred,' she said, clearly disconcerted, 'must you be so... business-like, so unfriendly?'

'I don't *feel* unfriendly, so I'm sorry if I sound it. I'm just not the ardent lover I was, having learned to my cost that there's no future in it.'

'Plainly, this isn't going to be easy,' she said, 'but I really would like us to meet if we can.'

'As I told you, I'm free at any time from this evening until Sunday evening. It'll be business as usual on Monday.' He added, 'Weather permitting, of course.'

'I'd rather not think about that.'

Fred thought briefly. 'If I pick you up at twelve o' clock tomorrow,' he said, 'I'll take you to lunch and then we can talk while we digest. If I like your suggestion, we'll discuss it at leisure.' He cocked an eye. 'If it ends in hurt and misery, we shall part, because disappointed people often say things they later regret, and there's no profit in recrimination. In that way, if you've achieved nothing else, at least you'll have had lunch.'

She closed her eyes, patently unhappy with his attitude. 'You sound so cold,' she said.

'Coldness is only absence of warmth, and you know how that came about.'

'I suppose I do, but yes, I'll agree to your suggestion.'

'Very well. Twelve o' clock, then.' He touched his cap. 'Until then.'

** ** **

An unscheduled meeting on Saturday morning with Wing Commander Bryant in the Squadron Office provided Fred with a degree of amusement.

'It's good to see you back, Fuller,' said Bryant, and it was clear that he meant it.

'Thank you, sir. It's quite a relief to be back, and my wireless operator agrees with me.'

'Of course. How was he…. I was going to say "under fire", but you know what I mean?'

'He was excellent, sir. He and I may well tour the music halls as a singing double act after the war. That's if all else fails, of course.'

'Really?'

'We sang every song we knew to keep ourselves awake through the night, and we invented quite a few verses too.'

'I've warned you in the past, Fuller,' said Elliot, 'about your familiarity with the lower deck.'

'Unlike you… sir, I was promoted from the lower deck, and therefore enjoy some affinity with the excellent men whose task it is to help fight this war. It was also necessary on the night in question for Beresford and I to co-operate in preserving our lives.'

Bryant laughed. 'It certainly was.' He picked up his hat and gloves and said, 'As I said it's good to have you back, and I imagine everyone agrees with me.'

'Well,' said Fred, smiling benignly at Elliot, 'almost everyone.'

'Get some rest, Fuller,' said Bryant.

'I will, sir. I'm just about to enjoy a leisurely lunch.'

'In the wardroom?'

'No, sir, further afield.'

** ** **

Agnes was ready when he called. She buttoned up her coat and took his arm to walk down the path to the Sunbeam.

She asked, 'What do you think of the peace treaty between Germany and Russia, Fred?'

'It's quite worrying.'

'Why?'

'Because the troops Germany has been deploying in the east will now come home to swell the Kaiser's ranks on the Western Front.'

'Oh dear, I hadn't thought of that.' She took her place on the passenger seat and arranged her skirts.

He started the engine and climbed in beside her. 'The only consolation is that we have the Americans on our side. We've yet to see what they can do, but they keep promising great things.'

'We just have to keep our fingers crossed.'

'That expedient may help to some extent,' he agreed. 'I don't think it's been tried up to now, but you never know.'

After an awkward silence, she asked, 'Where are we going?'

'The Corunna Hotel. My imagination doesn't stretch any further than that.'

'It's familiar,' she said, 'friendly and familiar.'

'I'm glad you approve.'

They drove the rest of the way in silence.

When they were seated in the restaurant, Agnes asked, 'How is the Beresford boy after the incident?'

'You know,' he said, 'apart from Wing Commander Bryant this morning, you're the first person to ask about Beresford. He's all right. He'll fly with me again on Monday.'

'What actually happened?'

'The oil feed pipe broke, and the engine seized.'

'What does that mean?'

'Without oil to lubricate the moving parts, the engine overheated and moving parts expanded so that they could no longer turn; the engine simply couldn't function any longer. It just stopped.'

'I see.' Whether she did or not, she abandoned the subject and studied the menu instead. 'According to the waiter, most of these items are unavailable.'

'That's war for you.'

She made her choice, and they gave their order to the waiter.

'It must be demoralising to be a waiter in these times,' she said, 'having to tell people that things are no longer available.'

'I imagine they become hardened to it after a while.'

'I imagine so. Tell me, though, what it was like, sitting in a seaplane and waiting for someone to come and find you.' She seemed desperate to foster some kind of conversation.

'We spent the time waiting for light. No one was going to find us in the dark.' Then, because she'd expressed her interest, he thought it only polite to satisfy her curiosity. 'It was cold and wet. The sea kept hitting the floats and showering us with what felt like freezing water. When that's been happening for some time, there's an awful temptation to give way to tiredness, and that's fatal.'

'Fatal?'

'Oh yes, the body gives in to cold and exhaustion. That's why it's necessary to fight the temptation and stay awake.'

'It can't have been easy, staying awake all night.'

He laughed at the memory. 'Beresford and I sang music hall songs to keep ourselves awake,' he told her. 'We talked as well. I know quite a lot about breeding cattle now.'

'Do you?'

'Not really,' he laughed, 'but I know more than I did before I spent the night with Beresford. I also learned that, as smallholders, Beresford, his father and his brother could have avoided military service, but they wanted to do their duty as they saw it.'

'Life's been cruel to them.' She placed her hand on his. 'Thank goodness you were both spared.' Then, as the thought occurred to her, she asked, 'How did you know that business about staying awake?'

'It was an old fisherman who told me that when I was a boy.'

'So the others in your squadron don't necessarily know about it?'

'I don't suppose they do.'

'Don't you think something should be done about letting them know?'

'I think you may have a point there, Agnes.' With so many things to attend to, he'd never really considered it. 'I'll see if I can get to see the wing commander and put it to him. I think survival training is important, although you have to remember that survival at sea won't be necessary after this month.'

'Why not?'

'There'll be no need to fly over the sea,' he told her confidently. 'General Trenchard would tell you that, although I may be doing him an injustice. He may not write off the sea altogether as a potential battleground while he has enough highly-trained soldiers in his new air force to carry out naval reconnaissance and tackle the U-boat problem. They must be capable of it. I mean to say, it's only like trench warfare, but with rather more water and a good deal less mud.'

'You feel very strongly about the Air Force Act, don't you?'

He waited until the waiter had delivered their first course. Eventually, he said, 'I'm a part of something great and glorious that, I fear, is about to be trampled underfoot. I told you some time ago that the formation of a central air force was probably, if regrettably, the only way forward, but it was always going to be difficult, creating a composite of two services, each with its own traditions, language and way of life. I must say I can only wonder why this government has handed the job of combining the two to a man who has already made his divisive attitude known.'

'Do you really know that?'

He nodded. 'It's common knowledge.' He leaned forward confidingly to say, 'I could be disciplined for saying this, but when you consider the way Haig and the General Staff have been using and abusing our troops on the Western Front, and the fact that the Navy is the domain of that posturing jackass Beatty, do we really need a third buffoon to take command of the central air force?'

After a while, he felt he'd probably aired his views sufficiently, because he changed the subject, saying, 'After all that, I believe we came here because you had a suggestion to make.'

'We came here because you decided we should. I asked you to call on me so that I could put my suggestion to you, and I shall be happy to do that when you've taken me home. When a delicate matter has to be discussed, public exposure in a hotel dining room comes a poor second to the privacy of my sitting room, wouldn't you say?'

'If that's what you prefer.'

** ** **

Fred placed the tray of coffee things on the low table and took his seat at the end of the sofa.

'Fred,' said Agnes, joining him on the sofa, 'don't you think you could be a little less withdrawn and just a shade more receptive?'

He considered the question and said, 'My feelings for you haven't changed. How could they after only a few days? My reserve is my defence, nothing more hostile than that.' He took a cup of coffee from her. 'Thank you.'

'Are you afraid I might hurt you again?'

'Let's say that I'm nursing the bruise. It's bound to heal eventually if it's allowed to do so, but if it's subjected to repeated blows, the healing might well take longer.'

'I can understand that.' She was looking down at her hands the way she had on their last meeting, before she'd given him her decision. 'Don't you think, though, that the same risk might apply to me?'

To give himself time to think about her question, he got up and put another log on the fire. Taking his place again on the sofa, he said, 'It may well apply to you, but if that's the case, it makes it all the more curious that you should want to meet me again.'

'I suppose it must seem odd.' After a little reflection, she said, 'When one of the ratings told me you were missing after a patrol, I was distraught. How I kept my feelings to myself, I really don't know.'

'How did it come about,' he asked, 'that a rating told you I was missing?'

'Your steward gave me your letter. He said he'd found it in your cabin, but that he hadn't seen you since the previous morning, and then another rating overheard him. He was the one who told me you were missing.'

It made sense. No one had been indiscreet, except that the unknown rating might have been a little more tactful.

'Part of me wondered if you might have been distracted by thoughts of what had happened between us,' she went on, 'and you'd been unaware of whatever danger it was that caused your misfortune. That possibility was horrifying enough, but my worst fear by far was simply that you wouldn't survive, and I couldn't bear that.' In her distress, and apparently without being conscious of it, she'd laid her hand on his sleeve and was now gripping his arm.

'You know I survived,' he said, 'and I can set your mind at rest about your distraction theory. Believe me when I tell you that, in ditching in the Channel and bobbing around all night in a flimsy seaplane, I never gave your rejection a single thought. I was far too busy trying to preserve our two lives, Beresford's and mine.'

'I'm glad.' She blinked to dismiss the tears that had formed during their conversation, but with little success.

'Here.' He gave her the white handkerchief from his breast pocket. 'I survived, so there's no need for guilt or conjecture.' Although their relationship was effectively over, it still distressed him to see her so unhappy.

'Something is needed, Fred.' She sniffed as further tears formed.

'A good blow is what you need,' he suggested, pointing to the handkerchief. 'Go on. See if you can bring down the walls of Jericho.'

'Suddenly you're warm again,' she said, 'much more your old self.'

'I was always clay in the hands of a tearful woman. Come over here and tell me what's on your mind.' He opened his arms to welcome her. It seemed there was no other course to take.

She gave her nose a final blow before joining him.

'Not bad,' he said, 'but not in the same class as the bugler who annoys everyone on the base with his wretched Reveille.'

'We're at a crossroads, you a'd I,' she said.

'Have another blow,' he suggested.

She did, quite successfully. 'A crossroads,' she repeated.

'I must confess, it looks to me more like a *cul de sac*.'

'Please listen.' She settled comfortably with her head against his shoulder.

'I'm listening.'

'On the one hand, you don't want to stay in England.'

'True.'

'Whereas the idea of leaving everything and moving to New Zealand terrifies me.'

'We established that the last time I was here.'

'Bear with me,' she said, stroking his hand. 'We've already tried a third option, which was to go our separate ways.'

'Do you mean there's a fourth option?'

'Yes, there is, and it's the suggestion I mentioned.'

'After all this time, you'd better trot it out before you forget what it is.'

'What?'

'You mentioned it some time ago, in your note.' In truth, he'd waited so long that he thought she might have forgotten it already.

'All right, I'm coming to it. The war's not going to end for quite some time, so we don't need to make a decision immediately. All kinds of things might happen between now and then.'

'What kinds of things?'

'The way we feel about various matters, how we feel about each other…. Anything, really.'

'What are you suggesting?'

'That we continue as we were, and just see what happens.'

He thought about it and said, 'I'm half-convinced.'

'It's a start.'

'It is, but the other half needs to be convinced. When you say we could change our minds about how we feel about things, what do you have in mind?'

'It's impossible to say, because it's all in the future. Just as an example, though, you might change your mind about staying here, or I might change mine about moving to New Zealand. Because it's in the future, we just don't know.'

'We may decide we no longer belong together,' he said.

'It's possible.'

'But I hope we shan't.'

'No, that would be awful.'

She was looking straight into his eyes, and when that happened, he had no control. Nature dictated and found him readily obedient. He bent and kissed her.

'You see,' she said, 'neither of us knew that was going to happen. That's what's so wonderful about the future. It's all so uncertain.'

15

Wing Commander Bryant was quick to see the need for survival training across the service.

'Write me a report that I can send through the appropriate channels, Fuller. With all the fuss and palaver leading up to the first of April, I can't see anything happening in a hurry, but something could eventually come of it.'

'Aye, aye, sir. In the meantime, I should like to speak unofficially to our own chaps, if I'm allowed. For the time we have left to us as a naval air service, I'd like to give them the benefit of my knowledge and experience.'

'You want to speak to the whole wing? I should say so. I'll get that organised straight away. How much time do you need with each squadron?'

'No more than half-an-hour, sir.'

'Excellent.' Bryant leaned forward confidentially and said, 'I know that many of you are feeling rather low about the first of April, but it mustn't affect your efficiency as pilots and observers.'

'It won't do that, sir, even though I speak for the rest when I say that I see the Air Force Act as necessary, even inevitable, but deeply regrettable.'

Bryant nodded in unofficial agreement. 'Any officer is at liberty to refuse to serve in the new air force,' he said, 'but don't forget that it would mean forfeiting the right to hold a commission in any other branch of the service.'

'We're all aware of that, sir.'

'In any case, most of you hold temporary commissions for the duration of hostilities. Regardless of how long this war will last, your discomfiture will be short-lived compared to mine and that of any other

RN officer who feels that he's been cast adrift.' He smiled weakly. 'We'll just have to make the best of a bad job. Given time, I'm sure the new service can be a success, but it's going to be an uphill struggle.' He added, 'By the way, you didn't hear me say any of that.'

Fred picked up his cap to leave. 'I didn't hear you say what, sir?'

'Never mind.' Bryant smiled and said, 'Carry on, Fuller.'

'Aye, aye, sir.'

** ** **

'As far as I know, the only character in the squadron who's looking forward to next month is Elliot.'

'Is he actually looking forward to it?' Agnes handed Fred a cup of tea.

'Thank you. Yes, he intends to make his mark in the new air force. Little does he realise it, but he's already made a name for himself in the RNAS. Admittedly, it's not a name his mother would be prepared to boast about, but he'll still be remembered by it.'

Agnes's thoughts were of gentler things. 'I'm so glad we're no longer avoiding each other,' she said.

'I wasn't avoiding you. I just didn't come looking for you.'

'You know what I mean. Kiss me and reassure me.'

'All right, if you'll do the same.' He kissed her slowly and with much feeling. 'Now it's your turn,' he reminded her.

'If you remember, I was taught that a lady should never take the initiative. Still, I'm not the innocent I was.' Having made her point, she kissed him in much the same way as he'd just kissed her.

'You're certainly not,' he agreed, 'and I'm thankful for it.'

The suggestion of a frown creased her forehead. 'What need have you to be thankful?'

'If you were completely passive, as you were taught to be, there would be little pleasure in it for me or, I suspect, for you. As things have turned out, we can share the fun.'

' "Fun" is a nice word,' she said. 'It sounds like something that doesn't have to be enjoyed seriously.'

He laughed at the idea. 'What kind of thing do you have to enjoy seriously?'

'Pastimes, you know. Bridge and Whist.'

'Yes, I prefer our kind of fun to either of those things.' He studied the flames flickering around the log in the grate, letting his thoughts choose their own route. Eventually, he said, 'In your current circumstances, I imagine you're relieved that you never started a family.'

'It would have made my life more difficult,' she agreed, 'but it was most unlikely.'

'Because you were only together for a short time? I'm not so sure. I've known it happen after one... after a single...'

'I know what you mean.'

'I'm sorry, I didn't mean to embarrass you.'

'Or yourself, presumably.' She laughed nervously. 'There are ways of avoiding accidents, you know.'

'Oh, I know.'

'Of course.'

He searched his mind for a change of subject, wishing he hadn't made the remark in the first place, but she rescued him by pouring another cup of tea and asking, 'Will you have to wear a different uniform after the first of April?'

'I believe a new one has been designed, and word has leaked out that it wouldn't look out of place in the foyer of a kinema theatre, but we have dispensation to wear our existing uniform until it becomes too worn to be smart. Hopefully, by the time mine becomes worn and shabby, the war will be over and I'll be back in familiar tweeds.'

'I hope it's not as awful as you imagine,' she said, kissing him.

'Things seldom are. I'll keep you informed.' He returned her kiss, questing playfully for a while, but then growing increasingly insistent, until she broke away.

'Let me rest for a minute,' she said, adding by way of entreaty, 'please.'

'You've no need to plead,' he assured her. 'Rest at your leisure.'

'When you kiss me like that, it... affects me.'

'I know.' He stroked her hand, telling himself that they'd already ventured beyond all recognised bounds. Further intimacy was out of the question.

** ** **

'As you all know,' Fred told the assembled squadron, 'my wireless operator and I recently spent an anxious night in the English Channel. We were wet and extremely cold and tired, which makes it more than likely that the reason for our survival was that I knew something about the danger of exposure to the elements.' He saw Elliot raise his eyebrows in an indication of boredom, a gesture that the wing commander, seated next to him, was quick to notice.

'I owe that knowledge to a fisherman I knew when I was a boy in Lymington. A ship had run aground in a storm further along the coast, and one of its lifeboats had been brought ashore. It was filled with passengers, all of whom were dead. Now, you may well ask, as I did at the time, why had they lost their lives when they'd been adrift at sea for only one night? It wasn't through hunger or lack of drinking water. I'll tell you why they perished. It was from exposure to the elements.' Elliot was still looking sceptical, but he was unlikely to go aloft, anyway, so he was safe enough. The others weren't and they were entitled to Fred's advice.

'They would be soaked to the skin and very cold,' he went on. 'When that happens, the body's first reflex is to shiver. This is to generate warmth, but success in that endeavour is most unlikely in an open boat. The next stage, however, is the dangerous one. This is where tiredness takes control of the body quite quickly, so that the victim is hardly aware of what is happening. Soon, he begins to feel less cold, and his saturated clothing ceases to matter any longer as he descends into warm, inviting and blissful sleep. The body's functions close down, and unconsciousness leads painlessly to death.' He looked around the squadron, satisfying himself that everyone except Elliot was waiting for the good news.

'Here is the advice I received from the fisherman I mentioned. From the very beginning, gentlemen, you have to resist that tiredness. Make yourselves stay awake, if necessary, by hard, physical effort. Make yourselves think, as well. It's very important that you're mentally alert as well as physically active, because mental relaxation leads, as you know, to drowsiness and then to sleep.' He wondered how the next piece of advice might be received by the more traditional officers in the squadron.

'Beresford, my wireless operator, and I talked well into the night. He told me about cattle breeding, and I told him about life in New

Zealand. We played word games, too. I'm sure you know the kind of game I have in mind. Then, when tiredness at its worst came stalking us, we sang.' He saw some of his colleagues smile, and Elliot's eyebrows made a repeated gesture of condescending boredom, but he continued.

'We sang music hall songs, as many as we could remember, and when we couldn't remember the words, we invented them. I wouldn't like to recall how many verses we managed of "Mademoiselle From Armentieres", but you can imagine that most of them were unfit for repetition in mixed company.' That last observation brought forth ribald laughter. 'I'm sure you can all think of your own diversions, gentlemen. The only rule is that you don't allow yourselves or your crewmembers to fall asleep until you're each safely tucked up in a rescuing vessel.' He took a step backward and asked, 'Have you any questions?'

'Yes.' Elliot rose to his feet. 'You're advising commissioned officers to indulge in parlour games with ratings. How can you expect any respect from them after that?'

'If the only alternative were to maintain the accepted distance between a junior rating and my exalted self, I should expect none whatsoever, unless – and this is pure conjecture – naval discipline also exists in the Life Hereafter, in which case I should expect him to salute me on his or my arrival.' He waited for the squadron's laughter to cease, before going on to say, 'As for respect, Squadron Commander Elliot, if I were to order my wireless operator to climb the ensign mast and sing two verses of "Hearts of Oak" clad in naught but seaboots and a sou'wester, he would do it without hesitation.'

'Oh, Elliot,' said the wing commander, chuckling, 'you walked into that one.' Turning to the squadron, he said, 'I think we all owe Flight Commander Fuller our thanks for his time, his effort and, quite possibly, our lives, should we ever have the misfortune to ditch. Thank you, Fuller.'

'Yes,' said George Makepeace enthusiastically, 'good on yer, Fred!' His endorsement gave rise to similar messages of appreciation from members of the squadron.

** ** **

A few days later, Wing Commander Bryant assembled both squadrons in the wardroom. None of the officers summoned had any inkling of what it was about, except that the likelihood was that it would be connected with the first of April.

When everyone was present, Bryant told them to sit and smoke if they wished.

'The fact is,' he said, 'I've been promoted to wing captain and given a new appointment. The news came very suddenly, and I shall be leaving you later today. I'm afraid there has been no time in which to hold individual meetings. I must say, however, that I have thoroughly enjoyed commanding this wing, I'm very proud of your achievements, as you should be, and I wish you all the very best of luck, both now and after the first of April.'

There was a chorus of good wishes from the two squadrons. Bryant was a popular officer and many had appreciated his efforts in curbing Elliot's oft-misguided zeal.

'By virtue of his seniority, Squadron Commander Elliot will be Acting Wing Commander for the time being, at least until his promotion is confirmed or another appointment is made. Flight Commander Fuller, by the same token, I should like you to take over as Squadron Commander.'

** ** **

'Not only are we now under the command of a malevolent half-wit, but I am henceforth grounded and expected to command the squadron from my ivory tower.'

'Are you to be promoted?' It seemed important to Agnes.

'Yes, I'll become Squadron Commander Nuisance, and you'll be even more confused, because I'll still have only two rings. That's because I have less than eight years' seniority, but I'll have two stars as well.'

'Maybe the new service will adopt a more straightforward system of ranks.'

'Yes, I'll be a captain, then, with three pips.'

'Gosh, rapid promotion.'

'No, Agnes,' he said, shaking his head resignedly, 'not a captain, RN. Until the RAF decide on a new structure, they're adopting Army ranks – the new service will be, after all, an Army acquisition – and a captain is the equivalent of a lieutenant commander.'

'All I know,' said Agnes doggedly, 'is that you're a lovely man, and no number of rings and stars can take that away from you.'

'Agnes,' he said, taking her in his arms, 'if they all thought as you do, there'd be no problem.'

'If women had been given a say in matters,' she said seriously, 'there most likely wouldn't have been a war.'

'You're probably right.' He kissed her, ostensibly to confirm his agreement, but chiefly because he couldn't resist the temptation.

'And you're the first man I've met who agrees with me. James was horrified when I said that. He said that women had absolutely no business meddling in politics. It was one of the few arguments we had, although we spent so little time together, it would have been impossible to disagree about much else.'

'Let him rest, Agnes. He was expressing the opinion shared by most men in this country, including those who have only just been given the vote. I have to admit that I only began to see those things differently after I'd lived in Enzed for a while.'

'Of course.' She kissed him enthusiastically, considering her initiation had been so recent. After some time, she asked, 'Am I overdoing it?'

'You've not even begun to overdo it,' he assured her.

'Good. That gives me some leeway.' She kissed him again with undiminished appetite.

16

Fred was no stranger to administration; he'd been used to sharing that burden with Aunt Amelia and the rest of the staff, but it wasn't the job of work he'd returned to England to do. He'd been accepted into the RNAS on the strength of his flying experience, and now he had to watch wistfully through the Squadron Office window as his old flight took off and returned.

'Would a cup of tea help, sir?' The leading Wren writer had appeared at his elbow almost without his realising it.

'Would it help with what?'

'Would it help you feel better, sir, about doing this instead of that?' She gestured towards his desktop and then the window.

'Is it so obvious?'

'You're like a caged bird, sir,' she confirmed, 'but we're all pleased to have you with us, for all that.' She checked herself quickly and said, 'I hope you don't mind my saying so, sir.'

'I don't mind in the slightest, Leading Wren Stubbs. I'm flattered, and a cup of tea will probably help enormously, especially when it's offered along with your genuine good wishes. Thank you.'

'You're welcome, sir.' She left the office to attend to it.

Life was being particularly unfair, and not simply with regard to the recent change in his professional fortunes. Leading Wren Stubbs was an attractive, intelligent and personable young woman, whose readiness to embrace adventure had led her in 1917 to join a new and therefore unknown women's service. Had circumstances been different, she might even have been game to make a new life abroad. Unfortunately, however, and in spite of her undoubted charms, Fred wasn't in love with her. Agnes remained the object of his devotion, and she still needed to be persuaded. He put aside pointless conjecture and concentrated on the U-boat sighting reports in his tray. Apart from two that had proved too distant for aerial attack, the sightings had been at the opposite ends of the Channel. Presumably, British air presence was persuading U-boats to remain submerged as they passed through the Dover Strait, and that was gratifying in itself, but the allies were still losing ships in the approaches to Portsmouth and Southampton. Fred was expecting the order at any time that would divert aircraft from Dover to Portsmouth.

While he was pondering the subject, Leading Wren Stubbs placed a cup of tea on the blotter in front of him.

'Leading Wren Stubbs, you're an angel with blue serge wings. Thank you.'

'You're welcome, sir.' She smiled at the compliment and returned to her desk to continue typing patrol reports.

A grunt at Fred's side alerted him to the arrival of a visitor. He looked up into the uncompromising stare of Acting Wing Commander Elliot.

'Time for tea, I see,' said Elliot.

'Yes, it's a floating event. Sometimes, when we're particularly busy, we go without tea until we can tolerate its absence no longer.'

'Do you think that the courtesy might be extended, on this occasion, to a senior officer?'

Fred looked searchingly around the office before shrugging at his own foolishness. 'Of course,' he said, 'you were referring to yourself.' Beaming across at the other occupant of the office, he said, 'Leading Wren Stubbs, will you pour a cup of tea, please, for Acting Wing Commander Elliot?'

'Aye, aye, sir.' There was little enthusiasm in her voice, but she smiled at Fred as she left the office.

'Fuller,' said Elliot with quiet menace in his tone, 'we've spoken on this subject before now—'

'You and I have discussed so many things, Elliot, 'I feel that we know each other intimately, although not too intimately, I'm relieved to say.'

'I'm referring to your inability to issue a coherent order. Must you speak to Wren ratings as if you're about to proposition them?'

'Is that how it sounds to you, Elliot? I'm simply treating them as human beings, firstly, because that's what they are and because they're entitled to it, and secondly, because if I'm civil towards them, they tend to repay the compliment by going about their duties with diligence and enthusiasm.' He smiled with exaggerated patience. 'It's a well-proven practice.'

The explanation was lost on Elliot, who was formulating his next reproach. 'There is another matter on which we've spoken recently,' he said, 'and that is your loutish reluctance to address me as "sir".'

'And of course, it means so much to you, doesn't it... sir? Rest assured, good sir, I shall make an effort, especially as you're now an acting wing commander.'

Leading Wren Stubbs placed a cup of tea in front of Elliot and returned without a word to her duties. Elliot merely lifted his cup and tested the tea for temperature.

'Thank you, Leading Wren Stubbs,' said Fred. Then, meeting Elliot's disapproving glare, he said, 'Nursery training dies hard. I was taught at an early age that "manners maketh man".'

However Elliot felt about that principle, he made no reference to it but said instead, 'I'll come straight to the point of my visit, Fuller.'

Fred thought he had a novel way of coming straight to the point, but he allowed him to continue.

'Portsmouth have asked for reinforcement. I wanted to send your squadron, but Wing Captain Forbes insists, for some reason, that I send ninety-eight squadron.'

'I'm sure the good wing captain knows best,' said Fred piously.

'By Jove, Fuller, I'd as soon send you, if only to get rid of you.'

Fred whispered chidingly, '*Pas devant les servantes.*'

'Of course.' Elliot glanced at the leading Wren and muttered, 'Heaven forbid that I should be infected by your lack of professionalism, Fuller.'

'That would never do,' agreed Fred. 'Meanwhile, however, the problem of the missing pilot remains.'

'What missing pilot is that?'

'My goodself, now that I'm confined to this office. I wondered if you might have given some thought to the acquisition of a replacement. There's a perfectly good seaplane pining in its hangar for someone to make it feel useful and wanted.'

'You do talk nonsense, Fuller. I imagine you saluted your aircraft as it sank.'

'Of course I did, and any pilot with a soul would have done the same.'

'I despair.' Elliot picked up his cap and straightened his tunic to leave. Fred simply smiled at the welcome thought of Elliot in a state of despair.

** ** **

'I shouldn't keep moaning to you about my lot,' said Fred.

'Why not? I'm full of sympathy. I've met your superior officer once, and I was less than impressed with him.' The restaurant of the Corunna Hotel was almost as empty as its menu, making discretion easier than in times past.

'It looks as if the chicken cutlet is the chef's speciality tonight,' said Fred.

'It's the only item available.'

'I was being kind.'

'You are kind, too,' said Agnes, touching his hand across the table before returning to the subject of Fred's fortunes. 'I worry, Fred.'

'Don't,' he entreated. 'All the best doctors advise against it.'

'Be serious, Fred. You could find yourself in awful trouble if you go on teasing that Elliot man.'

Before Fred could respond, the waiter came to take their order.

'Believe it or not,' Fred told him, 'we've chosen the chicken cutlet.'

'A wise choice, if I may say so, sir,' said the waiter with not even a flicker of irony in his voice. 'Have you perused the wine list, sir? I regret to say that the wine waiter has recently been conscripted into the Army, but I shall be happy to attend to your wishes.'

'And you'll do it superbly well, just as the wine waiter will become, I feel sure, an excellent officers' steward.'

'He is hoping for such an appointment, sir.'

'I wish him well.' Fred decided on a 1912 Burgundy, the choice being rather thin.

The waiter thanked him and left them.

Agnes asked, 'How old do you imagine the wine waiter is?'

'He'll be close to the upper age limit, certainly.'

'What is the limit?'

'Forty-one, although there's talk of their raising it again. The politicians will do that happily as long as they don't have to lend a hand themselves.' After a little thought, he said, 'I hope the wine waiter is successful in becoming a steward. He'll be much better at that than he would be in the infantry.'

'Are they the foot soldiers?'

'That's right.'

'Why would they put him in that, rather than anything else?'

'Because that is the area of greatest need. More than anything else, they're short of cannon fodder.'

'That's not a nice way to describe them, Fred.'

He took her hand and stroked it with his thumb. 'I agree, but that's how they're used. When I was based in France, I took part in an offensive, and I saw the way they were deployed.' He looked at her sadly. 'Every now and again,' he suggested, 'you may like to offer up a special prayer for the PBI.'

' "The PBI"?'

'The Poor... Blooming... Infantry. They see more than their fair share of horror.' He gave her hand a squeeze and smiled to relieve the atmosphere. 'And with all that going on in France, Elliot is upset whenever I fail to address him as "sir". If I could work miracles, I'd bring this war to an end, obviously, but I'd derive great satisfaction, also, from giving Elliot a sense of proportion.'

The notion evidently appealed to Agnes, because she smiled broadly and asked, 'Why does he resent you so much, Fred?'

'I've already told you. He's jealous of my devil-may-care manner and matinee idol appearance.'

'Be serious, Fred. There must be something more important than that.'

'He thinks it's important.' He gave her hand another squeeze to show that he was being serious, and said, 'He's a professional officer, who'll still be serving after the war, if he's lucky, albeit in a new service and a comic-opera uniform. He'll have emerged from the war minus the one thing that would give him credibility.'

'What's that?'

'A decoration, albeit a DSC,' he explained, touching the uppermost ribbon on his chest.

Agnes frowned. 'You'll have to relieve my ignorance again, Fred. What is the DSC?'

'The Distinguished Service Cross. I found mine in a ha'penny lucky bag, but Elliot hasn't been so lucky.' He brushed aside her protestation before she could make it. 'The other bone of contention, as far as he's concerned, is that because of the time I spent over the Eastern and Western Fronts, I am what is boyishly known as an "ace", which means that I've shot down at least five enemy machines.'

'And he hasn't?'

'He may have shot down a few, but he's jealous of my twenty-three.'

'Twenty-three?' She evidently found the number staggering.

'Don't be impressed, Agnes. There's an RFC type called Mannock, who'd chalked up, at the last count, more than sixty. Incredibly, he's still alive.' In response to her quizzical look, he explained, 'The RFC work them to death, literally. You'll have heard of Albert Ball, I imagine?'

She nodded. 'Yes, he was rather famous.'

'Deservedly so, but he didn't deserve his untimely end. He was killed when he was probably too exhausted to see the enemy coming. That's the kind of pressure they put on their people, and it's not going to change on the first of April, when we're all part of the same circus.'

** ** **

Later, at Agnes's house, she returned to the same subject. 'I know you're frustrated at being grounded,' she said, 'but I really can't share your vexation.'

'That's too bad of you.'

'Seriously, I can't, and it's simply because I know that all the time you're working at the base, you're safe. If you were still flying, I'd never stop worrying.'

'I wish I hadn't told you about Ball and the others.'

'It wasn't just that, Fred,' she said, taking his hands with hers. 'I've felt the same since your night in the Channel, when I feared you'd been killed.'

'A desk warrior can receive a terrible stab wound from an India tag,' he told her.

Her expression told him that she knew he was being less than serious, but she nevertheless asked, 'What is an India tag?'

'Some people call them Treasury tags, loops of string with a metal ferrule at each end, used to keep documents together. I believe they're used at the Treasury as well as at the India Office. That's why there are so many casualties among civil servants.' He shuddered in mock horror.

'I don't believe a word of it.'

'Neither should you,' he confessed, leaning forward to kiss her.

'You're leading me astray again,' she said as she responded to his attentions.

'As long as our future's uncertain,' he promised, 'I shan't make demands.' He kissed her again and then paused in thought. ' "Demand" is an unpleasant word, isn't it? I always think it suggests something stronger than an innocent request. For me, it has a table-thumping association, possibly accompanied by menaces, and I'd never menace a lady.'

She'd been looking at him uncertainly, and now she said, 'I'm relieved to hear it.'

'Are you really, Agnes?'

'No, I know you much better than that.'

'Good.' It was time for him to leave, and he preferred to do it in an atmosphere of affection and trust.

17

If only for the relief that contrast affords, Fred moderated his behaviour towards Elliot for the time being, even addressing him without obvious irony as "sir". For his part, Elliot appeared at first wary, and then puzzled, perhaps not wishing to be drawn into a disarming sense of wellbeing that might, without warning, discard its guise and reveal itself in its true form, inflicting shame and embarrassment. Eventually, however, he seemed to accept the situation at face value and became almost genial towards Fred.

For his part, Fred continued to fret. Each time he watched his old flight take to the sky, he felt a stab of regret because he was no longer with them. He'd considered the possibility of requesting a demotion to his old rank, but Elliot refused to entertain such a move, on the grounds that it would be seen as an act of self-indulgence, and Fred had to admit that it amounted to nothing less. Meanwhile, the flight continued to be short of one pilot. That was until a signal came through from Arthur Reynolds, Fred's old flight lieutenant. It had been difficult to read, and Fred suspected that the wireless operator had been hurt. It read simply: *Ditching. EA. 10, 40.* Thereafter, the signal became unreadable. All they knew was that the aircraft had been overcome by enemy action and, if it were still afloat, it was somewhere east of Dungeness, at ten degrees, forty minutes of latitude. Of longitude they had no idea, but local shipping had been informed.

Fred looked at the clock. The flight would be returning in about fifteen minutes, but only an hour of daylight remained. Thoughts of Arthur and his wireless operator combined with the memory of his night at sea continued to torment him as he waited for the flight to return. So far, no other aircraft had made a transmission, so the likelihood was that no one had seen Arthur go down. Even so, he still wanted to hear from 'B' Flight.

In due course, the four remaining aircraft returned, and Fred met them at the hangar. They reported that they had been attacked by Hun scouts, and that Sopwith Camels from Guston had successfully repelled the attack. As he had suspected, no one had seen Arthur's aircraft ditch.

'If I can take the spare One Eight Four, I can be over Dungeness in no time, sir,' Fred told Elliot. 'If he's still there, I can get a fix on his position and be back here before nightfall.'

'No, Fuller.'

'In that case, sir, first light is at oh six hundred. 'Will you let me start the search then?'

'You know the rule as well as I do, Fuller. Leave it to "A" Flight.'

'But they have their normal reconnaissance to do, sir. I could leave them to do that while I concentrate on finding G104.'

'Absolutely not. Rules are made to be observed.' Elliot was becoming impatient.

'And aircrew are expendable, I suppose.'

'That was an impertinent remark, Fuller.'

'I don't care, but I do care about the members of my squadron.' He'd been polite to Elliot for long enough.

** ** **

He called briefly on Agnes to explain why he was returning to the base.

'Poor men,' she said. 'I hope someone finds them.'

'I might have found them if Elliot had let me try.'

Presumably unable to think of anything else to say, she simply hugged him. 'Let me know what happens,' she said.

'I will.' He kissed her and left.

Back in the wardroom, the others were similarly on edge.

'I hope they're following your advice, mate,' said George Makepeace.

'I just hope they're still alive.'

'If they are, we'll find 'em in the morning.'

Fred was still grappling with the injustice of not being allowed to fly. 'The flight's down to four pilots,' he said. 'How can it be expected to recce a stretch of the Channel that calls for six?'

'It can't, mate. You'll just have to wait for those in authority to realise what's happening. I daresay Elliot will change his tune soon enough when that happens.'

** ** **

Fred was up in time to see 'A' Flight become airborne. The morning was hazy but bright, so visibility over the Channel would be good. Fortunately, the night had been quite mild. He could only wait.

The flight circled until the scouts arrived from Guston, and then they flew over the Channel before going to their respective areas. Fred wasn't feeling at all hungry, but he went to breakfast all the same. It was something to do until a message came from the wireless office.

He was still at the breakfast table when a rating came to the wardroom door, asking for him.

Fred went to the door. 'What is it?'

'A signal, sir, from seaplane G one oh six.' He handed the signal form to Fred. It read: *G104 sighted.* It gave the position and ended with, *Pilot waving. Seems OK.*

'Wait there,' Fred told him. 'I'll show it to the Acting Wing Commander.' He took it back to the table and tapped Elliot on the shoulder. 'This has just come in,' he said.

Elliot read the signal. 'Excellent.'

Fred waited, and when Elliot continued to eat, he asked, 'Aren't you going to send the machine's position to the searching vessels?'

'I'm eating, Fuller. I'll do it when I've finished breakfast.'

The other officers at the table looked up in surprise, but it was Fred who spoke. 'These poor buggers haven't eaten since yesterday lunchtime, and they've just spent the night in the Channel in open cockpits. If you feel that it's too much trouble, Elliot, I'll draft the bloody signal myself.' Before Elliot could say a word, Fred and the telegraphist were on their way to the wireless office.

** ** **

Arthur was delivered that evening by the sloop that had picked up him and his wireless operator. The latter was delivered to the mortuary, having bled to death from a flesh wound sustained in the attack.

'I dressed it with what we had, Fred. Bandages are one thing, but they're not waterproof, and there was no shortage of seawater in our cockpits. I reckon he died at some time between oh four hundred and oh four thirty. One minute, he was advising me on the training of terriers – he was sounding very weak – and the next, I couldn't get a sound out of him.'

'You did your best, Arthur. I wanted to come looking for you when the flight returned, but I was refused permission. If a ship could have reached you in the night, he might still have been alive. Who was he?'

'A lad called Berry. He was a good lad, too.'

For one heart-stopping moment, Fred thought he was going to say 'Beresford', but he told himself it was tragedy enough that Berry had lost his life. 'Rest up, Arthur. I'll tell the steward not to call you in the morning.'

'Thanks, Fred.' Arthur's eyes were closing, but he managed to say, 'Thanks, as well, for your lecture on survival. It saved my life. It was a pity about Berry.'

Fred walked over to the Wing Office. He didn't hurry, because he wanted time to think about what he was going to say to Elliot.

He found him dictating a letter, so he waited until he'd finished. When the Wren writer had returned to her office, he said, 'A word with you, *Acting* Wing Commander Elliot.'

'Damn it, Fuller. Do you have to emphasise the word "Acting" in that way?'

'I don't *have* to emphasise it in that particular way. I do it simply because it's the way that makes the most sense. Now, have you spoken with Flight Lieutenant Reynolds?'

Elliot glared at him. 'Not yet. I do have other duties to perform, Fuller. I'll speak to him when I can.'

'Having neglected the matter so far, you should wait until tomorrow morning, Elliot. The poor bugger needs his rest.'

Elliot gave him a sour look, but declined to comment.

'Have you written to the rating's next of kin?'

'Of course not. You don't seem to realise how much I have to do.'

'I'm quite busy, myself, but I'll do it.' With heavy emphasis, he said, 'That way, it'll mean something.'

Elliot laid down his pen with deliberate calm and asked, 'Is there anything else whilst you're in this holier-than-thou mood?'

'As far as I can see, Elliot, Jack the Ripper was holier than you. I can't recall ever hearing that he refused to allow a search that might easily have saved a man's life. Also, there's no record of his having refused to send vital information to the ships involved in a search, because he hadn't eaten the last rasher of bacon on his plate.'

Elliot seemed about to explode. 'How dare you, Fuller! That's gross impertinence!'

'I can be much more impertinent than that. Under the circumstances, I'm being quite reasonable.'

'You really have gone too far this time. I thought you'd mended your ways, but I was mistaken. I'm going to throw the book at you, Fuller.' In his fury, he seemed unaware that he'd showered his desk with saliva.

'Go on, Elliot. Have me charged with whatever takes your fancy, but don't be surprised when higher authority hears how you mishandled the search for an officer and a rating, and how a leisurely breakfast was more important to you than their lives. You're a disgrace to your uniform, Elliot, and I'll be happy to make that known to any flag officer.' He picked up his cap. 'I'm going to the squadron office to write to the poor grieving relatives of the rating whose life meant so little to you. That's where I'll be when you decide to have me manacled and thrown into a cell. Meanwhile, I'm prepared to obey your orders, so I should remove "mutiny" from the list you have in mind.'

** ** **

Fred wasn't surprised when he heard nothing during the next hour. Even Elliot was capable of recognising the stalemate that existed between them.

By contrast, when Leading Wren Stubbs brought him a cup of coffee at 1100, it was clear she had something on her mind.

'Something's troubling you,' said Fred. 'If it's not deeply personal, maybe you'd like to blow the gaff.'

'No, sir, it's not really personal.' She seemed almost relieved to be asked. 'We heard about Leading Telegraphist Berry this morning.'

'Did you know him well?'

'Quite well, sir. He was very popular.'

'I'm sorry, my dear. If we could have reached them sooner, he might have stood a chance.'

She was clearly poised to speak, but looked timidly uncertain.

He asked her, 'Were you involved at all with Berry?'

'No, sir, it was nothing like that. He was actually seeing a girl in the galley.' She seemed to brace herself before continuing. 'One of the girls heard you talking to Wing Commander Elliot this morning, sir.'

'I'm sorry,' he said soberly. 'I should have been more careful. I realise how unpleasant it must have been for her to hear something of that nature.'

She was quick to reassure him. 'Oh, no, sir. She's just concerned that you might be....' She searched for a word and fell back on the familiar service slang. 'We thought you might be in the rattle, sir. You're more popular at this base than you might think, and we....' She left the rest unspoken, but the message was clear. Then, remembering herself and the disparity in rank, she said, 'I hope I haven't gone too far, sir.'

'Leading Wren Stubbs, that's the kindest thing I've heard today, and you certainly haven't overstepped the mark. Having said that, I'd advise you against making a practice of sharing your convictions with other officers. They might take a more rigid view than mine.'

She smiled in her relief. 'I wouldn't dream of it, sir.' She returned to her desk.

Ten minutes or so later, the telephone buzzed and Fred picked it up. 'Acting Squadron Commander Fuller.'

'Fuller, yes.' The voice was Elliot's and he sounded uncertain as to how to proceed. Fred decided to help him.

'Yes, sir. How can I be of assistance?'

'Will you come to my office?' He sounded remarkably unlike the raging tyrant who'd promised Fred all the torments of hell earlier that morning.

'By all means, sir.' Fred put down the telephone receiver and smiled reassuringly at Leading Wren Stubbs. 'I'm summoned to the inner *sanctum*,' he told her. '*Nos morituri te salutamus*. We who are about to die—'

'I know, sir. *Bona fortuna*.'

'You're a great comfort to me, Leading Wren Stubbs. Try not to worry.'

He walked to Elliot's office in a philosophical frame of mind. He wasn't guilty of mutiny, so he couldn't expect the death penalty. He would possibly be reduced in rank, but that would be no real disaster. Satisfied about that, he arrived at the Wing Office and knocked on the door.

'Come in.'

Fred opened the door and entered to find Elliot wearing his cap. He saluted him accordingly.

'Take a seat, Fuller.' He sounded remarkably calm.

Fred removed his cap and took the other chair.

'I've just walked around the base,' said Elliot. 'I find that it helps me think more clearly.'

Fred waited for him to continue.

'Shall we go outside?'

'If you find that helpful, sir.'

'I must confess, I do.' He picked up his cap and led the way. 'It's possibly the fresh air that makes the difference.'

'I shouldn't be at all surprised, sir.'

They walked on in silence. In spite of Elliot's earlier enthusiasm for the mental stimulus of outdoor activity, he was strangely reticent. Neither did he appear at all conscious of his surroundings. Fred might have expected the towering splendour of Dover Castle to inspire great thoughts, but Elliot remained unforthcoming.

Eventually, however, as they walked downwards to the seaplane hangar, he spoke. 'Fuller,' he said, 'your behaviour earlier this morning was disgraceful. You can't deny that.'

Rather than deny it or defend it, Fred remained silent, waiting patiently for Elliot's next utterance.

'At the same time, I have reflected on my actions leading to the rescue, and I'm prepared to admit that I could have handled the whole business better than I did.'

'It's noble of you to say so, sir.'

'Quite, but it doesn't excuse your tantrum, Fuller.'

'Hardly a tantrum, sir. I'd be more inclined to call it a candid assessment of the situation as I saw it.'

For the first time since his telephone call, Elliot revealed his impatience. 'Damn it, Fuller,' he said, 'can't you see I'm trying to find a way forward?'

'Presumably one that's unlikely to expose you as uncaring and incompetent.'

Elliot stopped, so that Fred felt obliged to do the same. 'I believe you're enjoying this, Fuller.' He accompanied his words with the familiar glare.

'That's just where you're wrong, sir. How can I possibly enjoy a situation in which an innocent young man is now lying on a mortuary slab, and a good friend is recovering from sixteen hours' exposure to the elements and the uncertainty inevitably associated with it?'

Elliot walked on, checking after two strides that Fred was still with him. 'What I'm saying, Fuller, is that it would be the best outcome by far, for the sake of this base and for your sake and mine, if we simply reached an agreement.'

'That you don't have me court-martialled, and I refrain from broadcasting your shortcomings?'

'All right, if that's how you want to phrase it. Can we shake hands on it?'

The sound of feminine footsteps caused Fred to turn and look. Two Wrens from the airframe workshop hangar, were approaching. When they drew level with the two officers, they saluted. Fred returned their salutes and offered Elliot his hand. 'They need to see this,' he said, adding, 'for the sake of morale.' Looking at his watch, he said, 'It's lunchtime. Shall we go to the wardroom?'

Elliot looked relieved. 'Yes,' he said, 'we should.'

** ** **

'The next time I saw my secretary,' he told Agnes, 'I told her all was well.'

'That's good. She was concerned about you.'

'You know, I was more than surprised when she told me she already knew. Two Wrens saw Elliot and me shaking hands, and the gossip spread through the base like whooping cough.'

Agnes arranged herself more comfortably and said, 'That's two good things. They found the missing pilot, and you're no longer under threat. It's just awful about the rating who died.'

'It is,' he agreed. 'I've written to his mother. He has no father.'

'There's hardship everywhere you look.'

'But,' said Fred, 'it's an ill wind.'

'What is?'

'The one that blows no one any good.'

'I know that,' she said impatiently. 'Who could possibly benefit from the rating's death?'

'He was a leading telegraphist. He leaves room in the establishment for another leading hand, and I've persuaded Elliot to put forward Beresford's name.'

'You clever man.' She underlined the compliment with an enthusiastic kiss. 'You know,' she said, 'when I do that, I feel ever so slightly disreputable, like a wanton woman.'

'I don't think you feel like a wanton woman. The last time I felt a wanton woman, she didn't feel at all like you.'

'I don't think I want to hear about it.'

'You shouldn't. It might give you ideas.' He kissed her until he felt her begin to stir. More than that was tantalising, possibly for them both, and Fred was certainly aware of his needs.

18

On Thursday came news of a new enemy offensive on the Somme and two sinkings in the Channel. The German offensive was worrying enough; dense and widespread fog in Northern France was providing the advancing enemy with natural cover, creating further difficulties for the allies, but the development in the Channel was of more immediate concern.

The ships had been stragglers in the same convoy and were both sunk, quite brazenly, off Margate when the main convoy was in the region of Dover. A destroyer and a sloop had been detached to search the area, but they had failed to detect any U-boats in the vicinity. In all, it was both alarming and embarrassing.

'It's not surprising that they're picking off the stragglers,' said Fred. 'The escorts will be with the main part of the convoy. While we're keeping watch ahead of the convoy, the U-boats will be free to surface almost at will.'

Elliot had to agree. 'We can only extend our search pattern,' he said.

' "B" Flight is still short of a pilot,' Fred reminded him.

'I know.' After a moment's thought, he said, 'I'm going to ask them to notify us when ships fall astern of a convoy, and then we can keep an eye on them. Also, I'll ask if you can be allowed to fly, albeit temporarily.'

It was good news. With G117 re-engined and airworthy, the flight would have five machines available. Fred resolved to let Beresford know as soon as Elliot gained the necessary permission.

** ** **

Possibly in response to a belated sense of urgency after a third ship was reported sunk off the Thanet coast, permission came sooner than expected, and Fred was able to collect Beresford, who was surprised but no less willing, from the wireless office and to join the flight in the hangar.

A convoy straggler had been reported in the Ramsgate area, and Fred elected to shadow that himself, leaving the rest of the flight to watch over the convoy. The widespread fog reported in France and Belgium ended abruptly approximately halfway across the Channel, resembling a gigantic doorstep when viewed from above.

Fred located the straggler in Sandwich Bay, and from that moment, concentrated on the seaward side, reasoning that only a fool would take a U-boat close inshore, where it could so easily run aground.

The remainder of the patrol was simply tedious; the straggler was steaming at maybe six or seven knots and making a great deal of smoke, which hampered Fred's task, and he was relieved in both senses when Hanson of 'A' Flight took over from him an hour or so later.

He reported to Elliot on his return.

'I followed the ship until my relief arrived,' he said. 'Unless things have changed recently, a U-boat can remain submerged for a maximum of two hours, which means that if it doesn't show by the end of "A" Flight's patrol, either, it's found some magical place to surface unseen, or it wasn't there in the first place.'

'The Hun captain seems able to read our minds. We send up a patrol, and he makes himself invisible. This damned fog doesn't help, either.'

'I think that's the answer.' Fred had thought of little else since his fruitless patrol, and it was the only explanation that made sense. 'My guess is that he's disappearing beneath the fog to surface and charge his batteries, and then lurking on the edge of it until he spots a target.'

'And there's not even a hint of wind,' said Elliot. 'Even a moderate sou'westerly would disperse the damned thing, but the latest forecast is, believe it or not, for persistent fog.' He glanced up at the bulkhead clock and said irritably, 'Oh well, it's too late now. We can only try again in the morning.'

** ** **

From various experiences, both good and bad, Fred knew that women were generally intuitive. Agnes was particularly so, as she demonstrated that evening.

'Something is weighing heavily on your mind, Fred. I can tell.'

'I'm sorry. I shouldn't inflict my problems on you, and especially here.' They were in the restaurant of the Ambassador Hotel, which currently offered rather more choice than the Corunna. Fred looked up as the waiter approached their table.

'If you were considering ordering coffee, sir, I regret very much to inform you that we have none available.'

Fred smiled at his discomfiture and said, 'It's not your fault that we're at war. Will you just bring me the bill, please?'

'Certainly, sir.'

When he'd paid the bill, they went out to the motorcar. 'When you make such delectable coffee, Agnes, there's no hardship in leaving the restaurant early. Quite the reverse, in fact.'

She waited for him to start the engine and take his seat before asking, 'Are you going to tell me, now, what's troubling you?'

'I don't want to depress you.'

'I'll be unhappier still if you don't tell me. I'll think of you going about your duties with a face as long as a fiddle, and know that I failed to give you comfort of any kind.'

'Bless your kind, deserving heart, dearest Agnes. You're a comfort in yourself.' He turned into Snargate Street and joined what little traffic there was.

'Aren't you going to tell me?'

'All right, I shall, but it's not terribly interesting. I'm simply disappointed with the way rationing's been organised, and the fact that, despite my best efforts and those of my fellow U-boat hunters, the Huns are still sinking our ships.'

'The war news isn't very comforting,' she agreed, 'but you mustn't take it all on your shoulders.'

'Maybe not.' Even so, the subject of his current preoccupation was largely his responsibility, but he was unable to share it with her. He just hoped that he or someone from 'A' Flight would find the damned U-boat in the morning and deal with it, directly or indirectly, before it could do more damage than it had already. Meanwhile, the fog was set to linger. Even the weather was on the side of the Hun.

As they pulled up outside Agnes's house, she asked, 'Are you going to come in? I really don't mind if you're down in the mouth.'

'I'm sorry.' Under cover of darkness, he kissed her. 'I'll try not to be a wet blanket.' He stopped the engine and got out.

'It's all the same to me,' she said, taking his arm. 'If you can't let your feelings become known to me, who else is there?'

'There's absolutely no one,' he agreed. 'You are my sole confidante and comforter.' He considered that and found it lacking. 'Of course, you're much more than that.'

'Am I?'

He waited for her to unlock the door. 'I thought I'd made my feelings towards you quite apparent,' he said.

'Even so,' she hinted, taking his coat and cap, 'being told about them makes them infinitely more special.'

'Lead me to your kitchen, and I'll lavish flowery words of courtship on you.'

'I hope you're not going to treat it as a joke.'

'There's no joke,' he promised, taking her in his arms. 'I love you, Agnes. It's as serious as that.'

'And I love you.' Her eyes glistened.

They kissed with increased zeal Eventually, Fred said, 'You were waiting for me to say it, weren't you?'

'I was too shy to take the initiative,' she said, 'and I still say it's not a woman's place to do that.'

'You're quite right, as always. Let's make some coffee.'

'Would you like cognac as well?'

'Thank you, but I shouldn't. I'm flying in the morning.'

For a moment, her mouth fell open. 'You're flying again?'

'There's a shortage of pilots in the squadron, and… I'm the last resort.'

'Oh, Fred,' she said, putting down the percolator and taking his hands in hers, 'I really thought you'd finished with that.'

'There's nothing to worry about. The area's patrolled by scouts from Guston, although we see very little of the Hun. When we do, though, they wish they hadn't come calling. The Sopwith Camel's a fearsome machine.'

She buried her face in his tunic. He stroked her hair soothingly and said, 'I intend to be very careful indeed.'

'You'd better be.' Her voice was muffled by the cloth of his tunic, but she sounded no less determined.

'Let's make some coffee and talk about pleasanter things,' he suggested.

'You really are the limit, Fred.' She accepted a kiss nevertheless. 'You told me something wonderful tonight, and then you let slip that you were flying again.'

'Both those things were beyond my control, but let's concentrate on the first thing I told you.'

'Yes, let's.'

When the coffee was ready, Fred carried it, as usual, into the sitting room, where the fire appeared to be beyond salvation. 'It's quite warm tonight,' he said. 'Unless you're feeling cold, I shan't try to revive the fire.'

'No,' she agreed, 'let's sit close instead.'

'I shan't argue with that.' He watched her pour two cups of coffee and took the one she offered. 'Thank you.'

She stared into her cup until he said, 'A penny for them.'

'I just wondered if tea and coffee were grown in New Zealand. I was about to ask you.'

'No, they're not. The climate's too cold to grow coffee, and I don't know why they don't grow tea, even though it's very popular. At all events, we import them both.'

She nodded slowly, as if she found the information difficult to digest. Then, she asked, 'Are there lots of dangerous creatures?'

'No, there aren't. Very occasionally, a shark will put in an appearance, but they don't come close inshore, and we have no venomous snakes. They prefer to live in Australia.' As she settled her head against his shoulder, he asked, 'Are you weighing up the pros and cons?'

'I'm sort of weighing them up, but don't press me, Fred. Whichever course I choose, I must make that choice in my own time.'

'Of course you must.'

She swivelled her eyes to look up at him again and asked, 'Are you feeling any happier now?'

'Just now? I couldn't be happier, but it's not surprising, because that's the effect you have on me.'

'I know you mean that.' She demonstrated her trust by joining him in a long, searching kiss from which she eventually emerged a little breathless.

'Are you all right?'

'Yes.' She looked away and said, 'I'd like to do much more for you, but not as things are.'

'Don't give it another thought.' He thought about it quite often, but he had to be realistic.

'It's not a moral problem, I mean, because we're both single, or that I'm afraid of… you know, becoming pregnant. I just feel that to… to offer that…. Oh dear. What's the word I'm looking for?'

'Favour?'

'Yes, I feel it would give rise to certain expectations on your part regarding our future, and that would be unfair of me. Do you see what I mean?'

'Yes, I do.' As a reason for reluctance to engage in sexual intercourse, it was certainly novel, but he knew what she meant and, despite his immediate frustration, he appreciated her reasoning.

'That doesn't mean I can't go on loving you,' she assured him hurriedly.

'I should think not.'

'It could become a hurdle in time to come, but we don't know yet.'

'That's the wonderful thing about the future,' he said, quoting her words on an earlier occasion, 'it's so uncertain.'

'Yes, it is.' She still seemed keen to avoid misunderstanding, because she said, 'I realise how important it is – the thing I mentioned – for a man. At least, I think I do, and I don't want you to feel that I'm treating your needs lightly.'

'The suspicion never entered my head.' He thought he'd better clear up something else while the subject was under discussion. He said, 'At its best, you know, it's at least as important for a woman as for a man.'

'Is it?' Her face was a mixture of coyness and disbelief.

'That's the whole idea, that the pleasure is shared. At least, it should be. I learned that some years ago.' It was a lesson he was unlikely to forget. He'd been particularly fortunate in enlisting the services of Isabella, an otherwise consummate professional, who, in a rare moment of tenderness, had taken the innocent youth from England quite literally to her bosom and assumed responsibility for his sexual enlightenment.

It was even fair to say that she'd applied herself to the task as if it were a sacred trust, and Fred cherished the memory appropriately.

Still sceptical, Agnes said, 'I felt that I wanted something to happen, and when it did, I wasn't ready for it to happen, and then it occupied a matter of seconds.' She made a gesture of distaste and said, 'It seemed almost sordid.' Guiltily, she said, 'I hope that's not an awful thing to say.'

'Not if that was how it seemed to you.' He felt obliged to add, 'I feel flattered that, in the light of that experience, and in more definite circumstances, you'd feel so inclined. I assure you I'd make every effort to make the occasion far more rewarding than the one you recall.'

'I believe you.'

'You should.'

She nodded, seemingly still struggling to make sense of her unfortunate introduction to the marital bed, because she said, 'I found myself wondering why it felt so important in the first place.'

'It doesn't have to be like that.'

'What do you mean?'

It was a direct question, which made it impossible for him to prevaricate. 'Ideally, you can be ready for it to happen, and it doesn't have to be over so quickly, although accidents, of course, do sometimes occur.'

'That's been my experience, brief though it was.' She turned her face away in shame and said, 'I feel terribly disloyal, telling you this. I don't know why I did.'

'Disloyalty has nothing to do with it. I think you're just confused by the urgency and the anti-climax. Irony and confusion are, by definition, near neighbours.'

She sat in silence, looking down at her hands, as was her habit, before saying, 'I don't know what you must think of me. I've never discussed this sort of thing with a man – with anyone, really – except the doctor I had to see about… you know, about… precautions.'

'I told you when we first met, that people talk to me. Do you remember how I told you about a Maori girl who hadn't spoken for two years? I've still no idea why people do it, but they do.' He took her hands and held them. 'As for wondering what I think of you, I just think you've had a series of unfortunate experiences, and it's good that you spoke to me about it. I imagine you'll feel much better once the dust has settled.'

'I hope so. It was the oddest thing. I just started talking to you about something I'd have hesitated to discuss with my mother.'

'Did you ever discuss it with her?'

She shook her head firmly. 'No, you're the first and hopefully the last.'

'Don't hold it against me, Agnes. Remember, it's none of my doing, just a strange property I have.' He stood up.

'Must you go so soon?'

'I'm afraid so. I need to sleep if I'm to function properly tomorrow.' He kissed her. 'I'll be in touch.'

19

E lliot greeted Fred in the hangar the next morning with a report of two convoy stragglers off the Thanet coast, one near Broadstairs, the other off Margate.

'The hunting ground our friend seems to have made his own,' remarked Fred.

'Well, now it's ours as well. Good hunting, Fuller.' Since their confrontation and subsequent reconciliation, Elliot had been almost friendly towards Fred.

'Thank you, sir.' Fred waited until Beresford was in his cockpit, before climbing into his. The armourer carried out a final check on the torpedo slung beneath the fuselage and declared himself satisfied, and an air mechanic stood in front of the propellor, going through the cockpit drill and finally swinging the propellor once. The new Renault engine burst into life.

Fred made the sideways signal with both hands for the chocks to be removed from the floats and, when he was satisfied that everyone was safely out of the way, opened the throttle to take the seaplane down the ramp and into the calm waters of Dover harbour. He taxied as far as the Eastern Fortress before changing to full throttle as he cleared the harbour entrance. The Renault engine was running smoothly, and the seaplane was up to take-off speed in what seemed hardly any time at all. Fred pulled back the stick and left the Channel waves behind him as he climbed into the sky.

When he'd gained sufficient height, he made a gentle banking turn to port to approach the eastern peak of the Thanet coast. As he continued to climb, he fancied that the bank of fog had thickened since the previous day, and now appeared almost solid. He spared a thought for the unfortunate souls standing up to the Hun offensive beneath that immense cowl of swirling vapour, and then returned his concentration to the task in hand.

Soon, he spotted a ship, probably a collier, as coal was the main cargo of the east coast convoys. It had passed Broadstairs and was making its way laboriously towards Dover. Astern of it was another, similar kind of ship that seemed to be maintaining its distance from its neighbour. Fred tilted his wings to let them know he'd seen them, and then made for the fog bank. If the U-boat could use it as cover, he reasoned, so could he. A surfaced U-boat ran on diesel engines that made so much noise that its crew would be unable to hear an aircraft engine, and they certainly wouldn't see their attacker.

He flew figures of eight over the fog, always keeping the two ships in sight, and waited patiently.

His first intimation that the enemy was at hand came with a confident and insistent tapping on his shoulder. He looked round and saw that Beresford was pointing downwards and to starboard. Following his wireless operator's gloved finger, he spotted the surfaced U-boat. It was just emerging from the fog. He'd been right all along. He waited until the U-boat was clearly visible and about to launch a gun attack on the leading ship, and then opened the throttle in a straight dash towards the collier. He had to get between it and his target, because to attack from the other side would risk missing the U-boat and hitting a friendly ship instead.

As he neared the end of his high-speed manoeuvre and began a banking turn towards the U-boat, it became obvious that the enemy had seen the seaplane, because the crew were elevating the gun as fast as they could. There was no time for them to dive. Instead, they were going to fight it out.

Fred continued to dive with shells bursting above him as the gunners searched for the correct elevation and, when he reached the optimum height for a torpedo attack, about twenty feet above the waves, he held his course. Shells continued to explode, but there was no other way of making an accurate torpedo run.

A shell burst close on his starboard side; ominously, the enemy gunnery was improving all the time. The U-boat came within range, and Fred looked down for somewhere to launch the torpedo. He gritted his teeth as another shell exploded, and he heard the *twang* as its shrapnel sliced through a landing wire on his starboard lower wing. If the torpedo were to land on the peak of a wave, it might go anywhere, but now he found the ideal place in a trough between two large waves, and he grasped the torpedo release. As he did, another shell burst beside the seaplane, creating a ball of fire that seemed to envelope everything around it. Fred was conscious of the sudden heat, then of the void where the starboard lower wing had been, of the flames from the starboard mainplane, and finally, of the joystick, now loose and useless, as the seaplane plunged downward. After that, he became oblivious to everything.

** ** **

Lieutenant Commander Owen Price, commanding the sloop *HMS Crocus*, was convinced he'd heard an explosion to westward. The noise seemed to come from the area around Thanet, where so many luckless ships had recently met their end, so he wasn't surprised.

'It's quite likely that another straggler's been sunk,' he told his first lieutenant, 'so we'll have to investigate.'

They continued to search the horizon, a task made more difficult than usual by the thick fog spilling over from the continent, until a lookout reported, 'One, no, *two* ships fine on the starboard bow, sir.'

Price lifted his telescope and searched the bearing. 'You're right,' he said. 'They might know something.' Turning to the voice tube, he called, 'Bridge, wheelhouse.'

The answering call came. 'Wheelhouse, sir.'

'Steer one point to starboard.'

'One point to Starboard, sir. One point of starboard wheel on, sir.'

'Very good. Full ahead together.'

'Full ahead together, sir.' There was the distant clang of the telegraph as the quartermaster relayed the order to the engine room. 'Both engines full ahead, sir.'

As they drew closer to the aftermost ship, its captain began signalling on his foghorn. Morse code had never been one of Price's strengths, but it presented no difficulty for the signalman.

'From the merchant ship, sir, "U-boat sunk by aircraft at 0710. Crew in water. VMR forbidden to stop." '

'Thank you, "Bunts". He very much regrets, and I'm not surprised. The aircraft most likely saved his bacon.' Glancing at the bridge clock, he said, 'It looks as if we missed the main event by less than fifteen minutes. No wonder the explosion was so loud.'

The port lookout called, 'Men in the water, sir, port beam, about one hundred yards.'

'I see them. One of them is waving. Wheelhouse.'

'Wheelhouse, sir.'

'Stop engines.'

'Stop engines, sir.' There was another clanging on the telegraph, and then, 'Both engines stopped, sir.'

'Bunts, make to the merchant ship…' He squinted through his telescope. 'Make to *SS Pullen*, "Will pick up survivors. Thank you. Please make full report of incident." '

'Aye, aye, sir.' The signalman began flashing the message by light to the merchantman, and Price called to the upper deck, 'Lower the sea boat and pick up those survivors.' To himself, he muttered, 'I hope they are survivors.'

** ** **

Elliot waited for 'B' Flight and, particularly for Fred, to return. There had been no further reports of ships being sunk, so the likelihood was that the U-boat had evaded the patrols yet again. With the forecast that the fog was set to last at least for the next two days, it was too frustrating for words.

Eventually, the flight began to return, and Elliot was able to question the first pilot ashore, who turned out to be Flight Sub-Lieutenant Jameson.

'Any luck, Jameson?'

'None whatsoever, sir.

'Did you see anything of Squadron Commander Fuller?'

'I'm afraid not, sir, but I was patrolling out towards New Romney and Rye.'

As the rest of the flight came ashore, he questioned them and remained no wiser. He returned to his office, frustrated and quite possibly short of a squadron commander.

From his office, he noticed that an ambulance was approaching the

Eastern Fortress. It seemed rather odd, so he dismissed it from his mind as he continued to wait.

** ** **

Almost half-an-hour later, a telegraphist came to Elliot's office with a signal from Commander-in-Chief, Dover. It read, 'U-boat sunk at 0710 by aircraft. S/Cdr Fuller and L/Tel Beresford picked up by *HMS Crocus*. Fuller and Beresford in Dover Union Infirmary. Fuller critically injured. Beresford only slightly.'

So that was the reason for the ambulance on the Eastern Pier. *Crocus* must have dropped Fuller and the rating. Either, it was very sporting of her captain, or Fuller was so badly injured that he needed urgent medical attention. Elliot picked up the telephone and asked to be connected with the Dover Union Infirmary.

** ** **

There was a huddle of junior ratings in the canteen, which could only mean news of something that affected them all. Agnes looked up at the clock and said to Doris, 'Those boys will be in trouble if they're late returning to work.'

'I'll remind them, Mrs Morley.'

'Thank you, Doris.' Agnes had quite enough to do without rounding up errant ratings as well.

Doris packed them off, closing the door behind them. 'One of their friends is missing,' she said.

'Did they mention a name?' Agnes knew some of them by name.

'A boy called Beresford, Mrs Morley.'

Once again, Agnes felt the cold rush of blood to her hands and feet. 'Beresford? Did they mention an officer as well?'

'No, I don't think so. At least, they might have, but not in my hearing.' She paused almost guiltily. 'You know one of the officers, don't you, Mrs Morley? But it's not bound to be him. It stands to reason.'

'Carry on with the cleaning, please, Doris.' She walked into the kitchen and closed the door behind her. 'No,' she said desperately, 'it can't happen again. Surely, it can't.'

** ** **

A Worthy Scoundrel

Albert Beresford was frustrated. All he wanted was to check on Squadron Commander Fuller, to see if he was conscious yet, and to find out how bad his injuries were, but he'd been told he mustn't leave his bed, and on no account was he to attempt to find Mr Fuller. As for not leaving his bed, he couldn't understand why he was in bed when there was nothing wrong with him. He'd been given a warm bunk in the sick bay of *HMS Crocus*, and he was as right as rain, which was more than could be said for Mr Fuller. He was brooding about the injustice of it when he received an unexpected visitor. The sister was telling his visitor that he should think himself lucky he was allowed to visit outside visiting times, and that he mustn't over-tire the patient. Clearly, she didn't know how important Wing Commander Elliot was, or she wouldn't speak to him in that way.

'Hello, Beresford,' said the visitor. 'How are you feeling?'

'Very well, thank you, sir, except they won't let me see Mr Fuller.'

'No, I gather he's still unconscious, and that's why I want you to tell me what happened this morning.'

'Well, sir, we went after that U-boat, as you know, and we found it. It had been lurking under the fog. It was all set to start shooting at one of the stragglers, but Mr Fuller put a stop to that. He came roaring in on it and turned so that we were coming at it from the direction of the merchantman. I expect that was so that we didn't hit it by accident. The only trouble with that was that it gave the Huns more time to see us, and they were shooting at us all the time Mr Fuller was making his approach. Well, there was shells bursting all around us, and just as Mr Fuller launched the torpedo, we got a near miss on the starboard side that wrecked our starboard wings and sent us diving into the sea. That was the end of G117. All the same, sir, what's one seaplane against the sinking of a U-boat? My worry, though, is for Mr Fuller. Have they told you anything, sir?'

'No, Beresford, they haven't. Apparently, they only give information about patients to close relatives.' He looked thoughtful and said, 'That was a very useful account you gave me of the engagement with the U-boat, Beresford. What I don't understand, though, is how both of you survived the crash.'

'Oh well, sir, just before the aircraft hit the sea, I dived overboard. I'm a good swimmer, sir, although I say it as shouldn't. It comes of living by the sea, and I dived the safest way, facing aft. That way, you don't hit the water hard with your head, if you get my meaning, sir.'

'Yes, I can see that.'

'Well, I swam back to the aircraft, which was going down, sir. I unfastened Mr Fuller's safety belt and pulled him out just as it was taking him under.'

'That must have taken considerable effort, Beresford.'

'Well, I'm a farmer in peacetime, sir, and you have to be strong for that. Anyway, I pulled Mr Fuller free of the machine and blew up his inflatable jacket to keep his head above water, sir. Then, I'm happy to say, *HMS Crocus* arrived.'

Wing Commander Elliot smiled and shook his head in amiable disbelief. 'I'm very impressed, Beresford,' he said. 'I'm impressed by lots of things. Firstly, by the attack you made on the U-boat, then by the way you rescued your officer under very difficult conditions. Mainly, I'm impressed by your loyalty to Squadron Commander Fuller.'

'Mr Fuller's the best kind of officer, sir. He's been very good to me, and I'll look forward to flying with him anytime. That's if he'll only get well again. That was an awful crash when he hit the water.'

'Yes, Beresford, we'll have to keep our fingers crossed for him. Meanwhile, I can tell you that your leading rate has come through, although you'll be a leading telegraphist for only two days.'

'Will I, sir?' Albert was used to disappointments, but this was premature.

'Yes, after that, you'll be a corporal in the Royal Air Force.'

Albert's relief was mixed. 'That's not so bad, sir, but I'll miss being in the Andrew.'

The officer sighed. 'Another one. Will it sweeten the transition if I tell you that I'm making a recommendation on your behalf? At the very least, you'll be mentioned in dispatches, but I hope for something more than that.'

'That's very generous of you, sir. Thank you.'

At that point, a nurse came on the ward to say, 'You've had quite enough time with this patient, Commander. You'll wear him out.'

Wing Commander Elliot picked up his cap and gloves and said, 'I think you'll find he's made of sterner stuff than that, sister.' Turning to

Albert again, he said, 'Make a quick recovery, Beresford. Well done, again.'

'Thank you, sir.' He watched the officer go and thought to himself how much better things would be if Mr Fuller could also make a quick recovery.

20

For the second time in as many months, Agnes endured a form of purgatory. She knew that if she made enquiries at the wardroom, she would be no wiser, as operational information was closely guarded. If she could catch one of the officers on his own, she might find out something, but she'd seen no one so far. One squadron had been sent elsewhere, and there were consequently fewer officers on the base. Instead, she had to wait until the next stand-easy and hope that some rating might be able to end the suspense.

In the event, the news came sooner than she'd expected, when Steward Little arrived early to speak to her.

'I thought I'd get here before the others, ma'am, in case you hadn't heard.'

'Heard what?'

'About Mr Fuller, ma'am. He was shot down this morning, but he was picked up, along with Beresford, by a sloop or a destroyer, I'm told. They're both in the infirmary, and Mr Fuller's injured. That's all I know, ma'am.'

Her relief was guarded. 'Do you know how badly he's injured?'

'No, ma'am. It's not the kind of thing they tell us. I'm sorry, ma'am.'

'Don't be sorry. It's not your fault, and I'm grateful to you for coming to see me.'

'It's no trouble, ma'am.' He took a threepenny bit from the pouch on his belt and asked, 'Could I have a cup of tea and a slice of bread-and-dripping, please?'

'By all means, but you can put your money away, Steward Little. I owe you this.'

She poured the tea, cut a generous slice of bread and spread beef dripping on it, still in a state of uncertainty. She had no idea of the extent of Fred's injuries, but at least, she knew that he'd somehow survived the incident. 'You said they were in the infirmary. Which infirmary is that?'

'The Union Workhouse Infirmary.' He inclined his head roughly in the direction of Buckland Bottom, as if she were unsure of the way.

'Thank you. I'll go there this evening and see what I can find out.'

'When you do that, ma'am, I hope you'll find him improved. If it's not a lot of trouble, could you tell him everybody sends their regards? He's a popular officer.'

'Of course I will.'

Ratings began to arrive, bringing their conversation to an end, and Agnes went about her duties only half-aware of what she was doing.

** ** **

Shortly before twenty-past six, she arrived at Reception.

'Good evening,' she said. 'I've come to visit a patient who was brought in this morning. His name is Squadron Commander Fred Fuller.'

The nurse leafed through several documents before finding the name. 'A lot of patients were admitted today,' she explained. 'A hospital ship filled with casualties arrived from France.' She searched further until her efforts were rewarded. 'We have him down here as "Lieutenant Fuller".'

'He's actually a squadron commander, but the RNAS do things differently. He only looks like a lieutenant.'

'It's all the same to us. You'll have to speak to Sister Andrews,' she said. You'll find her on the second floor, on Ward Six.'

'Thank you.' Agnes took to the stairs, unsure of what she might find, but determined to see Fred.

A sign on the second floor landing told her that Ward 6 was straight on, and she continued down the corridor until she came to an office. The sign on the door read: *SISTER*, and a board inserted into in the parallel grooves beneath it carried the name *Andrews*. Agnes knocked on the door. On hearing a stern 'Come', she pushed it open. 'Good evening, Sister Andrews,' she said. 'I've come to visit Squadron Commander Fuller, who was admitted this morning, and I was told to speak to you.'

'That's right. What is your relationship to....' She looked at her list of patients and asked, 'What is your relationship to Lieutenant Fuller? I can only imagine he's been recently promoted.'

'Yes, he has.' There was no need to go into the details.

'And your relationship?'

Agnes told her, crossing her fingers behind her back.

'I see. Well, the fact is that he's not yet regained consciousness. He sustained multiple injuries, mainly fractures and concussion. Did you know that?'

'I only knew he was injured.'

'Ah well, by all means look in on him, but you mustn't touch him. You might try speaking to him gently, although there's no guarantee he'll respond. I'm sorry I can't be more encouraging than that.'

'Not at all, Sister. Thank you.'

'I'll take you to him.' She got up from her desk just as a man in a white coat appeared in the doorway.

'Sister Andrews,' he said, 'I've examined Lieutenant Fuller, and he can be moved. You can go ahead and make arrangements for tomorrow morning, if not before then.'

'Thank you, Dr Clark. You can leave that to me.'

'Thank you, sister.' Clearly busy, he went on his way.

Agnes asked, 'Where are you sending him, sister?'

'He'll go to the Royal Victoria Hospital in Folkestone. There's a bed for him there, and the latest development in France means that we're currently short of them. Also, they have facilities at the RVH that we lack. Please come this way.'

'I believe you also have a naval rating called Beresford.'

'We had. He was discharged this afternoon. As I told you, we need the beds.'

Agnes followed Sister Andrews through the ward until they came to Fred's bed.

'In the normal way, he would have been taken to a hospital for officers,' explained the sister, 'but his injuries have ruled that out for now. I'll leave you with him, Miss....'

'Morley.'

Agnes sat by the bed to look more closely. Fred's face was cut in places and horribly bruised. Elsewhere, his arms were in plaster casts, and a tent-arrangement had been placed over his legs. He was a pitiful sight. She looked around to ensure that they had privacy, and decided that no one was within earshot. 'Fred,' she said softly, 'it's me, Agnes. I'm not allowed to touch you, but I can tell you that I love you.' Tears came to her eyes, and she brushed them away impatiently. 'Get well, Fred. Please get well again. I'll come to see you in Folkestone. Thank goodness it's not somewhere silly and I can still visit you. Please get well, Fred. I love you.'

She felt a hand on her shoulder and looked up. Blinking her tears away, she saw Sister Andrews, who said gently, 'There's been a change in the arrangements, Miss Morley. We're going to move him now.'

Agnes was suddenly aware of two nurses and two porters with a stretcher. She asked, 'Is it safe to move him?'

'He'll take no more harm than he has already,' the sister assured her, stroking her shoulders whilst otherwise looking professional and detached.

Fresh tears were forming, and Agnes made a request that, at one time, she would never have considered in public. 'Am I allowed to kiss him?'

'Yes, very gently.'

Agnes leant over his body and touched his lips with hers. 'I love you, Fred,' she said. 'Just be well again.' She felt the sister's hands drawing her away from the bed.

'It's time for you to go, now, Miss Morley. You'll be able to visit him at the RVH.'

'Thank you, sister.' She made her way through the ward and downstairs, where she sought the privacy of the ladies' conveniences so that she could make herself less tear-stained and more in charge of herself. When she came out and went to the entrance, she was confronted by a line of ambulances, all waiting to disgorge their patients. It seemed that there'd never been a worse time to be injured.

** ** **

Agnes spent a wretched night, worried beyond reason, but impatient at the same time to hear that Fred had regained consciousness. However, with no telephone, the only way she could discover that development was by visiting him, and that was impossible until the next evening.

Eventually, tiredness took pity on her, and she slept.

In the morning, she opened the canteen as usual and went about her duties, appearing as far as possible to be her habitual, calm self.

She was surprised when Leading Telegraphist Beresford came to the canteen at a little after nine.

'I thought you'd be in the Sick Bay,' she said. 'How are you?'

'I'm fine, thank you, ma'am. There's nothing to worry about. Henry Little said he'd told you about Mr Fuller, and I just wondered if you'd managed to find out anything at the infirmary. They wouldn't tell me a thing.'

'I visited him last night. He was still unconscious, and he must have broken nearly every bone he possessed, but they've moved him to the Royal Victoria Hospital in Folkestone.'

'So soon?'

'Yes, I was surprised, but they need the beds urgently for casualties arriving from France.' She lifted the teapot, having brewed one for Doris and herself. 'Would you like a cup of tea?'

'Yes, please, ma'am.' He opened his belt pouch to find the money.

'No, this one's free.... What's your Christian name? I can't call you "Beresford".'

'My name's Albert, ma'am.'

'Albert, can you tell me exactly what happened yesterday morning?' It was important for her to know.

'Yes, ma'am. We sank a U-boat. The only trouble was that the U-boat got us before it sank, and the seaplane ditched in a hurry. I dived overboard just before it hit the sea, and helped Mr Fuller out of his cockpit, and then a ship came and picked us up.'

She looked at this modest rating in something akin to wonder. 'You saved his life, Albert.'

'Any bloke would have done the same, ma'am. I think I owed it to him, but I'd have done it anyway, him being such a good officer, and I wouldn't say that of all of them.'

'Nevertheless, I'm very grateful to you, Albert.'

He shrugged modestly. 'It's all in a day's work, ma'am. One thing was strange, though.'

'What was that?'

He looked a little uneasy. 'Can I speak between ourselves, ma'am?'

'I'm the very soul of discretion.'

'Well, Wing Commander Elliot came to see me in the infirmary, and he asked me all about it. He was really friendly and concerned, and he's going to recommend me for something.'

'It's no less than you deserve, Albert.'

'Thank you, ma'am, but I've never known Mr Elliot be like that before. He's always been really strict and stand-offish, and I know he hasn't always got on with Mr Fuller, but he was full of praise for him yesterday.'

It was a mystery. Agnes could think of one possible explanation. 'Maybe,' she said, 'you have a special quality, an ability to bring the best out of people.'

'Oh, I don't know about that, ma'am.'

'I think it's possible.'

** ** **

Fred's eyelids felt as if they were glued together. He tried raising a hand to rub them, but he couldn't move his arm. That attempt at movement, however, sent a wave of unbelievable pain shooting through the whole of his body; at least, it seemed so. He screwed up his eyelids and forced them to open, closing them immediately to shut out the bright daylight.

Someone was wiping his forehead, and a gentle voice said, 'Welcome back, Lieutenant Fuller. Would you like a drop of water?'

In what came out as a croak, he said, 'I'm Squadron Commander Fuller, and I'd like a glassful, please, at least.'

'I'm sorry if we got your rank wrong, Mr Fuller, and I'm afraid you can only have sips of water. We've been waiting for you to regain consciousness so that you can consent to an operation to mend your leg.'

Fred opened his eyes again and narrowed them. 'This is all wrong,' he said. 'The last I knew, I was in a seaplane over the English Channel.'

'You were shot down,' said the nurse, 'but a ship picked you up. Everything's going to be all right. Now, just have a little sip of water before I tell Sister you've regained consciousness.'

The water did no more than moisten his mouth, but he was in no position to complain, and it seemed he was in the hands of people who had his best interests at heart. The nurse took the vessel away, and Fred surrendered once again to unconsciousness.

At some time, he opened his eyes again and received the same treatment. On this occasion, however, a business-like woman with a board and a pen came to his bedside.

'We're pleased to see you conscious again, Lieutenant Fuller,' she said.

'Everyone keeps demoting me. I'm Squadron Commander Fuller of the Royal Naval Air Service.'

'Of course you are,' said the woman as soothingly as she could, 'and you have an injured leg that needs to be repaired. We need your consent to operate. Will you give us your consent?'

'Why not? You know more about it than I do. Where am I, anyway?'

'You're at the Royal Victoria Hospital in Folkestone.'

'You amaze me.' He didn't even try to make sense of it. 'Do you want me to sign something?'

'I doubt if you can,' she said gently. 'Both of your arms and your upper body are encased in plaster. If you will give your consent before witnesses, I can sign for you, unless there's someone else, your wife, perhaps?'

'No, Sister. Until I find one, you may as well stand in for her. Wheel in the witnesses.'

'Volunteer Nurse Hebble and I are your witnesses. Are you sure you want us to operate?'

'I think I said so, Sister.'

The sister looked at her form and said, 'I just have to check that you are who we think you are. You are Lieutenant Fred Fuller of the Royal Naval Volunteer Reserve?'

'No, I'm Squadron Commander Fuller of that same service.'

The sister made a note to that effect. 'What is your address, Mr Fuller?'

' "Davies' End", Queenstown, South Island, New Zealand.'

'What?'

'You'd better use The Seaplane Base, Dover, Kent.'

'Who are your next-of-kin?'

'Mr and Mrs James Davies, of the address I gave you in New Zealand.'

'That's awkward.'

'In that case, let's try Miss Agnes Morley.' He gave her Agnes's address in Whitfield. It was no more than wishful thinking on his part, but it might satisfy the inquisitive sister.

'Thank you, Lieut... Squadron Commander Fuller. I'll leave you to rest.'

'Thank you, sister. I can feel another sleep coming on.'

'It's nature's balm, Mr Fuller. It will help you recover.'

21

Fred was awake by the time Agnes arrived for visiting, although he didn't see her at first. He was still wrestling with his curiously bonded eyelids when he felt her lips on his.

'Agnes,' he said, 'there was a time when I thought I'd never see you again.'

'And I can say the same about you.' Her eyes were wet. 'What were you thinking of?'

'Oddly enough, being shot down wasn't part of the plan. It was just something that happened. What I don't understand was how I came to be rescued. I only remember being in my cockpit when we hit the sea.' He'd turned the question over repeatedly when he was sufficiently awake, but without success.

'Albert Beresford saved your life, and I'll always be grateful to him for that.'

'Beresford? I didn't know his Christian name. Did he pull me out?'

'Yes, and he kept your head out of the water until a ship came and picked you both up.'

'Well, blow me down. How is he? Have you seen him?'

'He came to the canteen yesterday morning to ask me about you. They didn't keep him long in hospital.' She remembered something else. 'Wing Commander Elliot went to see him in hospital, and told him he was recommending him for a medal.'

'A well-deserved one, I'd say.' As an afterthought, he said, 'That was very forthcoming of Elliot, wasn't it?'

'Oh, there's more,' she said, looking like someone with a secret to share. 'Albert says that Wing Commander Elliot was particularly friendly and full of praise, both for him and for you.'

159

That made Fred think. 'Is it Christmas, by any chance? I've lost track of time.'

'No, today is Easter Sunday, the thirty-first of March.'

'In that case, I can rule out a visit by three spirits. I wonder what or who can have performed the miracle.'

'I have a theory.'

'Trot out your theory, my love, but first of all, give me a kiss. I've had none since....'

'The last one you got from me. At least, I hope so.' She leaned over him and kissed him gently. 'My theory,' she said when she was back in her seat, 'is that Albert Beresford has a special facility for inspiring the best in people.'

'He's a good lad,' agreed Fred, 'but maybe Ellison just decided to turn over a new leaf. He's working hard at becoming a ringmaster in this new circus of theirs.'

'Just be thankful he's being nice, Fred.' She surveyed the plaster casts and asked, 'Have they told you how long you're likely to be out of commission?'

'No, but my guess is that I'll be out for Christmas.'

'I hope so. I have plans for you at Christmas.'

'Don't over-excite me, Agnes. I can't cope with it inside this suit of armour, and it'll be worse after tomorrow.'

'Why?' She seemed genuinely alarmed.

'They're going to operate on my leg – I don't know which. I haven't looked at them yet – and they're going to put something called a plate into it to support the bone. Speaking of plates, I'm ever so hungry. I haven't eaten since breakfast yesterday.'

'I expect they're starving you because of the operation. They'll probably give you something after it's all over.'

'I hope so.' Mention of the operation reminded him of his conversation with the sister. 'By the way,' he said, 'you're now my next-of-kin. My aunt and uncle are too far away to do the job.'

'Right. What does it entail?'

'They'll let you know if I die under anaesthetic, although I'll try very hard not to.'

'You horror. Is that all it means?'

'No. there's the good bit.'

'Tell me about the good bit.'

'Is there any chance of a kiss?'

'I think so.' She leaned forward as before and administered the desired favour.

'The good bit comes when I'm almost fit and healthy, free of plaster casts, pain and everything else.'

'I'm listening.'

'It's an important part of my recovery.'

'Don't keep me in suspense, Fred.'

'That's when I'm going to monopolise you. We're going to be inseparable, locked in each other's arms, until you decide you can't live without me.'

She sighed. 'You're being naughty. I've already told you, I have to decide in my own time.'

'All right, but a man can dream.'

'Oh, Fred,' she said, smiling for sheer pleasure, 'I'd allow you most things for the delight of seeing you safe, conscious and, hopefully, out of this war for a very long time.'

'I love you, Agnes.'

'I know.'

A wrinkle of concern crossed his features. He asked, 'We did sink that U-boat, didn't we?'

'You did.'

'What a relief. I wouldn't want to bow out of the war before I've done something useful. Hey, maybe the U-boat is the reason why Elliot's behaving like Scrooge on Christmas morning.'

A bell rang and a voice said, 'Visiting time is over, ladies and gentlemen.'

Agnes kissed him again. 'I'll be back tomorrow evening,' she said. 'Just remember to keep your promise.'

'Promise? Oh, when I'm under anaesthetic. Yes, I'll give it my whole attention.'

'I love you, Fred.'

'I love you, Agnes.' As she waved to him, it occurred to him that he probably meant those words more than ever.

** ** **

161

'Someone was saying, 'Come on, Commander Fuller. Spit it out. You don't need it anymore.'

There was something large and solid in his mouth, and he quite agreed that he'd be better without it, but it was taking some dislodging. With a little more persuasion on the part of his unknown helper, the object fell from his mouth, leaving behind only dryness and the memory of it. He didn't worry about it for long, however, because sleep claimed him almost immediately.

How long he'd slept, he had no idea, but he awoke with an incredible pain in his left leg. It was so painful that it eclipsed completely the pre-existing pains in the rest of his body.

Seeing that he was awake and in some distress, a nurse brought Sister to him, and she gave him an injection that dulled the pain and caused him, once again, to sleep.

** ** **

He hadn't expected to see anyone from the base, so the appearance of Elliot, and particularly in his new, sky-blue uniform, took him quite by surprise.

'Congratulations, Fuller. Really well done.' Elliot realised that handshaking was out of the question, so he sat down without ceremony and asked, 'How do you feel?'

'Bloody awful, sir. By the way, are there any seats left in the balcony for second house?'

'Oh, not you as well. They're going to change the uniform again, you know. They've had a barrage of complaints.'

'I'm not surprised.'

'They say the Czar bought the cloth for his Palace Guard.'

'Did they give it the thumbs-down, too?' Fred couldn't imagine anyone doing otherwise.

'No, the revolution had made it surplus to requirements, so the British Government bought it for the new RAF uniforms, and now they wish they hadn't.'

'Not everyone's as sporting as you, sir. Speaking of uniforms, though, because I was trawled in wearing two rings, everyone's been calling me "Lieutenant". I'm tired of telling them I'm a squadron commander.'

'You're not even that now, Fuller.'

'No?'

'You're a captain in the Royal Air Force.'

Fred groaned. 'I woke up wondering where I was, and they told me I was in hospital in Folkestone. I'm not really. I've died and gone to hell.'

Incredibly, Elliot was laughing. 'I've recommended Beresford for the DSM,' he said finally.

'Good, he deserves it.'

'I've also recommended you for a bar to your DSC.'

'Incredible. Thank you, sir.'

'There's quite a lot of hardware flying around. His Majesty has decided to honour certain officers late of the RNAS and the RFC, and I'm to receive the OBE.'

'Congratulations, sir. Quite right.'

'Thank you.' Ellison was quite clearly taken aback by Fred's approval.

'I can see it's made you happy, as well, sir, and rightly so.'

'Quite, and someone else who's happy is the Commander-in-Chief.'

'What has His Majesty given him, sir?'

'I don't know. He's happy because you sank that blasted U-boat.'

'Mm.' Looking back over the past few days, Fred had to say, 'I suppose the only people who are not so happy are the Boche, but they tend to take life seriously, anyway. It comes of having no sense of humour.'

As usual, Elliot was non-committal; he never knew whether or not to take Fred seriously, and Fred gave him no help. 'You know, of course, don't you,' he said, 'that Marshall Foch has been made Supreme Allied Commander?'

'Yes, sir. It's an appointment that I intend to celebrate as soon as I recover the use of my arms. At all events, it has to be a step in the right direction.'

'I hope so, and you're likely to be in plaster for some time.'

'As distinct from being plastered for days on end, yes, sir.'

Elliot winced. 'I see your experience hasn't taken the edge off your sense of humour, Fuller.'

'No, it takes more than a few eighty-six millimetre shells to wipe the smile off my face, sir, and I'm going to need my sense of humour in days to come.'

'I fear so, Fuller,' said Elliot, standing up, 'but I must leave you. The war continues regardless of individual misfortunes.'

'Inhuman bastards, the Boche,' agreed Fred.

'Well, I suppose so. Is there anything I can send you?'

'Just my number five uniform, if you will, sir. I should be able to wear it again one day.'

'Yes, I realise you're not in sympathy with the way things have turned out. I'll have it sent over. Let me know if there's anything else you need.'

'Thank you. That's very noble of you, sir.'

'Well, good luck, Fuller.'

'Thank you, sir, and thank you for the recommendations. Congratulations, as well, on your OBE.'

'Thank you. Goodbye, Fuller.'

'Goodbye, sir. I'm afraid you'll have to see yourself out.'

Elliot departed as seriously as he'd arrived, and he had not been gone long, when Fred received another visitor.

'George, come and take a seat. You'll have to excuse the sporadic howls of pain.'

'Congratulations on the U-boat, Fred, you old bastard. How are you, apart from being in agony?' George Makepeace took the seat Elliot had vacated.

'Thanks, George. I'm grateful to be alive. You know I owe that to Telegraphist Beresford, don't you?'

'*Leading* Telegraphist Beresford, he is now.' He checked himself and said, 'Well, *Corporal* Beresford. Yes, Elliot told us all about it. He was so pleased, anyone would think he'd carried out the whole operation himself.'

Fred smiled at the thought. 'I'm pleased about Beresford's hook, and I think I know what's put Elliot in such a good mood.'

'His OBE?'

'Yes, Other Buggers' Efforts. That's Elliot, through and through. You'll have seen his new uniform, I expect?'

'Strewth, yes.' George laughed. 'He looks fit to lead a circus into town.'

'I thought that was what was happening.'

'Yes, you know that secretary of his, the Wren with the red hair?'

'Don't tell me he's got her bare-back riding already.'

'No, he only gave her a bottle this morning for saying "Aye, aye, sir". The correct receipt is now "Very good, sir" or simply, "Yes, sir". We also have to adopt the Army salute and "make every effort to refrain from using naval terminology".'

Fred sighed in disgust.

'One thing that hasn't changed is our dependence on the weather. It's raining heavens hard out there, which is why I was allowed to come and see you.'

'I'm glad you did, George. Who else could have cheered me up with stories about four hundred years of naval tradition being thrown overboard, or should I say, "by the wayside"?'

'We'll find out soon enough, what to call it.' George was studying the plaster cast over Fred's left leg. He asked, 'How far does this thing go?'

'Up to my neck, as you can see.'

'What about when you need to point Percy at the plumbing, mate?'

'They've left holes in the plaster for that. The only trouble is, they have to go fishing with a button hook to find him.'

'I expect that's when your pride does a nose-dive. I mean, the old fella can't be at his best in these circumstances.' He was trying to look sympathetic, but his face creased into merriment, so that before long, they were both laughing, at least until Fred gritted his teeth and let out an expression of pain.

'Aagh!'

'What is it, mate?'

'It hurts when I laugh.'

George was immediately apologetic. 'An' I thought I was cheering you up. I'm sorry, mate.'

'I expect you meant well, George.'

The bell sounded to end visiting, and George consulted his watch. 'Quite right,' he said, 'it's time to make way for the First Dog Watch, and I don't care who hears me say it.'

'Thanks for coming, George.'

'Keep you spirits up, mate.' He grinned and said, 'Trenchard wouldn't know *that* was naval terminology.'

** ** **

After a welcome cup of tea, sleep gave Fred a welcome respite from pain, at least until dinner was served at six o' clock. Unable to move his arms, Fred had to be fed, on this occasion, by a friendly and cheerful VAD nurse.

'Down the little red lane,' she said, introducing a forkful of cottage pie into his mouth, and then rewarding him enthusiastically by saying, 'Well done, Lieutenant Fuller.'

'I'm Squadron Commander Fuller,' he corrected her. 'Actually, I'm supposed to be Captain Fuller, now, but I'd rather be Squadron Commander Fuller.'

'We can't always have what we want in this world, and my instruction was to help Lieutenant Fuller with dinner.' She appeared to be little more than twenty years old, but she wielded her authority with the air of a genial nanny.

'Lieutenant Fuller can't be here, Sister, so you'll have to feed me instead.'

'You mustn't call me "Sister".'

'Why not?'

'Sister doesn't like it.'

It made sense. 'What should I call you, then?'

' "Volunteer Nurse Barlow" or just "Nurse Barlow". Now, come on, eat up.'

After swallowing another forkful, he said, 'I'd rather call you "Florence" after Florence Nightingale.'

She shook her head disapprovingly and said, 'You mustn't do that. There must be no familiarity between a nurse and her patient. Come on, a little bit more.'

He obliged her by finishing the cottage pie.

'There, you managed it in the end.'

'I did it for you, Florence. Will you do something for me?'

'What do you want?'

'I want you to bring a button hook and the necessary utensil, and draw the screens round my bed.'

'What do you mean?' She was evidently very new to hospital routine.

166

'I need to do a jimmy riddle before visiting time, Florence. Will you oblige me, please?'

She stared at him before realisation came. 'Oh, you need to pass water.'

'Good girl, you've got the idea.'

'Very well.' She took the plate and fork and disappeared, leaving Fred to think of a suitable greeting on her return, until he was confronted, not by Florence, but by an older nurse with a stern and forbidding countenance. She carried the requisite equipment in one hand, leaving the other free to pull the screens round his bed. Fred closed his eyes and tried to think about other matters as she arranged the plumbing. Inhibition hindered progress at first, but desperation then took the upper hand, and the object was achieved. Thank you, nurse.' He spoke with much feeling.

When the nurse folded back the screens, he saw that visitors were already seated at some of the beds. The process of relief had taken longer than he thought, and now Agnes came to his bedside. Without a word, she bent over him and kissed him.'It feels strange,' she said, 'doing it with all these people around us.'

'I was just thinking the same thing a few minutes ago.' He decided to take her observation seriously. 'I imagine we're invisible as far as they're concerned,' he assured her. 'Their attention will be centred on the person they've come to visit, so please ignore them and do it again.'

She obliged. 'It still feels strange,' she said afterwards, 'but I don't mind.'

'Aren't you glad you learned to take the initiative?'

'I am, really.'

'I love you, Agnes, especially when you take the initiative.'

She gave him an admonishing look and said, 'Don't be awful. Instead, tell me what's happened today.'

'This morning, I had an operation on my left leg, and then they starved me until dinnertime this evening, when I was fed by a nurse dressed in a strange uniform and a little brief authority. I think she wants to control men when she grows up, but she can be quite sweet, so I hope she'll think again.'

'Is she very young?'

'A mere child.'

'She has time to think about her future. What else happened?'

He put on a thoughtful look. 'It's difficult to remember things when you're here, Agnes. Just having you here drives all other thoughts from my mind.'

'Fiddlesticks.'

'All right. Elliot came. He's recommending Beresford for the DSM, and me for a bar to my DSC.'

'What does that mean?'

'As I already have a DSC,' he explained, 'I'd look silly with two, so I'll get a bar to wear on the ribbon of my first one, and I'm determined to wear it on my naval uniform.'

'Oh yes,' she said, remembering, 'today was the big day, wasn't it?'

'The end of civilisation, yes. I'm supposed to be a captain, now, although I'll hold out against that for as long as I can.'

Agnes shook her head sadly. 'It's you against the establishment,' she said. 'You can't win.'

'In that case, I'll go down fighting.' In spite of his brave words, he felt, and was, completely helpless. 'Will you put your hand on mine? Either hand, I'm not choosey.'

'Of course.' She rested her hand gently on his where the plaster cast ended.

'You're truly wonderful, Agnes, coming to see me like this every day.'

'Who says I'm going to come every day?' She smiled at his crestfallen expression and said, 'I'll come whenever I can.' Then, possibly sensing a need, she kissed him again before asking, 'Did you discover the reason for Mr Elliot's good humour?'

'I think so. He's been awarded the Order of the British Empire. He'll finally receive a medal.'

'Don't be awful, especially when he's trying to get one for you.'

'I reckon that would have been in the pipeline sooner or later. I gather the Commander-in-Chief is cock-a-hoop about my U-boat.'

'You could become famous, Fred. You won't forget about me then, will you?'

'You know the answer to that question.'

'Yes, I was teasing.'

'How dare you?' Then, by loose association, he remembered his other visitor. 'George Makepeace came as well.'

'I'm glad. Who is George Makepeace?'

'Flight Commander of "A" Flight. I suppose they'll want to call him a lieutenant, now. Anyway, he's a good friend, an Aussie from Brisbane. Between us, we've made Elliot's life a trial in the past.'

'You do surprise me. Did he bring you any news?'

'Yes.' Fred smiled at the memory of it. 'Elliot reprimanded his Wren secretary this morning for saying, "Aye, aye, sir". He didn't even give the poor girl time to adjust to being in the Army.'

Agnes wrinkled her brow. 'The Army? I thought it was called the Royal Air Force.'

'To all intents and purposes, the RFC has taken over the show, and that means that we have to keep our feet on the floor, not the deck, and we must salute the way the Army do. In short, we must shed our naval past and become good soldiers. I just want the war to end before I have to get into that theatrical costume and behave like a pongo.'

'Is the uniform very theatrical?'

'It's worthy of a fifth-rate Viennese operetta. *Major* Elliot was wearing his today. I gather he's been ragged about it already.'

'I suppose that's the price he has to pay for being keen.'

'That's putting it politely. There's "keen" and there's "downright reckless".' He sighed as another thought occurred to him. 'I'm going to be in this suit of armour for months on end, Agnes, and then, when it comes off, I'll have to do all kinds of exercises, they tell me.'

'Be thankful you're still alive, Fred. I am.'

'That's just it. How long will you go on waiting for me to do something useful again?'

Agnes narrowed her eyes. 'That depends on what useful thing you have in mind.'

'I'm helpless. I'm no use to you. That's what I'm saying.'

She leaned over his body to kiss him again. 'Maybe it's my turn to be of use to you,' she said.

22

THREE MONTHS LATER

Mr Ernest Brotherton, consultant orthopaedic surgeon, was most likely a highly-qualified and skilful man. So thought Fred as he lay on his back, looking upward at the man who controlled his immediate future, so why, he wondered, didn't he attend to the hairs growing down his nose? They seemed almost to be in competition with those protruding from his ears.

Mr Brotherton perused the final X-ray before handing the collection back to Sister Godfrey, who placed them in their envelope and handed them to a more junior nurse so that she could put them safely away. Fred had seen the chain of command operate in the hospital since his admission, and it still amused him. Mr Brotherton's next words, however, were better than amusing.

'Those plaster casts can come off, now, Captain Fuller.'

For a moment, Fred thought he'd misheard the surgeon, and then the words registered. 'You say they can come off?'

'Absolutely. Your fractures have healed satisfactorily, including the two I plated, and you're now ready for physiotherapy.'

'What absolutely magnificent news! Thank you, Mr Brotherton. I've waited a long time to hear those words.'

'A little over three months, actually. Now, you mustn't get too excited. You won't be able to do very much at first, but regular physiotherapy will soon get you active again.'

'Even so, Mr Brotherton, I'm delighted. Thank you again.'

'Not at all, Captain Fuller.' He smiled a little wistfully and said, 'The news isn't good for everyone, I'm afraid. You'll be saddened to hear that the Bolsheviks have murdered the Czar and his family.'

'I didn't know them personally, but you're quite right. I do find that sad. There would be children among them, I imagine.'

'Five children,' confirmed Mr Brotherton. The rest of his firm tutted in chorus whilst Sister Godfrey and her nurses waited obediently to be addressed. Fred wasn't surprised. By that time, he knew the protocol.

'I've often thought that it's a mistake to take politics too seriously,' he said, 'considering the harm it can do.'

'On a lighter and more optimistic note,' said Mr Brotherton, brushing aside what he possibly saw as an irreverent remark, 'the German advance appears to have run out of steam.'

'That is good news.' Fred had never known his surgeon furnish a bulletin during rounds, and he wondered if it were something he usually kept as an accompaniment to the kind of momentous news he'd just given him regarding his plaster casts.

Later that morning, he was taken on a stretcher to a place of industry, where a man wearing a rubber apron and wielding a fearsome pair of shears cut the plaster away very expertly.

'Thank you very much for that,' said Fred. 'I only need something to preserve my modesty, and I'll walk back to the ward.' He attempted to swing his legs over the side of the plinth, realising immediately that he was incapable of the act.

One of the porters draped a sheet over his torso to cover his nakedness, and said, 'Not yet, you won't, Captain. Them muscles haven't done a stroke of work since they brought you in, and now they've forgotten how.'

'Oh well, I was foolish to expect too much all at once.'

Back on the ward, Sister Godfrey loaned him a suit of hospital pyjamas in the absence of his own, and Florence helped him into them.

She asked, 'How do you feel, Captain Fuller?'

'Much more human,' he told her, 'but I'll be even happier when I can move under my own steam.'

'You'll get there soon enough. Physiotherapy can work wonders.'

'In that case, I'll soon be able to chase you around the ward, Florence.'

'You'd better not, or Sister Godfrey will have something to say about it.'

'When I get my strength back, I'll chase her as well. I mean to say, fair shares and all that.'

'You're naughty.' Even so, there was fun in her eyes.

'I'm helpless, Florence. I can only joke about it.'

'And you have a lady who comes to visit you. Don't forget that.'

'That's right, Florence, a very special lady. I could never forget her.' He hoped he wouldn't get the chance.

Sister Godfrey came on the ward to see him in his new garb.

'Hello, sister. What do you think? Do I cut a dash in these pyjamas or not?'

'You'll probably look better in your own, Captain Fuller. Most men do, but it's good to see you out of those casts.'

'Thank you, sister. Do you think they'll send me back to my squadron soon?'

She shook her head sadly. 'There's no chance of that, Captain. After a spell of physiotherapy, they'll send you to a convalescent home for officers, somewhere in the country, and then you'll have to go before a medical board to determine whether or not you're fit for service. Be patient.'

Mention of a convalescent home made him think. 'Will the home be far from here?'

'It depends on where they have a bed for you, but most of our people have gone in the past to homes in Kent or Sussex.'

'Thank you, sister.'

He thought about that at odd moments during the day, because it was important.

** ** **

When Agnes arrived that evening, her eyes opened wide at the sight of him in pyjamas. 'Fred,' she said, 'this is wonderful.'

'I can't do much yet,' he said, 'but it's a start.'

She put her arms round him for the first time since the incident and kissed him enthusiastically.

'Agnes,' he said when she'd released him, 'do you remember when I asked you if you'd ever thought of learning to drive?'

'Yes, I think I said it didn't seem ladylike.'

'Neither is hugging men in public, but you do that readily enough, you shameless hussy.'

In her patient way, she asked, 'Why have you brought that up again?'

'I thought I'd ask, because I have to have physiotherapy next, but then they'll send me to a convalescent home.'

'What's phys...?'

'Physiotherapy? It's a series of exercises to build up strength in my wasted muscles. It's so that I can come home and make wild, passionate love to you.'

'Behave yourself.'

'I can't do it now, Agnes. You're safe enough because I need the physiotherapy first.'

'I see.' Indications were that she didn't, but she returned to the original subject and asked, 'What has that to do with driving?'

'Basically, I don't know where they'll send me to convalesce. If it's twenty or thirty miles distant, you could have a problem.'

'Yes, I could.' Now she looked very serious.

'That's why I'd like you to learn to drive. It's so that you can drive my Sunbeam. Always provided you can get the petrol, you'll be able to visit me.'

'That's all very well.' She was looking lost. 'Who would teach me to drive?'

'I've heard very good reports of the British School of Motoring, and you won't have to worry about the cost. I'll pay for it.' She continued to look uncertain, so he said, 'There's a motor car standing idle at the base, and there's no one I'd rather have drive it.' To reinforce his argument, he said, 'I'll put it another way. I love both of you, you and the Sunbeam, and I'd like to think of you operating together as a team.'

'You are silly, but seriously, it looks so complicated when you do it.'

'In no time at all, you'll be able to do everything I do... did. I can just see you driving it nonchalantly to wherever I'm going, leaping out and saying, "Here I am, darling, and I think one of the wheel bearings needs attention." '

She looked a little less helpless as she said, 'You have more faith in me than I have in myself, Fred.'

'Of course I have. I have the utmost faith in you, and you'll be in good hands at the British School of Motoring. I wouldn't entrust my beloved to an organisation that was less than truly excellent.' He held up his arms to seal the agreement, and they kissed on it.

'All right,' she said, 'I'll do it for you.'

** ** **

Over the next few weeks, Fred decided that learning to drive, and even to fly, had been child's play compared with returning to fitness. Two months' inactivity had left his muscles powerless, and the work required to restore them to their former state was more demanding than he could have imagined. A further complication was that the plaster had left his skin in a deplorable state, and that needed much attention. Eventually, however, the physiotherapist reported to Mr Brotherton that Captain Fuller was ready to receive further treatment at a convalescent home for officers.

He waited impatiently to learn about his destination, and soon he was rewarded. An ambulance was to take him and various others to a home in Willesborough, near Ashford. It was good news. He told Agnes about it that evening.

'I'll be going by ambulance,' he said. 'It makes sense, because petrol's not that plentiful, and it'll save you a journey.'

'All right, but you'll have to tell me exactly where it is. My sense of direction's quite.... No, that's not true,' she said hopelessly. 'I have no sense of direction.'

'It's on the main road between Hythe and Ashford,' he told her. 'I'll draw you a map.'

As if to put out of her mind the awful prospect of driving to an unknown destination, she asked suddenly, 'Isn't it wonderful that you're on the last leg, if you'll allow the pun, of your journey?'

'It's.... Yes, it's wonderful.' It would be wrong of him to inflict his impatience on her. 'How's the driving coming along?'

'I've been told I'm quite capable of driving on my own, but I feel more confident with someone beside me.'

'Good. Hopefully this war will soon be over and petrol will be more plentiful. Have you heard the news from France?'

'About Amiens? Yes, but there's one thing that puzzles me. What is a tank?'

'It's a vehicle that can cross difficult terrain and act as a shield of armour. It's enabled the allies to advance into enemy territory. I really believe we're on the brink of victory.'

'I hope so.'

'The war's not been at all good to you,' he said, taking her in his arms.

'Fred, someone will see us.'

'Kiss me and I'll let you go.'

'All right, but behave yourself.'

He released her. 'I'm going to take my uniform to Willesborough,' he said.

'Won't you have to wear hospital blue?'

'Probably, but I want to practise putting my uniform on. Actions that were automatic at one time make me feel awkward. It'll improve in time, but I want to work at it.'

'Why do you want to practise putting your uniform on?'

'So that I don't look like a half-wit at the medical board when I undress and dress again. I don't want them to think I'm helpless.'

She eyed him with disbelief. 'You're not really expecting to stay in the service, are you?'

'I'm hoping so. I don't imagine for a minute that they'll let me fly operationally again, but there must be something I can do. There may be a job for me at the Central Flying School.'

'Flying with untrained pupils.' She shook her head hopelessly at the danger that was obvious even to her. 'As if you haven't done quite enough already. Fred, I despair.'

'It may well come to nothing, Agnes, but I have to try.'

'Oh dear.'

23

Fred was sitting on the lawn, enjoying the September sunshine when he looked up to see Agnes coming towards him dressed in a substantial woollen coat of dark russet. She also wore brown kid gloves. He stood up to greet her, but she spoke first.

'Here I am, darling, and I think one of the wheel pairings needs attention.'

'The wheel *whats*?'

'It's what you told me to say when I arrived in your motorcar.' She let him put his arms round her and kiss her.

'I probably said, "wheel *bearings*", but I'm no less delighted to see you. Take a seat and let me see if I can arrange some tea for us.' He picked up his canes to make the journey across the lawn.

'Fred, you mustn't, even with two sticks.'

'I have to exercise. It's official.'

He was saved the task, however, when a nurse came over and asked Fred if he and his fiancée would like tea.

'We certainly should. Yes, please.' He waited until the nurse was safely out of earshot, and said, 'I wonder what could have given her that idea.'

Agnes looked at him innocently. 'That we would like tea?'

'No, that you're my fiancée, and now I think of it, I haven't seen you wear your wedding ring recently. I didn't like to mention it until now.'

She shrugged matter-of-factly. 'When I came to visit you at the infirmary in Dover, before ever they would let me see you, they asked me what my relationship was to you, because only close family were allowed to visit seriously ill patients. I couldn't say I was your sister or anything so dishonest, so I told them I was your fiancée. They could see my engagement ring, and they let me in. I suppose the information travelled with your records to Folkestone and then to this delightful residence.'

'Where was your wedding ring at the time?'

'Clutched in my other hand, and then I left it at home. It was the first time it had been off my finger since my wedding day.'

'I'm very touched that you did that.' Now that her gloves were off, he looked closely at her left hand. 'I'd like to buy you a new engagement ring,' he said,

'I know, but nothing is yet certain, as we've said so many times.'

'You really intend to keep me guessing, don't you?'

Their conversation was halted for the moment, when the nurse returned with a loaded tea tray and placed it on the table beside them.

'Thank you,' said Agnes, 'you're very kind.'

The nurse gave her a friendly smile and said, 'Not at all. It's just hospitality.' She smiled again and returned to the house.

Agnes lifted the teapot lid to examine the contents. 'I'll leave it for another minute,' she said, replacing the lid. Then, as if their conversation had never been interrupted, she said, 'I'm not being deliberately cruel in keeping you waiting like this, but you must recognise the enormity of the decision you want me to make.'

'All right. It was easier for me, I had no choice.'

'And it all came about because you kissed a girl.' Her eyes teased him.

'It was an excuse for my family to rid themselves of me, and nothing more than that. Men have been cast adrift for far worse offences.'

'What kinds of offence were they?'

'Drinking or gambling to excess, wanting to marry the wrong kind of girl, being obliged to marry the wrong kind of girl, associating with the wrong people....' He paused to reflect. 'Given time to develop my wayward habits, I might have committed any of those transgressions.'

'No, you wouldn't,' she told him confidently.

'How do you know I wouldn't?'

'Because you're a gentleman. At least, you've always behaved like a gentleman when you've been with me.'

'Hm.' He considered the compliment and said, 'Yes, maybe I have been a little restrained. As a remittance man, I'm not truly worthy of the name.'

'Are you thinking of repenting your upright behaviour and pursuing a life of debauchery?' She asked the question whilst pouring tea for them both.

'It's an option. You be surprised at some of the ideas that occur to me as I wait for the Admiralty to remember my existence.'

'The news from France as well as Palestine is most encouraging. The war may not last beyond the year, and then the Admiralty will have no further need of you.'

'It could all be over before Christmas,' he agreed. 'That has a familiar sound, now I think of it.'

'Honestly, darling, is it so important to you that you return to the war? I pray that it will be over before you can, because I have an awful feeling about this.' She reached out for his hands to emphasise her words. 'You've had two lucky escapes,' she said, 'and you want to go on tempting fate.' A naval officer walked past them, raising his cap to Agnes with his one remaining arm.

'Something has happened, actually,' said Fred, feeling in his inside pocket. 'I'd forgotten about this.' He produced a letter, which he handed to her.

'Do you want me to open it?'

'Please do.'

She opened the envelope and took out the letter from the Admiralty. 'How marvellous,' she said. 'This Admiral, not an Air Force officer, is actually coming here on Friday, the twenty-seventh to give you your medal.'

'Bar,' he corrected her. 'I suppose it's because I was a naval officer at the time of the incident. I don't really know. I'm just glad they're keeping it in the family. There are several others here, as well, who'll receive theirs at the same time.'

'It says you can have two guests if you wish.'

'I'll be happy with one,' he told her. 'That's if you'd like to come and you can get leave.'

** ** **

At 1120 on the morning of the 27th, recipients of the decorations, mainly the DSC, were ushered with their guests into what, in peacetime, was the drawing room of the house, to await the arrival of Vice-Admiral

Sir Nicholas Townson. They had not long to wait, because the admiral and his flag lieutenant arrived almost on the stroke of the half-hour. He made a short speech, and then two officers were called to receive the Distinguished Service Order. It was then the turn of those who were to receive the Distinguished Service Cross, and these were listed in order of seniority, which meant that Fred was among the first.

The flag lieutenant read, 'Captain Fred Fuller, DSC and bar, Royal Air Force.'

Proud in his naval uniform, Fred stepped up and favoured the admiral with the naval salute.

'Good morning, Fuller. Still in navy blue, I see.'

'Good morning, sir. Yes, I've nailed my colours to the mast.'

The admiral smiled broadly before changing the subject. 'That was a splendid operation you carried out, Fuller, sinking that U-boat.'

'Thank you, sir. It had been an awful nuisance.'

Congratulations, Fuller.' He attached the bar with a crown at its centre to the ribbon of Fred's DSC and said, 'Carry on.'

'Aye, aye, sir.' Fred saluted again before returning to Agnes's side.

'I'm allowed to take you out for lunch,' said Agnes when the admiral's party had left.

'Are you really?'

'I asked permission when I arrived. I must have you back here for your afternoon nap by two-thirty. I've heard of a nice restaurant in Ashford, but I'd like you to drive us there and back.'

He smiled at her unsureness. 'Have you an address for this restaurant?'

'Yes, it's in Hythe Road.'

'But that's the main road outside this place. Surely, that's no threat.'

'All the same, I'd prefer you to do the driving.'

'You really are a shrinking violet, but don't worry. I'll drive.'

They signed themselves out and walked out to the car. Fred held the passenger door for Agnes and then started the engine. Even as he swung the handle, he realised how weak he still was. He took his seat, put the motor in gear and stopped what he was doing. 'I'm sorry, darling,' he said, taking it out of gear and letting the clutch in, 'you'll have to drive. I tried pushing the clutch out and I know I can't keep it up over a journey.'

'All right, but you'll have to be very patient with me.'

'Am I not always patient with you?'

179

She looked almost forlorn. 'You have been, but you've never been with me when I'm driving.'

'Agnes, you've nothing to worry about. Concentrate on driving, and I'll look out for the restaurant.'

The gearbox snagged as she went into first gear, but he ignored it.

'I'm sorry, I don't usually do that.'

'What don't you do?'

'I don't make an awful noise when I change gear.'

'That's nothing. Don't worry about it.'

She drove to the end of the drive and looked both ways before pulling out into the main road.

'It's only about half a mile or so further along this road,' he told her.

'Thank goodness for that.'

He made no comment. A little later, he said, 'It's the place set back from the road, with the green paintwork. You can see it from here.'

'I can see it.'

As they approached the restaurant, Fred noticed the apron of ground in front of the building. 'If you go forward a little,' he said, 'you'll be able to reverse up to the front wall.'

'I'm hopeless at reversing.'

'Just do as I say, and you'll be all right. Pull in here.' He waited until the vehicle was stationary, and said, 'Look to see if anyone's behind you.' He turned and looked through the rear screen. 'No, the road's clear. Go into reverse and then turn your wheel hard left. I'll tell you when to stop.' He watched her reverse painstakingly slowly. 'Straighten up and... stop now.'

'Oh.' It was a sigh of relief.

'Well done, darling. That was excellent. I told you the BSM would teach you well.' He could see her shaking. 'I'm sorry,' he said. 'I wouldn't have put you through that if I could have driven, but just let me tell you something important. With more experience, you'll be an excellent driver.'

'I was so worried. I didn't want to damage your motor.'

'And you didn't. Let's go inside and find out if they have a table.'

The waiter found them a table at the front, where, as Fred pointed out, Agnes could survey the scene of her latest triumph.

** ** **

It was a good meal as far as shortages allowed, but the main treat for Fred was simply that he was back in civilisation, at least for a spell. Not surprisingly, though, as they sat at their table with the unexpected luxury of coffee, Agnes was still preoccupied with her driving.

'You're very kind about it,' she said, 'but I know I lack confidence.'

'That will come with experience,' he told her. 'I wasn't terribly confident when I first took over the controls of an aeroplane, but it came quickly enough.'

'Someone wrote a letter to the newspaper, saying that women shouldn't be allowed to drive.' Her expression seemed to suggest a measure of agreement with the correspondent.

'That argument's hard to support, considering the number of women driving military vehicles and ambulances, some of them in France.'

'I suppose so, but I've always thought that driving is a man's thing.'

'But you've just proved otherwise, which makes you all the more wonderful in my eyes. I wouldn't have considered it possible, but you've surprised me.'

She smiled at his silliness, but it was evident that a more serious matter occupied her mind. 'Fred,' she said, 'are you serious about flying again?'

'Yes, it's the only thing I can do.'

She considered his reply only briefly and said, 'It's not the actual flying that frightens me, it's the idea of you flying in time of war. I may be superstitious, but I'm convinced that falling into the sea.... What do you call it?'

'Ditching, and the first time, I put the machine down in a controlled landing. I didn't ditch.'

'But you were in danger. I'm just saying that those two incidents should be a warning to you.'

'The first time was due to engine failure, Agnes. It had nothing to do with war.' He thought someone should introduce an element of logic into the conversation.

'The second incident was sufficient warning on its own.'

'I wouldn't care to repeat it,' he conceded, now that Agnes's fixation had moved to the U-boat incident. Women seldom played fair in an argument.

'But you want to fly again, and you may well repeat it, or something like it.'

'I've told you, there's little likelihood of them letting me fly operationally again, but there must be some way I can make myself useful.'

Agnes sighed. 'We're going around in circles with this argument,' she said. 'Let's put it behind us, at least for the time being.'

24

OCTOBER

The following week, Fred was surprised to receive two letters. The first was from the Air Ministry, ordering him to attend a medical board on the following Friday at the Royal Naval Hospital in Portsmouth. He could only imagine that the RAF hadn't yet laid claim to a hospital at that early stage in its life, and that the Army hospitals were too busy dealing with casualties from France. He made a note of the date and opened the other letter, postmarked *Lymington, Hants*. He recognised the handwriting immediately, but couldn't imagine why his brother might want to communicate with him, so he opened the envelope to find out. The letter was dated the 30th September.

Dear Frederick,

I appreciate that this letter must come as something of a surprise to you, so I shall try to explain things as clearly and as succinctly as I can. I learned of your location, by the way, from an account in The Times, *detailing your recent, commendable adventures. I should, at this stage, offer my heartiest congratulations on the bar to your Distinguished Service Cross.*

It was during a period of grief, when my mind was in turmoil following Father's death, that I stopped your remittances, and I regret most deeply having done so. I have therefore decided that the time for reconciliation is overdue, and I intend to pay you a visit on Tuesday, 8th October, with a view to reaching a new understanding. I trust you find the proposed date agreeable. Should it be, for any reason, inconvenient, please contact me at the above address so that we might make alternative arrangements.

Wishing you a rapid and complete recovery from your injuries, I remain your affectionate brother,
Ralph.

Fred read it again by virtue of its unexpected content, and returned it to its envelope. It posed two important questions. What had persuaded Ralph to make the overture, and why had he left it six years after callously discontinuing the payments? Perhaps his visit might provide the answers. Meanwhile, Fred was expecting a visit from Agnes, and that pleased him a great deal more.

** ** **

Tea on the lawn was now a memory, and Fred and Agnes sat in a bay window of the old morning room, drinking tea, thankful that they were indoors and out of the wind and rain. The advantage was practical, but not exactly cheering. For four years, the house had been utilised but uncared-for. Even the morning room's velvet curtains were showing wear, and the Axminster carpet was almost threadbare in places.

Agnes was reading Ralph's letter. She reached the end and asked, 'What do you think about it?'

'I think it's completely out of character, unless he stands to gain something from such a development, in which case, it's entirely typical of him.'

'You know him. I don't.' Her tone was neutral, almost detached, as if she were preoccupied with something else.

'Believe me, Agnes, I would advise you against getting to know him.'

'Is he a dangerous man to know?'

'He succeeded in having me exiled. He's as dangerous as that, but I have an advantage over him now, and that is that he knows nothing of my life in Enzed and possibly imagines me to be as impecunious as I was when he and my father arranged my passage eight years ago.'

'Is it so important?'

'I don't know what he has in mind, but I imagine that, having inherited the estate and become wealthy, he believes he has the upper hand. He may well be surprised.'

She seemed to tire of the subject, because she asked, 'Have they given you a date for your medical board?'

'Yes, it's next Friday, in Portsmouth.' He thought he could see what she was thinking, because he said, 'I've decided to see out the war in a desk job. That's if they have one to spare.'

She nodded, surprisingly unmoved by his decision. 'I've given an awful lot of thought, recently, to the question of whether or not we have a future together.'

Finding her tone less than encouraging, he said, 'I thought you might.'

'I'm glad you've made the decision not to go on flying. Your safety really does mean a great deal to me.'

'But?' He braced himself.

'You're right. There's a "but", and it's a big one. You see, your decision, although welcome in itself, makes no difference to mine.'

'I don't understand. You've been adamant that you didn't want me to fly again, and now that I've decided against it, you're unimpressed.'

She put her cup down on the table, silent for the moment, as if the words were hard to find. Then, she said, 'You misunderstand me, Fred. My difficulty is that you asked me some time ago to leave behind the life I knew, and take up a new one with you on the other side of the world.'

'That's right.' It had been the case all along. He'd understood that perfectly.

'You've been expecting all that,' she said patiently, 'but you've never made any attempt to address my fears, whether about New Zealand or your continued aerial escapades. You expect so much, but you yield nothing.' Before he could speak, she went on. 'You may as well know that, after a great deal of thought, I was beginning to feel that I could face the enormity of moving to New Zealand. That was no longer a problem, but then you told me you were determined to serve again as a pilot, as if your future were yours alone to decide.'

'I've already said I'm content to take a desk job.'

She shook her head impatiently. 'It's not about the actual flying. The real problem is your insensitivity towards my feelings. You tell me you're a fair-minded man, who disapproves of the inequalities of our culture, you embrace a society that shuns those differences, and yet you

185

want everything to be in your favour. Even if I accept that you're the patriarchal figure that is so much a feature of our society, and I'm just a weak and feeble woman, I wonder what kind of life we'd have, with you completely unprepared to consider my needs and concerns.'

He'd naturally been aware of her objection to his flying; she'd made it very clear, but the argument she was advancing now had come as a total shock. In genuine disbelief, he asked, 'Is that really how it seems to you?'

'I'm afraid so.'

'Agnes, your feelings *are* important to me. Everything about you is important to me. I never realised you felt this way.'

'It took a little time for the idea to crystalise, so maybe it wasn't so obvious earlier, but that is how I feel.'

Fred looked around the room. Happily, everyone else was either occupied in conversation or involved in some absorbing pursuit such as chess or whist. It seemed that their disagreement was still a private one. 'I just don't understand. All the time you've been visiting me, either in hospital or at this place, and you've been harbouring this resentment.'

'As I've already told you, Fred, it took me a while to realise fully how I felt, but the reason I spent so much time by your side was that I loved you. I still do, possibly more than you realise, but I also have serious reservations, and if you believe as the poets do, that love is blind, then you and they have a great deal to learn.'

Now feeling completely drained, he asked, 'What do you want to do? Do you want us to go our separate ways now? This afternoon?'

She said quietly, 'I don't want us to part immediately after a quarrel.'

'Don't you? I must say I'm surprised, as that seems to be the agenda you brought with you today.'

She picked up her bag and said, 'I'll take your motorcar back to the base. That's unless you want me to leave it here. I can catch an omnibus back to Dover easily enough. At some time before you leave for New Zealand, it would be good for us to meet once again so that we can part on good terms. Don't you think so?'

He gave the suggestion only a little thought before saying, 'No, I don't. I think a clean break is better. Now I think of it, I've experienced a few of them in the past few months, so maybe I'm something of an expert. I have at least learned to tolerate the pain associated with them.'

He sighed heavily. 'At all events, we're parting because of a quarrel, and I don't see how denying the fact is going to make any difference to anything. Take the Sunbeam back to Dover by all means.'

She stood up to go. 'Let me see myself out, Fred.'

'Now, that I simply can't allow. I'll take you out to the motor.'

They walked to the front door, where Fred helped her on with her coat, waited for her to adjust her hat, and offered her his arm.

'You've no need to do this, Fred.'

'Yes, I have, unless you want to leave me feeling like a cad as well as the unfeeling despot who trampled on your feelings.' He walked to the motor, opened the door and held it for her. 'I'll start the engine,' he offered.

'Thank you.'

He waited for her to advance the ignition, and then swung the handle. The engine caught immediately, so that it seemed to Fred that even the motor could barely wait to make its escape.

'Goodbye, Agnes,' he said, holding the door. 'Have a happy life.'

'And you, Fred.' Her cheeks were wet. 'Be happy too.'

He closed the door and waited until she was at the end of the drive, and then he went inside. It was coming on to rain. The weather was in perfect harmony with his mood.

** ** **

Two days later, Fred travelled to Dover by omnibus. He was able to look up a great many people he'd known, including George Makepeace, now a captain commanding Fred's old squadron, and Leading Telegraphist Beresford. He spent some time with the latter, having made the arrangement with the officer in charge of signals.

'It's good to see you again, Beresford. I was very grateful for your visit when I was in hospital.'

'It was no trouble to me, sir, and I'm heartily glad to see you up and about again.'

It was small-talk, and that wasn't the object of the meeting, at least, as far as Fred was concerned. 'Beresford,' he said, 'you and I both know that I owe you my life, and I shall always be grateful for that.'

'I was only doing what was right, sir.'

'No, Beresford, you put your own life at risk to save mine.'

'Well, maybe I felt I owed it to you, sir.'

'Whether or not,' said Fred, taking a card from his wallet, 'I want you to take this so that you have my home address in New Zealand, and if there's ever any way in which I can help you and your family, you must let me know. People say these things, but this is a genuine offer.'

'Thank you, sir. An offer from you could never be anything but genuine.'

They shook hands, and Fred returned to the wardroom, where he was treated to lunch as a guest.

Once again, Major Ellison was on his most careful behaviour, so that Fred wondered if his attitude might have taken a permanent turn for the better.

'It's good to see you again, Fuller,' he said, handing him a glass of sherry. 'Have you had any word, yet, of your posting?'

'No, sir, my medical board is on Friday. I imagine a posting will follow that.'

'Yes, but it does seem rather pointless. I mean, you're RNVR, which means that when peace finally comes you're not likely to be around for very long. Chances are, they'll simply discharge you.'

'Well, we'll just have to wait and see, sir. Meanwhile, I imagine you're eagerly awaiting promotion to lieutenant-colonel, or whatever they'll decide to call you in this new circus, and an appointment elsewhere.'

Ellison laughed. The sound was not normally heard in that wardroom, and Fred wondered again about the change in his superior.

'You find the prospect amusing, sir?'

'Considering I've held the rank of major for less than a year, yes, I do. Also, why would they want to move me away from this establishment?'

'Can you really see the seaplane surviving much beyond the war, sir? The old guard of the RFC were always of the opinion that it was a waste of timber and canvas, and they, after all, are the establishment of the RAF.'

'You know, Fuller,' said Elliot putting down his empty sherry glass, 'you would do well to be a little less outspoken in your resentment.'

'What harm can it do me now, sir? As you said, they'll probably turn me out to pasture, or kick me out of the service altogether.'

'Well, yes, I suppose you have a point.'

It was pleasant to eat in the wardroom again, in the company of old colleagues and a few new ones, and when it was time to leave, Fred returned to another old friend, his beloved Sunbeam, because the main purpose of his visit had been to drive it back to the home.

He swung the handle twice, and it started. Other than his abortive attempt earlier, to drive to the restaurant with Agnes, it was the first time he'd driven it since before the U-boat incident, but it felt very familiar and welcoming.

He drove, by necessity, past the canteen, knowing that Agnes would be inside, a matter of yards away, but as distant as if he were already in New Zealand.

25

Ralph's visit provided one immediate benefit, in that it served as a merciful distraction when Fred needed one most. For the duration of their meeting over lunch at the Victoria Hotel, he was able to forget the awful pain of separation from Agnes. All too soon, thoughts of her would return to torment him afresh, but for the time being, he would concentrate on other matters.

Ralph had aged somewhat in the eight years they'd been apart, and his lean face was marked with lines, although Fred was at a loss to imagine who or what had been responsible for such a change. In all other respects, however, little about him had altered. In particular, and in spite of the mere two years' difference in their ages, he was as pompous as ever.

'I'm curious, Frederick,' he said. 'I am aware of your record of service in the Royal Navy, but how did you spend your time prior to the war?'

'I was, and still am, employed by the Queenstown Trading Company.'

'In what capacity?'

'As a director of the company.'

Ralph made no effort to conceal his surprise. 'Am I to understand that you have enjoyed some success in New Zealand?'

'I've been very successful, both financially, which I imagine is the kind of success you have in mind, and in a less material way. In short, I've been very happy, living in New Zealand.'

'You do surprise me.'

'I don't doubt it, Ralph. It's a kind of lifestyle you could never begin to imagine.'

Ralph took a hefty draught of his wine, possibly to adjust to a state of affairs he'd never expected. Then, he asked, 'You will have been in regular correspondence, I imagine, with Messrs Botham and Chorley as well as the stockbrokers who act for Coutts?'

Fred smiled. He'd often thought that "Botham" was an unfortunately appropriate name for someone who had taken to manufacturing saddlery. 'No,' he admitted, 'all business correspondence, apart from everyday banking matters, goes to my address in New Zealand, and you can imagine the difficulty involved in carrying the mails between Great Britain and the Antipodes in wartime.' At the same time, he wondered how Ralph knew that his affairs were handled by Coutts Bank. The remittances, for as long as they'd lasted, had been paid to his account at the National Provincial Bank.

'I can imagine that difficulty, Frederick.' He appeared to be thinking quite furiously. Eventually, he said, 'I've been aware for some time that Mother left you a block of shares in Botham and Chorley.'

'Have you really?'

'Yes, Father mentioned it frequently, and I assume that they are still in your possession?'

'You should never assume, Ralph. Assumption makes an ass of us all.'

'I'm aware of that. Are they still in your possession?'

'For what it's worth, yes, they are.'

For a moment, it seemed likely that Ralph might choke on his wine. 'You say, "For what it's worth", Frederick, and it seems you have no idea of what that block of shares really is worth.' His moustache quivered, as if it, too, could scarcely believe such apparent nonsense.

'None whatsoever. For all I know, any communications between the company and me could be at the bottom of the ocean.'

'But your bank statements…. Haven't you been aware of the dividend payments?'

'They go to my account at Coutts Bank. I left it there because they managed Mother's account, and the only address they have for me is in New Zealand. I deal locally with the National Provincial Bank, as you know.'

'So you've no idea?'

'Not until you give me a clue as to what I've missed.'

It seemed that Ralph was experiencing some difficulty in mustering the appropriate words, because his mouth had fallen open, but no words came out.

'Have a drink,' advised Fred. 'Maybe that will help.'

Ralph took him at his word and called the waiter to demand another bottle of the St Emilion. 'When Father died,' he explained, 'I spent some time with his solicitor, during which he commented on the unfortunate fact that neither Father nor I had followed Mother's example and invested in Botham and Chorley. Actually, the shares were left to her by Grandfather Fuller, so the example was not exactly hers, but I'm sure you see what he meant.'

'Are you saying that those shares have done particularly well?'

'That's exactly what I'm saying, Frederick. You are now a wealthy man.'

'I know.'

Ralph was puzzled again. 'You know? If you had no idea about the shares, how could you possibly know that?'

'You're right, Ralph. I'd no idea about the shares, but I acquired my wealth in New Zealand.' He opted for total honesty and said, 'Maybe I'm not exactly wealthy by your standards, but I'm still very comfortably off.'

The waiter returned to the table with a bottle St Emilion and asked Ralph if he would care to taste it, to which Ralph replied dismissively and in his familiar, autocratic way, 'No, just pour it.'

The waiter did so, offering then to pour a glass for Fred, who said, 'No, thank you. I have to drive.'

'Very good, sir.' The waiter left them to resume their conversation.

'You tell me you're comfortably situated, Frederick, but now, you are a great deal wealthier than you imagine.'

Fred looked around the restaurant, noticing for the first time the over-ornate wainscoting and dark-stained mahogany panels. It was Victorian bad taste at its very worst, and it seemed wholly appropriate for such a meeting. 'I really hadn't given the matter any thought,' he said. 'I've been a little preoccupied over the past few years, as you can imagine, but it stands to reason that the shares have done well. I imagine that no one in the leather industry can fail to have benefited from the war.'

'Exactly. The company was not involved in saddlery at the time of the South-African Wars, or the shares might have been even more valuable than they are now.'

'I suppose they might,' said Fred, 'but I imagine there were plenty who profited from it. It's just as well all those men didn't die completely in vain.'

The irony of Fred's observation seemed lost on his brother, who simply agreed with the sentiment. 'Yes.' he said, 'Now, when you've informed Coutts of your address in England, you'll be able to order a statement, and then you'll see what I've been telling you.'

'Yes, I know how everyday banking works, and I'll go and speak to them when I have a day to spare. Now that my medical board is imminent, you can imagine that there's plenty to keep me occupied.' He let Ralph digest that information, and then said, 'However, I'm sure you didn't make the journey from Lymington just to congratulate me on my windfall.'

'No,' said Ralph solemnly, 'I didn't. My purpose in writing to you and in making this journey, was to bring about a reconciliation between us and to facilitate your return to the family home after your regrettable absence.'

Fred considered his brother's words, unable to believe fully what he'd just heard. Ralph was keeping something back; there was a further fetch involved, and he was being particularly reticent about it. 'I have no regrets about my absence,' he said, 'and I have a very well-appointed home in New Zealand. When the Navy has no further need of my services, I shall return there and take up my life where I left it when war broke out.'

'But I'm offering to take you back into the family home, the home to which you belong.'

'And how would you gain from that?'

Ralph offered Fred a cigar, which he refused. 'I should have the satisfaction of ending a distressing and embarrassing quarrel, and bringing my brother back into the family.' He cut the end of his cigar and took out a box of matches, striking one and attending to the leisurely process of lighting the cigar.

'There's something else you haven't mentioned,' said Fred. 'I think there's a connection between my windfall and your allegedly earnest desire to see me at the family table.'

193

It was clear from Ralph's reaction that Fred's challenge had come just a little earlier than he would have preferred, and he continued to play with the cigar, presumably to gain time for his explanation. Eventually, he said, 'I stopped your remittances because I had to make economies after Father's death. He left substantial debts, I'm afraid, that came as a great shock to me. He'd never mentioned them, and I had no reason to suspect that anything was amiss.'

By this time, Fred knew the rest, but he kept quiet, preferring to hear the disagreeable story from his brother's lips.

'Knowing that you were now the owner of a substantial holding in Botham and Chorley, I thought you might care to help set Father's affairs in order, if only for the sake of the family name.'

Ralph looked more sinister than usual through a cloud of cigar smoke. It was an impression that Fred found entirely fitting. 'Your family is called Fuller-Davies,' he pointed out. My name is Fuller. I changed it legally. I've no doubt my solicitor notified you of the fact.'

'But you're still a member of the family,' protested Ralph.

'An outcast sent to live twelve thousand miles away.'

'Damn it, Frederick, I've asked you to come home.'

'So that I can repay the debts accumulated by the other man who sent me into exile?'

'The *other* man?'

'There were two of you behind it. You can't deny your part in the plot. Even so, you're suggesting that I repay those debts in order to restore the honour of a man who didn't even know its meaning.' He blew to dissipate the cigar smoke. 'I'll tell you something about honourable people, Ralph. When I arrived in New Zealand, the person you regard, if you think of him at all, as a very distant cousin and the descendant of another exiled member of the Davies family, took me in and gave me board, lodging and employment. More than that, he and his wife welcomed me into the family business and treated me as their own son. They are honourable people, and if they ever needed help, I would do anything I could to provide it. That is where my loyalty lies.' He took his napkin from his lap and put it on the table. 'Thank you for a very passable lunch, Ralph. I wish you a safe journey home. Goodbye.'

** ** **

About twenty-five miles away, Agnes's thoughts and feelings were still at odds with each other. She'd believed the things she'd told Fred, but now she was beginning to doubt her judgement. It was true that he'd seemed to take so much for granted, but it wasn't always like that. When she'd had to drive his car with him beside her, he knew why she was afraid. She'd expected criticism and recrimination, particularly when she clashed the gears, but he'd dismissed the event as unimportant. The truth was that, recognising her state of mind, he'd deliberately made light of it, and that wasn't the behaviour of a man who disregarded her feelings. There was also the time during the air raid in London, when he'd done everything he could to allay her fears. There was that curious conversation, as well, that they'd had the last time they were together before he was horribly injured. She was almost embarrassed to think about it. She'd actually spoken to him of her misgivings regarding the ultimate intimacy, and he'd told her gently that, at its best, the ecstasy she'd regarded as the man's preserve was a shared delight. She had to accept his word for it, because her brief experience had been very different. All the same, his argument hadn't been that of an insensitive man.

It was the second time they'd been estranged. It was true that Fred had initiated their first parting, but only in response to her refusal to contemplate emigration to New Zealand, and she'd been able to make good the damage, but this time it was final. She'd missed his departure from the base, but the empty space his motorcar had previously occupied served as a mocking memorial. She would never see him again.

** ** **

Fred elected to spend the two days before his medical board in London. He would need two days, because the bank had told him they would need to telegraph his office in Queenstown for confirmation that he was the Fred Fuller of that address, which, as everyone knew, was twelve hours ahead of Greenwich Meantime. He would need to provide the bank in London with various forms of identification and then cool his heels for twenty-four hours. He would have no difficulty in doing that.

His only difficulty for the moment was in coming to terms with the loss of Agnes. He'd been a fool, he knew, but no amount of self-recrimination was going to change the fact that he'd lost her, this time for good. He must settle for it and hope that the Air Ministry would post him to a station as distant as possible from Dover.

26

Fred had spent a miserable night in London. As a diversion, he'd gone to a revue called *Box o' Tricks* at the Hippodrome, at the corner of Cranbourn Street and Charing Cross Road. Whilst the entertainment was quite good in itself, it was unfortunate that anything to do with the theatre reminded Fred of evenings he'd spent with Agnes, either in London or in Dover, and he preferred to be spared the memory.

Coming out of the Hippodrome, he'd decided to walk to his hotel in Charing Cross Road, even though he could hear harsh words being spoken and even shouted. He could see some theatregoers brandishing their canes at the pathetic figures crouched in the doorways, who asked for coppers before the police came to move them on.

As he drew level with one doorway, he saw a roughly-painted sign that read, *Husband and 2 sons lost in France*. Another read, *Baby to support. Husband lost in trenches.* People were actually cursing them and threatening to beat them unless they vacated the public pathway. Fred felt in his pocket, where he knew he had change. He gave each of the two women five shillings, saying, 'Buy yourselves a hot meal. You look as if you need one.' Acknowledging their exclamations of gratitude, he moved to the next doorway, where a man in evening dress was raising his cane to beat its occupants. Fred parried it with his walking cane, causing it to fly out of the man's hand. 'Touch these women,' he warned, 'and you'll regret it. I warn you, I don't just hit bullies, I *thrash* them.'

'The absolute cheek of it,' said the woman by the man's side. 'Who does he think he is?'

'Yes,' said the man, but rather less boldly, 'what the devil do think you're doing, encouraging beggars?'

'Their husbands gave their lives in the war. What have you given? Go on, tell me what you've done in this war.'

'Infernal cheek.' The man and his wife moved on.

'Thank you, sir,' said one of the women tearfully.

'Yes, thank you, sir,' said her neighbour. 'They want locking up, his sort do.'

'I can think of worse things I'd inflict on him and his kind,' said Fred, taking out his wallet. 'Can you ladies share a ten shilling note? I seem to be short of change.'

'Can we...? We won't 'ave a lot of bovver doing that, sir. D' you mean it, sir?'

'Of course I do. Take this.' He handed the banknote to the nearest. It would probably buy them each four or five meals of some kind.

' "Ladies", you call us,' said the other. 'You're a saint. Thank you, sir.'

'I'm not a saint,' he told her. 'I'm a naval officer whose seen too many good men die in this war.'

'Well, God bless you anyway, sir.'

'And you, ladies, and your children.'

A voice of authority at his shoulder asked, 'Is there a problem here, sir?'

'The only problems of which I'm aware, Constable, are an ungrateful government and thugs in evening dress.'

'It doesn't pay to get involved, sir, if you don't mind me saying so.'

'Oh, but I am involved, Constable, as everyone in the civilised world should be.'

** ** **

Fred undressed, but instead of going straight to bed, he sat by the fire with a bottle of gin and a jug of water, thinking about the ugly scenes in Charing Cross Road, and not just his confrontation with the awful bully. Each doorway scene was ugly; the very fact that the widows sheltering in them were half-starved made them so. Had the policeman arrived a little earlier, of course, he could have arrested Fred for assault or whatever the offence was called, but he didn't care. He'd been angrier then than he could ever remember himself being. Even Ralph's attempted manipulation had only left him feeling cold and disdainful, but he would cheerfully have beaten the living daylights out of that bully.

That was the problem with British society. It needed people of passion to make things happen. He poured himself another glass of gin and continued to ponder the problem.

** ** **

His appointment with Mr Goodman at the bank was at 11:30, so he had a leisurely breakfast before setting out. The bank being in the Strand, it was necessary for Fred to pass several groups of distressed people along his route, and he dispensed help as he passed them, resolving to do so whenever the opportunity arose. There was no sign of the women he'd met on the previous evening, and he could only hope and imagine they were enjoying the benefit of his small gift.

He reached the entrance to Coutts and entered the magnificent banking hall, with its high ceiling, tiled floor, ornate balconies and crystal chandeliers. A uniformed servant asked if he might be of assistance.

'I have an appointment at eleven-thirty with Mr Goodman,' he told him. 'My name is Fuller.'

'Please wait here, sir.' The servant knocked on the door of an office that Fred remembered from the previous day as that of Mr Goodman's secretary. After less than a minute, she came out and, recognising Fred, asked him to follow her to Mr Goodman's office. His reception on entering was most effusive.

'Good morning, Mr Fuller. Come in and take a seat. Would you care for coffee?' His host was a large man both in height and in girth, whom wartime shortages seemed not to have troubled.

'Yes, please. That would be more than acceptable.' It seemed that the wardrooms and officers' messes were not alone in procuring luxuries unknown to the majority of the population.

Mr Goodman asked his secretary to make the necessary arrangements, and took his place behind a huge and ornate desk. 'We have received a telegram from your family in Queenstown, Mr Fuller, and I'm happy to say that the bank is now once again at your service.'

'It was remiss of me to keep you uninformed of my whereabouts, Mr

Goodman, but war has a way of concentrating the mind on immediate concerns, whilst others are easily forgotten.'

'Quite so, Mr Fuller, and may I take this opportunity to congratulate you on your recent decoration, which I'm sure was richly deserved?'

'Thank you, but let's attend to the matter of my account. I'd like to see a statement, if that can be arranged.'

'Of course.' Mr Goodman opened a manila file on his desk and took out a typewritten statement, which he handed to Fred, saying, 'I'm sorry we found it necessary to be so careful when you contacted us, but the bank's brokers informed us that an attempt had been made some time ago to gain fraudulent access to some shares that are in your name, and we were at great pains to prevent a similar wrong.'

'Not at all. I appreciate your concern for my property.' Fred had a vague notion that he knew the identity of the attempted fraudster, but he dismissed the thought for the moment and gave the statement his full attention. He examined the latest dividend payment and the current balance, and blinked, unable at first to believe what his eyes told him. Ralph's description of him as a wealthy man was no exaggeration.

Happily, at that point, Mr Goodman's secretary entered the office with coffee and, incredibly, biscuits. Her arrival afforded Fred an opportunity to come to terms with his recent surprise whilst she poured the coffee.

'Mr Goodman,' he said, will it be possible for you to acquire a valuation of my holding in Botham and Chorley?'

'I have one here.' He passed the document across his desk to Fred. 'The shares have always been good, but the war has caused them to appreciate in value to an extent that has, let's say, surprised the most experienced of brokers.'

If the balance of Fred's account had caused him to doubt what he saw, the valuation of the Botham and Chorley shares left him momentarily stunned. He digested the information as far as he could, and then looked again at the broker's note.

'The bank's brokers would advise you to acquire more ordinary shares as they appear on the market, but such occurrences are rare, as you might expect.'

'But when the war is over,' said Fred, 'the bough is likely to break and the baby to fall, surely.'

'There must inevitably be a decrease in yield, conceded Mr Goodman, but Botham and Chorley have built up a sound and diverse business.'

'They used to make ladies' handbags. I believe that was the case when my mother inherited the shares. Tack was a more recent venture, further encouraged by the war.'

' "Tack", Mr Fuller? I'm not familiar with the word.'

'Leather goods of the equestrian kind,' explained Fred. He tried his coffee and found its flavour rich and intense. Even wardroom coffee suffered by comparison.

'Are you going to be in town long, Mr Fuller?'

'I have to be in Portsmouth tomorrow for my medical board, but I should like to speak with someone at the Ministry of Pensions this afternoon, if I can. Otherwise, I shall have to make alternative arrangements.'

'I have a contact at the Ministry. Would you like me to speak to him?'

'That would be most helpful, Mr Goodman. I'm obliged to you.'

** ** **

Twenty-four hours later, Fred reported to Royal Naval Hospital Haslar in Portsmouth, where he was invited to remove his clothes prior to being X-rayed. The process took very little time, and he was shown promptly into a consulting room, in which two doctors were examining the X-rays, still wet from the developing process.

Presently, one said, 'Hm, I'm inclined to agree,' and then acknowledged Fred, saying, 'I'll leave you with Surgeon Commander Baird, Captain Fuller.'

'Thank you.'

As he swept out, his colleague extended his hand to Fred. 'Baird,' he said, 'orthopaedic surgeon.'

'I'm glad to meet you, sir,' said Fred, recognising that Baird was, after all, a surgeon-commander.

'You must have hit the water with some force,' he commented.

'The aircraft was out of control.'

'How on earth did your crewmember escape unhurt?'

'He tells me that just as the machine was about to hit the water, he dived overboard, but facing aft. In that way, he avoided the concussion he might have suffered by hitting the sea headfirst at possibly thirty or forty knots.'

'Incredible.' His expression said the same.

'He's a strong swimmer, sir.'

'Fortunately for him and for you, I believe.' Taking the last of the X-rays from the screen, he said, 'This whole journey's something of a waste of your time, Captain Fuller. We already had your previous X-rays, and there was never any likelihood of your flying again, considering your rank, but I suppose the Admiralty or the Air Ministry had to satisfy itself that you wouldn't be claiming a disability allowance.'

'Not a total waste of time, then.'

The surgeon commander consulted a document on his desk and said, 'You're due for leave.'

'Possibly overdue, sir.'

'Quite. Where's your home?'

'Queenstown, New Zealand.'

'Oh.' The surgeon looked surprised. 'You don't sound colonial.'

'I spent just four years in New Zealand before returning to serve in the RNVR, sir.'

'Quite. All the same, I don't think they'll let you go there.'

'Even now that I'm not troubling them for a disability allowance?'

'I don't think it would have made all that much difference, old man.' He shuffled the documents and placed them in a manila folder. 'Just out of interest, where will you spend your leave?'

'From here, I'll return to the convalescent home, and when my posting comes through, I'll report there immediately.' On reflection, he said, 'I have some business to transact in London. Otherwise, I'll hang around for while until I hear where my posting is.'

'I admire your spirit, Captain Fuller.'

Fred felt obliged to say, 'Well, I have spent the past six months in subsidised idleness.'

The railway journey from Portsmouth to Ashford was lengthy and tiresome, but it gave Fred an opportunity to plan ahead. For four years, he'd lived from one moment to the next, but now he could take a more distant view, and the knowledge gave him deep satisfaction.

** ** **

Almost two weeks after his return to Ashford, he received a letter from the Air Ministry, ordering him to take seven days' leave before assuming command of No. 206 Squadron, RAF, based at Walmer Aerodrome. In the final paragraph, he was informed that it was a non-flying appointment. That came as no surprise, unlike the location, which was basically next door to Dover.

27

A telephone call to RAF Walmer confirmed that there was currently no accommodation available for him, nor would there be until the day his appointment commenced, so he spent two days in London and then took a room at the Ambassador Hotel in Dover. After all, he told himself, it wasn't as if he would be living beyond his means.

The luxury of his hotel room was very pleasant at first. To begin with, the bed was infinitely more comfortable than the hospital-type single beds at the home, and what food was available was also of superior quality. Even so, he'd been looking forward, after his long absence from duty, to the wardroom camaraderie he remembered, and which was as yet denied him.

Now that Germany had rescinded its policy of unrestricted U-boat warfare, he'd wondered how life at the seaplane base might be affected, and now, fuelled by curiosity, he decided to drive up there and find out.

It was, he concluded, almost like coming home. George Makepeace was still there, and so were some of the others he remembered. Lunch in the wardroom was all that he remembered, and particularly when Elliot looked in to ask who'd parked a private motorcar on service property. When he caught sight of Fred, he remembered whose motor it was, and after an almost-friendly reunion, ordered him to move it.

George was the first to object. 'You can't expect the poor bugger to park outside the base and walk all the way in with those broken bones,' he said. 'I'll move it for you, Fred, and when you have to leave, I'll fetch it back for you. Just sit there, mate, and take it easy.' Everyone knew he was only taking a rise out of Elliot, but he pulled on his coat and left the wardroom all the same. When he returned, he told Fred, 'I've left it by the canteen. It's civilian property, so not even Wing Commander Elliot can raise an objection.'

' "Major Elliot",' Elliot corrected him. 'We're in the RAF now.'

'That's right,' said George, 'we're pongos now, but just you wait, Major Elliot. You'll soon have a new rank to get used to. It'll be "all change" again.'

It was true. The Air Ministry were looking into how they might make the RAF unique, with a new system of ranks that owed nothing to the Army or the Navy. Fred's current concern, however, was of a different kind.

'Thank you for doing that, George,' he said, 'but I wish you'd left it somewhere other than the canteen.'

'I know, mate. Don't worry, I'll go for it when the time comes.'

** ** **

The first of the junior ratings were making their way to the canteen, but some of them seemed to be gathered around a motorcar. It was quite normal for young men to take an interest in motor transport, whether it ran on two or four wheels, so Agnes thought nothing about it at first. It was only when the ratings were in the canteen that she recognised the Sunbeam, and it caused her to gasp at first. She wondered for a moment if he might be back at the base, but that was most unlikely. The strongest likelihood was that he'd sold the motorcar to one of his old friends on the base. After all, it would be of no use to him when he left for New Zealand. Seeing the motor, however, brought back the grief afresh, and she wished someone would take it away.

Her wish was granted an hour or so later, when the Australian officer, Captain Makepeace, climbed into it and drove it away. It confirmed her suspicion, but she hoped he wasn't going to park it there regularly. It would be too much for her to cope with.

** ** **

It had been an afternoon of fun, memories and friendly merriment, but Elliot had pointed out that Captain Fuller was no longer on the establishment, which meant that dinner in the wardroom was out of the question. There was a barrage of protest, but Elliot was used to being unpopular, so it made no difference. Fred took his leave of his friends and went out to the motorcar, which George had parked outside the wardroom in a gesture of defiance. It had begun to rain earlier, and the wind, which had been blustery, was now squalling and most unpleasant. He swung the starting handle and climbed into the Sunbeam readily.

He was about to take the direct route to the Main Gate, when he saw that a coal lorry had arrived, and the process of unloading the base's fuel had begun. More importantly for him, however, was the fact that the lorry was blocking his exit. He would have to take the road past the canteen. Taking a deep breath, he drove up the slope. The canteen was dark inside; Agnes must have closed for the day and gone home, an event for which Fred was thankful. He drove out to the main road, and was about to turn left towards the centre of Dover, when he saw a figure at the omnibus stop across the road struggling with an umbrella in the gusting wind. As he peered through the windscreen, which was partially obscured by rain, he recognised the unfortunate pedestrian with the umbrella. It was Agnes, the very person he wanted to avoid.

28

Fred had never considered himself fanciful, but he could only imagine that it was some mysterious agency over which he had no control that caused him to make the split-second decision to turn right across the road.

As he drew level with her, he stopped the motor, leaned across the passenger seat and opened the door. 'Get in,' he told her. 'I'll take you home.'

Agnes stared. 'Fred, what are you doing here?'

'Never mind that. Get in before you're soaked to the skin.'

She sank into the passenger seat and closed the door. 'I saw Captain Makepeace drive your motor away and I thought he must have bought it from you. I didn't realise you'd come back to Dover.'

Their combined breath was causing mist to form on the windscreen that even the draught from the side windows was unable to clear, so Fred wiped it with the duster he kept in the door pocket. 'No, George was just having a little fun at Elliot's expense. Anyway, how are you?' Now that the encounter had taken place, he was finding it easier to talk to her than he might have expected.

'I'm well, thank you, and you?'

'Fit for active service, but too senior to fly. In any case, as I told you, I'm happy to see out my time on the deck. They've put me in command of Two Oh Six Squadron at Walmer, believe it or not. I came over to the base just to see some old friends.'

'That was convenient, wasn't it?'

'Very convenient,' he agreed. 'I don't start until next week. I'm staying at the Ambassador in Dover.' He slowed down as the rain became heavier and the wipers struggled to cope.

'Very comfortably, I imagine. Where were you heading,' she asked, 'when you stopped to pick me up?'

'To the hotel.'

'You must have known you were driving in the wrong direction.'

'Oh, yes.'

'Did you do it because of the rain?'

'Yes.' It was interesting that she'd avoided asking openly if he'd done it for her benefit. He suspected that she was feeling a little vulnerable. 'I'm going to stop here, just until it eases.' He pulled into the side of the road and pulled the brake on. 'I stopped for you because if I hadn't, you'd have been half-drowned by the time you arrived home.'

'It was very kind of you.'

'Ah well, I don't find it all that unusual or surprising.'

'What do you mean?'

He turned as far as he could in the narrow, bucket seat and explained patiently. 'I don't find it unusually kind of me to prevent a lady from being drenched,' he said. 'As far as I'm concerned, it's normal behaviour. In fact, if you recall, I extended the same courtesy the day we met.'

In a small voice, she said, 'Yes, you did. You're a naturally kind man. I forgot that for a while.'

'The rain's not quite so bad now,' he said, engaging first gear and moving off. He concluded that his initial impression was correct, and that she was feeling vulnerable. He resolved, in the brief space of time they would be together, to treat her gently.

They had almost reached her home when he said quite conversationally, 'I can be thoughtless. I sometimes feel a headlong rush of enthusiasm and I forget the important things. I have been particularly thoughtless in your case, but it will surprise you to learn that your feelings were always important to me.'

'I can see that now, and the fault wasn't all yours.'

'Oh well, it's so much spilt milk,' he said, pulling up outside her house.

'And speaking of which, will you come in and have some tea?'

He hesitated. It wasn't what he'd had in mind. He'd intended leaving her at her door and driving back to the hotel, but the same mysterious agency that had made him stop for her, despite his proud intentions, prompted him again, and he made another quick decision. 'Thank you,' he said, 'I'd like that.'

They walked up the footpath, as they had so many times, and she let them into the house.

'Give me your coat and cap,' she said.

'No, let me take yours first.' He eased her coat off her shoulders. 'It's absolutely sodden.'

'Leave it here to drip. I'll find something in a minute to catch the drops.'

He took a coat-hanger and hung her coat on a hook behind the door. Mine's not bad,' he said, hanging it in the usual place. 'Do you want me to light a fire?'

'Yes, please. In the sitting room, if you will.'

After closing and fastening the shutters against the hideous weather, he built a fire while she made tea in the kitchen. After a while, she came to the sitting room to say, 'I have some muffins. Would you like one?'

'I had a hearty lunch in the wardroom, but why not? The fire's coming on nicely.' He wondered what had persuaded her to buy muffins. It seemed odd, so when she appeared with the tea things, muffins and toasting forks, he asked her, 'Were the muffins intended for a special occasion?'

She looked uncomfortable. 'No,' she said.

'I only wondered. Don't tell me if you find it embarrassing.'

'I always find myself telling you things, anyway. It just happens, as you know.'

'Go on, then. You know I won't make you feel uncomfortable.'

'I know you won't.' She smiled faintly. It was her first smile since their meeting at the omnibus stop. 'I was feeling so wretched about our parting, I'd been trying not to think about the times we spent together, but I found I couldn't avoid it. I was tormented by happy memories that made me desperately unhappy. I hope that doesn't sound as nonsensical to you as it does to me.'

'Of course not. Please go on.'

'Do you remember the first time you came here? I'd baked a cake, and I was dreading the result, but you advised me to tackle the problem head-on and cut into it, to defy what you called... I think it was something like "the ogre in the room".' It was clear that she remembered the occasion vividly.

'Yes, I remember it.'

'Well, I decided to face the current problem, to grasp the nettle, I suppose, and I bought the muffins... as a gesture of defiance. I thought that doing that would make it easier for me to cope.' She said hopelessly, 'It really does sound ridiculous, doesn't it?'

'Not in the least. It was a perfectly good reason for buying muffins. Let's start toasting.'

They sat by the hearth, as they had on his first visit ten months earlier, toasting muffins over the fire, which was now burning nicely. After a while, he said, 'Since we arrived here, I wondered about inviting you to dinner at the hotel. I remember how reluctant you were for us to part immediately after a quarrel, and I know I disagreed with you at the time, but it suddenly seemed a good idea.' He smiled hopelessly. 'Unfortunately, the weather is quite unambiguous in its dissent.'

'Yes, and I'm still damp and shivering.' She shuddered, as if to underline that disclosure, and asked, 'Will you be offended if I change into my night things and come down in my dressing gown?' A particularly fierce squall of rain pelted the windows, adding reinforcement, as if it were needed, to her request.

'Not in the least. You should get out of those wet clothes before you catch a chill. Don't worry,' he teased, taking her toasting fork from her, 'I shan't let your muffin go to waste.'

'Don't be awful.' She disappeared upstairs, leaving Fred to toast two muffins, a fork in each hand. Eventually, he judged them sufficiently done and transferred them to two plates. He also poured tea into both cups and waited for her to come down.

She came into the room in a nightgown, bedroom slippers and a saffron dressing gown, the whole ensemble demonstrating beyond doubt that her slender figure owed nothing to whalebone and laces.

'You're so clever,' she said, 'toasting them both at the same time.' Her expression changed to one of apology when she said, 'I'm afraid butter is impossible to find. This is the concoction we use at the canteen.'

'If it's good enough for Jolly Jack, it's good enough for me,' he said, spreading margarine on half a muffin.

'I'm glad we saw each other today, Fred, and not just because you drove me home.'

'So am I.' It was difficult to think of anything else to say. They were estranged, but on friendly terms. The situation was so unusual that words were inadequate.

'How was your meeting with your brother? Or am I prying?'

'There's no question of your prying, but you'll possibly be disappointed to learn that nothing's changed. At least, relations between us are very much as they were.'

'But I thought he was suggesting a reconciliation.'

'That's what I was supposed to believe, too.' He told her the story of Ralph's dishonest and clumsy attempt to persuade him to repay his father's debts. 'He even suggested that I should do it for the honour of the family. The bait, believe it or not, was that all would be forgiven and that I could take up residence once more at the ancestral home with a clean slate and my sins forgiven.'

'It sounds as if you decided against it. I'm not at all surprised.'

'I certainly did. I know where my home is and I know where my loyalty lies.' He put another log on the fire, creating a shower of sparks, and asked, 'How do you feel now? Are you any warmer?'

'Yes, much warmer, thank you, now that I'm dry again.' She brushed the matter aside, as though it were no longer a concern. 'So, the meeting was a complete waste of your time.'

'Not exactly. If I hadn't met him, I wouldn't have known about the windfall, and I needed to know, because of the very real risk that the bubble might burst when the Army stops ordering boots, saddles, reins, harnesses, belts and holsters. However, I was in London earlier in the week, and I instructed the bank's stockbrokers to sell the lot. Needless to say, they didn't linger on the stock market for long.'

'Didn't you know of their existence before your brother told you about them?'

'Oh, I knew about them. They were a long-running bone of contention in the Fuller-Davies household. You see, my mother inherited them before she met my father, and they married after the Married Women's Property Act was passed, so she didn't have to surrender them to him. Instead, they provided her with a fund that kept her in luxuries and ensured that she wasn't completely dependent on him. He kept badgering her to make them over to him so that he could, as he put it, "manage them more profitably", but she was more astute than he realised. She was no fool, believe me.'

'Oh, good for her.'

'Yes, in her will, she left them in trust for me until I reached my majority, so he couldn't touch them even after her death, although I suspect strongly that my brother attempted some kind of skulduggery more recently.'

'Do you really?'

'Someone tried to gain access to them, and I certainly wouldn't put it past him.'

She moved back from the fire and joined him, ruddy-cheeked, on the sofa. 'What was the name of the firm?'

'Botham and Chorley. It sounds like a music-hall turn, doesn't it?'

'I don't know about that, but they used to make beautiful handbags, cases, trunks and that kind of thing.'

'So my mother told me, and they may need to resort to that again when sanity is restored.'

'But they turned out to be a good investment, it seems.'

' "Good" doesn't describe it. I must say, I found it difficult to believe at first, but it sank in eventually. They're worth more than twenty thousand pounds.'

'What?' Her eyes opened in disbelief.

'And that's not counting the huge dividends that have accumulated in my bank account since I left Enzed.'

She was speechless for a spell, and then she said, 'You really are a wealthy man.'

'The richest man is the man who has enough, and I'm comfortably placed without those shares.'

'You told me that some time ago, I remember now.' The news was so unexpected that she was temporarily silent. When she eventually spoke, she asked, 'Have you given any thought to what you're going to do with your fortune?'

'Yes, I found that I had an array of choices.' He began to list them, counting on his fingers. 'I could simply live the high life. Champagne and caviar could have been my daily fare. That was one available avenue, but not one I cared to take. Another option was that I could comply with my brother's suggestion, but I didn't see why I should make good the name of a man who never did a thing to deserve it.' He touched his third finger. 'I could set myself up in England, and then I wouldn't have to worry about persuading any woman to come to New Zealand.'

'Oh, dear.'

He apologised at once. 'I'm sorry,' he said. 'That remark wasn't worthy of me.'

'That's all right, Fred.'

He went on to the next possibility. 'My fourth option might have been to try to cajole you into letting bygones be bygones, to marry me, but to live in England. It was tempting, but no. Although you still mean the world to me, I respect your reservations and your decision.' He touched his thumb. 'The fifth option is the one that truly appeals to me, because, frankly, I don't want a brass farthing of that fortune for myself.'

'Why ever not?'

'Because it represents the proceeds of war profiteering. It's been made on the backs of the thousands – probably millions – who've been killed or maimed in this war. It's tainted money, Agnes, the result of selfishness and greed. I suspect that those who exploited the situation are incapable of atonement, but the money can redeem itself by doing some good.'

She was staring at him mutely, waiting for more.

'When I was in London, having arranged to visit the bank, I went to see a revue at the Hippodrome, although I've no idea why, because I can honestly say that, whilst the entertainment had some quality, my own company was no substitute for yours.'

'Thank you, Fred,' she said quietly. 'In view of recent events, that's a lovely thing to say.'

And I mean every word of it. However, be that as it may, when I stepped outside and into Charing Cross Road, I saw a truly heart-rending sight. I saw half-starved women in doorways, begging for small change. As you know, the basic war widow's pension is sixteen shillings and threepence per week, with six shillings and eightpence for each child under the age of sixteen. Naturally enough, children grow out of their clothes, which have to be replaced, so when their mother has fed them and paid the rent, the only way she can buy clothes or pay for the materials to make them is by going without food and clothing herself. Even worse than that, some widows don't even qualify for a pension, and they have to fall back on the workhouse system. I learned all that at the Ministry of Pensions, and to say I was appalled does my feelings scant justice.'

Visibly troubled, she asked, 'What are you going to do, Fred?'

'I'm setting up a fund to be managed here in England by someone I can trust. I'm told that the Soldiers' and Sailors' Association does tremendous work, but it can't help every widow or fatherless child. More help is needed, and that most urgently. That, Agnes, is how that pile of money will redeem itself.'

Her tears were running freely, and he took the handkerchief from his breast pocket to give to her. 'I didn't tell you that to upset you, although I do feel that the people of this country need to be upset. They need to begin caring about those left to struggle.'

When she'd blown her nose, she was more collected. 'I'll send this back to you when I've washed it,' she said.

He put his hand on hers. 'I may have expressed myself a little too passionately. Unfortunately, that's how I feel. That night in London was a baptism of fire for me. I saw revellers in evening dress threatening those wretched widows with immediate violence if they didn't move on.'

'Oh, no.'

'Oh, yes,' he said in a fair imitation of the heartless carouser who'd earned his contempt on that occasion, 'Beggars are unsightly. Not the kind of thing one likes to see. They give the district a bad name, don't you know.'

Taking his hand between hers, she said, 'These tears are not just for the plight of those wretched women, or what you're about to do with the money, wonderful though that is, but for the fact that you care enough to do it.'

'It doesn't seem particularly wonderful to me, Agnes, because I shudder to think what kind of person I'd be if I didn't care. I suppose I'd be like those inhuman layabouts in top hats I saw brandishing their canes at hungry widows who didn't deserve it.'

'Don't, Fred,' she said, moving closer to him. 'You'll have me in tears again. You could no sooner behave like that than sup with the Kaiser.' As she spoke, the thought seemed to provoke another, and she said, 'I'm keeping you from dinner. I really don't feel like eating anything tonight, but I'm sure you do.'

'No, I ate well at lunchtime in the wardroom. I'm where I want to be, Agnes, ensuring that we part company on friendly terms.'

'Yes, we must, and I couldn't possibly be unfriendly towards you after what you've told me this evening.' Her red-rimmed eyes and the threat of further tears added eloquence to her words.

'Good, I'm pleased about that.'

Realising the state of her appearance, she said suddenly, 'I must be an awful sight.'

'Not in the slightest,' he assured her, giving her hands a squeeze.

'I must tidy myself up. Please excuse me.' She made for the stairs once more, and he forbore to argue, knowing how important such matters were to women. She no doubt wanted to look her best when they took their leave of each other.

As he pondered that thought, the wind and rain continued to hammer the windows with unrelenting malice, and a sudden down-draught caused the flames around the log to flare sideways before reaching once more up the fireback, seemingly undeterred by the interruption and leaving behind only a whiff of smoke.

Agnes returned after a few minutes, looking more cheerful for her efforts, and she resumed her seat beside him. 'I'm sorry about that,' she said, smiling. 'I only realised when I saw myself in the mirror what a woeful sight I was.'

'If you say so,' he said, taking her hands again and realising that there was nothing to be gained by delaying their farewell any longer. 'Given that we're about to part amicably,' he said, 'am I allowed to kiss you once more, for old times' sake?'

'Of course you are.'

He let his lips touch hers, having accepted that it would be for the last time, so he was surprised when she responded, not with the polite reserve he might have expected, but much as she had before the rift between them had occurred; in fact, they kissed fondly for some time, during which she became increasingly aroused, but seemed unusually content to let things continue.

After a while, he felt for the sash of her dressing gown ˗ no objection, loosened the bow and negotiated the fold intimate warmth and softness of her body through the fabric of her nightgown. Her reaction was to respond more eagerly to his kisses, and her quickening breath told him that his stroking excited her further. She gave a start when he cupped one breast with his hand, but her tension abated when he kissed her again, and her irregular breathing betrayed the obvious pleasure she felt when he massaged the taut nipple through the thin cotton fabric, gently running his palm over it in a slow, circular movement.

For some time, she seemed content to enjoy what for her must have been a novel experience, but then she spoke urgently in his ear. 'Fred,' she said, 'Let's go upstairs.'

'Are you sure?'

'Yes.'

'Absolutely sure?'

'Yes, come along.' They got up, and she led the way upstairs. When she reached the landing, she took an electric torch from the window ledge and asked, 'Will you turn the light on? I'll show you where it is.'

When he put a match to the gaslight, he found that the room was much as he might have expected it; its furnishings were unmistakably feminine, and the mahogany dressing table was host to the kind of paraphernalia that women seemed to find essential. With no fire in the grate, however, the room was also extremely cold.

Agnes carried out a quick and apparently successful search of one of the dressing table drawers and made for the doorway, clutching her hairbrush and some other precious object. She said, 'I shan't be more than a minute.'

Fred decided that the most useful thing he could do in her absence was to close the shutters to stop what draughts he could and make the squalling wind and rain less intrusive, although the weather wasn't currently his main concern.

Agnes returned after a few minutes, with her Titian locks loose about her shoulders. 'I'm afraid I can't offer you pyjamas or a nightshirt,' she said.

Trying not to smile at her innocence, he said, 'Don't worry, it's not essential.' It was his turn to apologise, however. 'Agnes,' he said, 'I came here with absolutely no idea that anything like this might happen, and I'm afraid I'm without the necessary equipment.'

She asked shyly, 'Do you mean precautionary measures?'

'Yes.'

'Don't worry, I've dealt with that.' She made no attempt to elaborate on that information, but removed her dressing gown, hanging it on a coat hook on the back of the door, after which she kicked off her slippers and climbed into bed, looking away coyly as Fred removed his tie, collar and shirt.

'Well done,' he said, 'but aren't you going to undress, too?'

There was a momentary hesitation, as if she'd not heard him or maybe failed to understand the question, and the latter turned out to be the case, because she said uncertainly and still with averted eyes, 'I am undressed. This is my nightgown.'

'I know, and it's a very elegant nightgown, but are you actually going to wear it?'

Her surprise and diffidence continued unabated. 'I was going to…. I'll… I'll remove it. That's… if you'd rather.'

'It's your nightgown, Agnes,' he told her soothingly, now wishing he hadn't mentioned it. Sensible of her dilemma, he had no wish to make her more nervous than she was already. 'It's your choice whether you wear it or not. It's rather cold in here, so keep it on if you'd rather.' He finished undressing, turned off the gas, and joined her between the cold sheets.

'I didn't know…. I mean, about my nightgown.' The fact that she was shivering was apparent in her speech. 'I'm afraid it's rather cold in here and, with firewood being in short supply, I've not had a fire recently.' No doubt because of her uneasy state of mind, the words rather tumbled out. 'I sometimes wear a bedjacket as well as a nightgown, but I shan't wear it tonight.'

'That's your choice.'

'Are you sure?' If anything, she was shivering more than ever.

'Yes, you must wear whatever makes you feel comfortable. I'm sorry if I unsettled you.' He took her in his arms, aware that her nightgown had become tucked up around her waist.

'I'll take it off in a minute.'

'That's up to you, honestly.'

The wind and rain continued to batter the window, the noise no doubt increasing her discomfort, but Fred wasn't convinced that her shivering was solely due to the coldness of the room, although he had to do something about that.

'Snuggle up and let me warm you.' He wrapped his arms around her, drawing her beneath the bedclothes to create a warm tent, and held her close, so that her shivers grew progressively fewer and eventually ceased altogether.

'I'll take it off now.' She broke away from him to haul up the garment and pull it over her head.

'I'm sorry,' he said, kissing her by way of apology and because he could only try to imagine how nervous she was. 'I really started something, didn't I? I was being thoughtless again.'

'It's all right. I was surprised, that's all. I've always... you know, kept it on... before... now.' Not surprisingly, references to previous bedroom encounters seemed to make her more nervous than ever.

'Are you feeling any warmer?' Her back felt warm to his touch.

'Much warmer, thank you.'

'Your feet are still cold,' he said.

'Yes, they are.'

'Warm them against me.'

'How?'

It was a good question, but ingenuity came to his aid. 'Turn over so that you have your back towards me, and then I'll snuggle up to you. We'll be like spoons, and then you can put your feet against my legs.' The situation was becoming increasingly bizarre, but if warming her feet was going to help put her at ease, that was what he would do.

'All right.' She turned on to her side, and he winced at the initial shock when she flattened her feet against him, because they were like ice. Her bottom was equally cold, and that was a shock, too, although the surprises were not all his.

'Something's sticking into me, Fred.'

'I'm sorry.' he arranged himself to accommodate her in a way that was unlikely to cause her further alarm or embarrassment. Then, with his arm around her middle, he held her close to transfer some of his warmth to her.

After a few minutes, she said, 'They're much warmer now.' She wriggled over again to face him.

'Good.' They kissed almost casually, until he felt that she was, at least, a little less apprehensive than she'd been.

'I love you, Agnes.' He kissed her to underline that statement.

'I love you, Fred.'

Presently, he became more playful, moving her abundant hair aside to kiss her throat, her neck, her cheek and then an ear, which he found deliciously cold. She shuddered when he kissed it again, and he asked, 'Do you like that?'

'I'm not sure. I think I do.'

He repeated the action several times, eliciting the same reaction, before moving downward gradually and by unhurried steps to her firm breasts, which, by contrast, he found warmly inviting. She reacted, surprised at first, but quickly abated as doubt gave way to cautious enjoyment. Then, he buried his face between them, kissing the intermammary cleft slowly and appreciatively as a prelude to sharing his favours with its neighbours. He felt her stiffen when his lips closed briefly on one nipple, but then she relaxed again, moaning softly in response to his attentions.

Moving upward once more, he traced the route with kisses until his lips found hers again, and she re-joined him readily.

'There's absolutely nothing to be afraid of,' he assured her.

'I'm not really afraid. I trust you, but it's a new experience. I mean, it's not, but it is, if you see what I mean.'

'I know, but believe me, you'll never be as nervous about it again.' He kissed her, cradling her breasts and kissing them again in turn, now that the strangeness she'd known earlier had given way to familiarity, and she made no demur. After a while, he moved his hand to her waist, stroking the smooth skin with his palm, while his outstretched fingers explored and gently massaged the area beneath her navel. Between kisses, she moaned softly at the pleasure it gave her.

When he arrived at the edge of her forest, she stiffened, and he felt an eyelash flicker against his cheek, so that, even in the darkened room, he was conscious of her heightened unease. 'It's all right,' he murmured, kissing her to reassure her. 'I shan't run away with it.'

It was hardly necessary for him to do more; the evidence of her arousal was there beneath his fingertips, but he continued all the same, causing her to cry out repeatedly in her helpless state, until she gasped urgently, 'Stop. Please.' Gathering herself again, she said, 'Just give me a moment.'

He gave her the respite she asked for, and then, when he knew she was ready to receive him, moved gently into the space between her trembling limbs. He was aware of the double catch in her breath when he entered her, and then, after a few seconds, the sigh of blissful realisation that what she was experiencing bore no resemblance to the clumsy incursions she'd endured in the past. Then, in what seemed no more than an instant, nature took control over her actions, and she began to move easily against him.

Although he knew the answer, he asked, 'Are you happier now?'

'Yes,' she said with the tremor of excitement in her voice, 'much happier.' She clung to him eagerly, her grip tightening as she responded to every sensation, her arousal intensifying, even as he paused to accommodate her eager, excited movements, until she gave a loud gasp, her breath shortened, and she stiffened and cried out, unable to contain her joy at the sensation that surged through her body.

** ** **

Fred opened his eyes to see the early streaks of light around the shutters. Agnes lay sleeping, her arm still across his waist. With some difficulty, he eased himself into position to move a lock of her hair and kiss her cheek, and the gentle movement was enough to rouse her.

'Good morning,' he said, kissing her on the lips.

'Good morning,' she said drowsily. 'There can be no better way to be woken than this.'

'It's a well-tried method,' he assured her.

She made no response to that, but said simply, 'Whether last night really happened, or whether I dreamt the whole thing, it was simply too wonderful for words.'

'I'm glad you enjoyed it.'

'I'll never forget it.'

'I'll always remember it, too, even when I'm twelve thousand miles away.'

She looked at him in sudden alarm. 'Don't say that, Fred,' she pleaded, 'after everything we said last evening, and then… last night.'

'Are you saying you've had a change of heart?'

Her expression changed to realisation and then reproof. 'You know perfectly well I have. You're just teasing. I told you the last time we met, that I'd come to terms with living in New Zealand, and now I'm even looking forward to it.'

He kissed her in celebration, but couldn't resist asking, 'Am I forgiven for being selfish, thoughtless and inconsiderate?'

'We're all thoughtless and inconsiderate sometimes, but last evening and… last night, you reminded me of the kind of man you really are, and selfishness had nothing to do with it.'

He gave an exaggerated sigh of relief. 'So I'm no longer cast into outer darkness?'

'No, you're not, Fred.' She kissed him to confirm it. 'Your days as an outcast are over.'

THE END

If you enjoyed this story, you may like to read *A Chance Sighting*, also by Ray Hobbs and published by Wingspan Press.

A Chance Sighting

'The plot has so much depth; it is far more than a love story.... the characters are rich and believable.' – *Readers' Favorite* ®

It is January 1944. Pilot Cliff Stephens and linguist Laura Pembury meet for the first time on a rain-swept night in Hampshire and are immediately attracted to each other. They meet again three times and their relationship blossoms. The future looks inviting until Cliff is posted missing over the English Channel.

Unknown to those searching for them, Cliff and his crew are picked up by a German patrol vessel. Meanwhile, a storm in the Channel leads to the search being called off, and Laura believes Cliff has been killed.

Now a prisoner-of-war in Germany, Cliff has no address for Laura, and the need for stringent security means he cannot write to her at the wireless station where she is based. It seems that their relationship is over.

Destiny, however, follows its own agenda.

CPSIA information can be obtained
at www.ICGtesting.com
Printed in the USA
LVHW100931071122
732535LV00004B/152